UNCANNY OF PLACE

Uncanny of Place

Cities, Streets, Shops, and Spaces
in Classic Speculative Fiction

Edited by

Chad Arment

COACHWHIP PUBLICATIONS
GREENVILLE, OHIO

Uncanny of Place
© 2024 Coachwhip Publications
Cover: Houses © Macrovector SLU; Tentacles © Kolonko

CoachwhipBooks.com

ISBN 1-61646-578-6
ISBN-13 978-1-61646-578-0

Contents

The Fall of the House of Usher

Edgar Allan Poe

(1846)

Son cœur est un luth suspendu;
His heart is a suspended lute;
Sitôt qu'on le touche il résonne.
As soon as it is touched it resounds.
J. P. de Béranger.

During the whole of a dull, dark, and soundless day in the autumn of the year, when the clouds hung oppressively low in the heavens, I had been passing alone, on horseback, through a singularly dreary tract of country; and at length found myself, as the shades of the evening drew on, within view of the melancholy House of Usher. I know not how it was—but, with the first glimpse of the building, a sense of insufferable gloom pervaded my spirit. I say insufferable; for the feeling was unrelieved by any of that half-pleasurable, because poetic, sentiment, with which the mind usually receives even the sternest natural images of the desolate or terrible. I looked upon the scene before me—upon the mere house, and the simple landscape features of the domain—upon the bleak walls—upon the vacant eye-like windows—upon a few rank sedges—and upon a few white trunks of decayed trees—with an utter depression of soul which I can compare to no earthly sensation more properly than to the after-dream of the reveler upon opium—the

7

bitter lapse into every-day life—the hideous dropping off of the veil. There was an iciness, a sinking, a sickening of the heart—an unredeemed dreariness of thought which no goading of the imagination could torture into aught of the sublime. What was it—I paused to think—what was it that so unnerved me in the contemplation of the House of Usher? It was a mystery all insoluble; nor could I grapple with the shadowy fancies that crowded upon me as I pondered. I was forced to fall back upon the unsatisfactory conclusion that while, beyond doubt, there are combinations of very simple natural objects which have the power of thus affecting us, still the analysis of this power lies among considerations beyond our depth. It was possible, I reflected, that a mere different arrangement of the particulars of the scene, of the details of the picture, would be sufficient to modify, or perhaps to annihilate its capacity for sorrowful impression; and, acting upon this idea, I reined my horse to the precipitous brink of a black and lurid tarn that lay in unruffled luster by the dwelling, and gazed down—but with a shudder even more thrilling than before—upon the remodeled and inverted images of the gray sedge, and the ghastly tree stems, and the vacant and eye-like windows.

Nevertheless, in this mansion of gloom I now proposed to myself a sojourn of some weeks. Its proprietor, Roderick Usher, had been one of my boon companions in boyhood; but many years had elapsed since our last meeting. A letter, however, had lately reached me in a distant part of the country—a letter from him—which, in its wildly importunate nature, had admitted of no other than a personal reply. The MS. gave evidence of nervous agitation. The writer spoke of acute bodily illness—of a mental disorder which oppressed him, and of an earnest desire to see me, as his best, and indeed his only personal friend, with a view of attempting, by the cheerfulness of my society, some alleviation of his malady. It was the manner in which all this, and much more, was said—it was the apparent *heart* that went with his request—which allowed me no room for hesitation; and I accordingly obeyed forthwith what I still considered a very singular summons.

Although, as boys, we had been even intimate associates, yet I really knew little of my friend. His reserve had been always excessive and habitual. I was aware, however, that his very ancient family had been noted, time out of mind, for a peculiar sensibility of temperament, displaying itself, through long ages, in many works of exalted art, and manifested, of late, in repeated deeds of munificent, yet unobtrusive charity, as well as in a passionate devotion to the intricacies, perhaps even more than to the orthodox and easily recognizable beauties, of musical science. I had learned, too, the very remarkable fact that the stem of the Usher race, all time-honored as it was, had put forth, at no period, any enduring branch; in other words, that the entire family lay in the direct line of descent, and had always, with very trifling and very temporary variation, so lain. It was this deficiency, I considered, while running over in thought the perfect keeping of the character of the premises with the accredited character of the people, and while speculating upon the possible influence which the one, in the long lapse of centuries, might have exercised upon the other—it was this deficiency, perhaps, of collateral issue, and the consequent undeviating transmission, from sire to son, of the patrimony with the name, which had, at length, so identified the two as to merge the original title of the estate in the quaint and equivocal appellation of the "House of Usher"—an appellation which seemed to include, in the minds of the peasantry who used it, both the family and the family mansion.

I have said that the sole effect of my somewhat childish experiment of looking down within the tarn had been to deepen the first singular impression. There can be no doubt that the consciousness of the rapid increase of my superstition—for why should I not so term it?—served mainly to accelerate the increase itself. Such, I have long known, is the paradoxical law of all sentiments having terror as a basis. And it might have been for this reason only, that, when I again uplifted my eyes to the house itself, from its image in the pool, there grew in my mind a strange fancy—a fancy so ridiculous, indeed, that I but mention it to show the vivid force of the sensations which oppressed me. I had so worked upon my imagination as really to believe that about the whole mansion and domain there hung an atmosphere peculiar to themselves and their immediate vicinity—an atmosphere which had no affinity with the air of heaven, but which had reeked up from the decayed trees, and the gray wall, and the silent tarn—a pestilent and mystic vapor, dull, sluggish, faintly discernible, and leaden-hued.

Shaking off from my spirit what must have been a dream, I scanned more narrowly the real aspect of the building. Its principal feature seemed to be that of an excessive antiquity. The discoloration of ages had been great. Minute fungi overspread the whole exterior, hanging in a fine, tangled web-work from the eaves. Yet all this was apart from any extraordinary dilapidation. No portion of the masonry had fallen; and there appeared to be a wild inconsistency between its still perfect adaptation of parts, and the crumbling condition of the individual stones. In this there was much that reminded me of the specious totality of old woodwork which has rotted for years in some neglected vault, with no disturbance from the breath of the external air. Beyond this indication of extensive decay, however, the fabric gave little token of instability. Perhaps the eye of a scrutinizing observer might have discovered a barely perceptible fissure, which, extending from the roof of the building in front, made its way down the wall in a zigzag direction, until it became lost in the sullen waters of the tarn.

Noticing these things, I rode over a short causeway to the house. A servant in waiting took my horse, and I entered the Gothic archway of the hall. A valet, of stealthy step, thence conducted me, in silence, through many dark and intricate passages in my progress to the studio of his master. Much that I encountered on the way contributed, I know not how, to heighten the vague sentiments of which I have already spoken. While the objects around me—while the carvings of the ceilings, the somber tapestries of the walls, the ebon blackness of the floors, and the phantasmagoric armorial trophies which rattled as I strode, were but matters to which, or to such as which, I had been accustomed from my infancy,—while I hesitated not to acknowledge how familiar was all this, I still wondered to find how unfamiliar were the fancies which ordinary images were stirring up. On one of the staircases I met the physician of the family. His countenance, I thought, wore a mingled expression of low cunning and perplexity. He accosted me with trepidation and passed on. The valet now threw open a door and ushered me into the presence of his master.

The room in which I found myself was very large and lofty. The windows were long, narrow, and pointed, and at so vast a distance from the black oaken floor as to be altogether inaccessible from within. Feeble gleams of encrimsoned light made their way through the trellised panes, and served to render sufficiently distinct the more prominent objects around; the eye, however, struggled in vain to reach the remoter angles of the chamber, or the recesses of the vaulted and fretted ceiling. Dark draperies hung upon the walls. The general furniture was profuse, comfortless, antique, and tattered. Many books and musical instruments lay scattered about, but failed to give any vitality to the

scene. I felt that I breathed an atmosphere of sorrow. An
air of stern, deep, and irredeemable gloom hung over and
pervaded all.

Upon my entrance, Usher arose from a sofa on which
he had been lying at full length, and greeted me with a
vivacious warmth which had much in it, I at first thought,
of an overdone cordiality—of the constrained effort of
the *ennuyé* man of the world. A glance, however, at his
countenance convinced me of his perfect sincerity. We sat
down; and for some moments, while he spoke not, I gazed
upon him with a feeling half of pity, half of awe. Surely,
man had never before so terribly altered, in so brief a
period, as had Roderick Usher! It was with difficulty that I
could bring myself to admit the identity of the wan being
before me with the companion of my early boyhood. Yet
the character of his face had been at all times remarkable. A cadaverousness of complexion; an eye large, liquid,
and luminous beyond comparison; lips somewhat thin and
very pallid, but of a surpassingly beautiful curve; a nose
of a delicate Hebrew model, but with a breadth of nos-
tril unusual in similar formations; a finely molded chin,
speaking, in its want of prominence, of a want of moral
energy; hair of a more than web-like softness and tenuity;
these features, with an inordinate expansion above the re-
gions of the temple, made up altogether a countenance not
easily to be forgotten. And now in the mere exaggeration
of the prevailing character of these features, and of the
expression they were wont to convey, lay so much of change
that I doubted to whom I spoke. The now ghastly pallor of
the skin, and the now miraculous luster of the eye, above
all things startled and even awed me. The silken hair, too,
had been suffered to grow all unheeded, and as, in its
wild gossamer texture, it floated rather than fell about the
face, I could not, even with effort, connect its arabesque
expression with any idea of simple humanity.

In the manner of my friend I was at once struck with an incoherence—an inconsistency; and I soon found this to arise from a series of feeble and futile struggles to overcome an habitual trepidancy, an excessive nervous agitation. For something of this nature I had indeed been prepared, no less by his letter than by reminiscences of certain boyish traits, and by conclusions deduced from his peculiar physical conformation and temperament. His action was alternately vivacious and sullen. His voice varied rapidly from a tremulous indecision (when the animal spirits seemed utterly in abeyance) to that species of energetic concision—that abrupt, weighty, unhurried, and hollow-sounding enunciation—that leaden, self-balanced, and perfectly modulated guttural utterance, which may be observed in the lost drunkard, or the irreclaimable eater of opium, during the periods of his most intense excitement.

It was thus that he spoke of the object of my visit, of his earnest desire to see me, and of the solace he expected me to afford him. He entered, at some length, into what he conceived to be the nature of his malady. It was, he said, a constitutional and a family evil, and one for which he despaired to find a remedy—a mere nervous affection, he immediately added, which would undoubtedly soon pass off. It displayed itself in a host of unnatural sensations. Some of these, as he detailed them, interested and bewildered me; although, perhaps, the terms and the general manner of the narration had their weight. He suffered much from a morbid acuteness of the senses. The most insipid food was alone endurable; he could wear only garments of certain texture; the odors of all flowers were oppressive; his eyes were tortured by even a faint light; and there were but peculiar sounds, and these from stringed instruments, which did not inspire him with horror.

To an anomalous species of terror I found him a bounden slave. "I shall perish," said he, "I *must* perish in this deplorable folly. Thus, thus, and not otherwise, shall I be lost. I dread the events of the future, not in themselves, but in their results. I shudder at the thought of any, even the most trivial, incident, which may operate upon this intolerable agitation of soul. I have, indeed, no abhorrence of danger, except in its absolute effect—in terror. In this unnerved—in this pitiable condition—I feel that the period will sooner or later arrive when I must abandon life and reason together, in some struggle with the grim phantasm, Fear."

I learned, moreover, at intervals, and through broken and equivocal hints, another singular feature of his mental condition. He was enchained by certain superstitious impressions in regard to the dwelling which he tenanted, and whence, for many years, he had never ventured forth—in regard to an influence whose supposititious force was conveyed in terms too shadowy here to be restated—an influence which some peculiarities in the mere form and substance of his family mansion, had, by dint of long sufferance, he said, obtained over his spirit—an effect which the physique of the gray walls and turrets, and of the dim tarn into which they all looked down, had, at length, brought about upon the morale of his existence.

He admitted, however, although with hesitation, that much of the peculiar gloom which thus afflicted him could be traced to a more natural and far more palpable origin—to the severe and long-continued illness—indeed to the evidently approaching dissolution—of a tenderly beloved sister, his sole companion for long years, his last and only relative on earth. "Her decease," he said, with a bitterness which I can never forget, "would leave him (him, the hopeless and the frail) the last of the ancient race of the Ushers." While he spoke, the lady Madeline (for so was she called) passed slowly through a remote portion of the apartment, and, without having noticed my presence, disappeared. I regarded her with an utter astonishment not unmingled with dread; and yet I found it impossible to account for such feelings. A sensation of stupor oppressed me, as my eyes followed her retreating steps. When a door, at length, closed upon her, my glance sought instinctively and eagerly the countenance of the brother; but he had buried his face in his hands, and I could only perceive that a far more than ordinary wanness had overspread the emaciated fingers through which trickled many passionate tears.

The disease of the lady Madeline had long baffled the skill of her physicians. A settled apathy, a gradual wasting away of the person, and frequent although transient affections of a partially cataleptical character, were the unusual diagnosis. Hitherto she had steadily borne up against the pressure of her malady, and had not betaken herself finally to bed; but on the closing in of the evening of my arrival at the house, she succumbed (as her brother told me at night with inexpressible agitation) to the prostrating power of the destroyer; and I learned that the glimpse I had obtained of her person would thus probably be the last I should obtain—that the lady, at least while living, would be seen by me no more.

For several days ensuing her name was unmentioned by either Usher or myself; and during this period I was busied in earnest endeavors to alleviate the melancholy of my friend. We painted and read together; or I listened, as if in a dream, to the wild improvisations of his speaking guitar. And thus, as a closer and still closer intimacy admitted me more unreservedly into the recesses of his spirit, the more bitterly did I perceive the futility of all attempt at cheering a mind from which darkness, as if an inherent positive quality, poured forth upon all objects of the moral and physical universe, in one unceasing radiation of gloom.

I shall ever bear about me a memory of the many solemn hours I thus spent alone with the master of the House

of Usher. Yet I should fail in any attempt to convey an idea
of the exact character of the studies, or of the occupations
in which he involved me, or led me the way. An excited
and highly distempered ideality threw a sulphurous luster
over all. His long, improvised dirges will ring forever in
my ears. Among other things, I hold painfully in mind a
certain singular perversion and amplification of the wild
air of the last waltz of Von Weber. From the paintings over
which his elaborate fancy brooded, and which grew, touch
by touch, into vaguenesses at which I shuddered the more
thrillingly because I shuddered knowing not why,—from
these paintings (vivid as their images now are before me)
I would in vain endeavor to deduce more than a small
portion which should lie within the compass of merely
written words. By the utter simplicity, by the nakedness
of his designs, he arrested and overawed attention. If ever
mortal painted an idea, that mortal was Roderick Usher.
For me, at least—in the circumstances then surrounding
me—there arose out of the pure abstractions which the
hypochondriac contrived to throw upon his canvas, an
intensity of intolerable awe, no shadow of which felt I
ever yet in the contemplation of the certainly glowing yet
too concrete reveries of Fuseli.

One of the phantasmagoric conceptions of my friend,
partaking not so rigidly of the spirit of abstraction, may be
shadowed forth, although feebly, in words. A small picture
presented the interior of an immensely long and rectangular
vault or tunnel, with low walls, smooth, white, and without interruption or device. Certain accessory points of the
design served well to convey the idea that this excavation
lay at an exceeding depth below the surface of the earth. No
outlet was observed in any portion of its vast extent, and
no torch or other artificial source of light was discernible;
yet a flood of intense rays rolled throughout, and bathed
the whole in a ghastly and inappropriate splendor.

I have just spoken of that morbid condition of the auditory nerve which rendered all music intolerable to the sufferer, with the exception of certain effects of stringed instruments. It was, perhaps, the narrow limits to which he thus confined himself upon the guitar, which gave birth, in great measure, to the fantastic character of his performances. But the fervid *facility* of his impromptus could not be so accounted for. They must have been, and were, in the notes, as well as in the words of his wild fantasias (for he not unfrequently accompanied himself with rimed verbal improvisations), the result of that intense mental collectedness and concentration to which I have previously alluded as observable only in particular moments of the highest artificial excitement. The words of one of these rhapsodies I have easily remembered. I was, perhaps, the more forcibly impressed with it, as he gave it, because, in the under or mystic current of its meaning, I fancied that I perceived, and for the first time, a full consciousness on the part of Usher, of the tottering of his lofty reason upon her throne. The verses, which were entitled "The Haunted Palace," ran very nearly, if not accurately, thus:

I.

In the greenest of our valleys,
    By good angels tenanted,
Once a fair and stately palace—
    Radiant palace—reared its head.
In the monarch Thought's dominion—
    It stood there;
Never seraph spread a pinion
    Over fabric half so fair.

II.

Banners yellow, glorious, golden,
    On its roof did float and flow;

(This—all this—was in the olden
    Time long ago)
And every gentle air that dallied,
    In that sweet day,
Along the ramparts plumed and pallid,
    A wingèd odor went away.

III.

Wanderers in that happy valley
    Through two luminous windows saw
Spirits moving musically
    To a lute's well-tunèd law,
Round about a throne, where sitting
    (Porphyrogene!)
In state his glory well befitting,
    The ruler of the realm was seen.

IV.

And all with pearl and ruby glowing
    Was the fair palace door,
Through which came flowing, flowing,
        flowing,
    And sparkling evermore,
A troop of Echoes whose sweet duty
    Was but to sing,
In voices of surpassing beauty,
    The wit and wisdom of their king.

V.

But evil things, in robes of sorrow,
    Assailed the monarch's high estate;
(Ah, let us mourn, for never morrow
    Shall dawn upon him, desolate!)
And, round about his home, the glory
    That blushed and bloomed

Is but a dim-remembered story
    Of the old time entombed.

VI.

And travelers now within that valley,
    Through the red-litten windows, see
Vast forms that move fantastically
    To a discordant melody;
While, like a rapid ghastly river,
    Through the pale door,
A hideous throng rush out forever,
    And laugh—but smile no more.

I well remember that suggestions arising from this ballad led us into a train of thought wherein there became manifest an opinion of Usher's which I mention not so much on account of its novelty (for other men[1] have thought thus) as on account of the pertinacity with which he maintained it. This opinion, in its general form, was that of the sentience of all vegetable things. But, in his disordered fancy, the idea had assumed a more daring character, and trespassed, under certain conditions, upon the kingdom of inorganization. I lack words to express the full extent or the earnest *abandon* of his persuasion. The belief, however, was connected (as I have previously hinted) with the gray stones of the home of his forefathers. The conditions of the sentience had been here, he imagined, fulfilled in the method of collocation of these stones—in the order of their arrangement, as well as in that of the many fungi which overspread them, and of the decayed trees which stood around—above all, in the long-undisturbed endurance of this arrangement, and in its reduplication in the still waters

---

[1] Watson, Dr. Percival, Spallanzani, and especially the Bishop of Landaff.—See *Chemical Essays*, vol v.

of the tarn. Its evidence—the evidence of the sentience—
was to be seen, he said (and I here started as he spoke),
in the gradual yet certain condensation of an atmosphere
of their own about the waters and the walls. The result
was discoverable, he added, in that silent, yet importunate
and terrible influence which for centuries had molded the
destinies of his family, and which made *him* what I now
saw him—what he was. Such opinions need no comment,
and I will make none.

Our books—the books which, for years, had formed
no small portion of the mental existence of the invalid—
were, as might be supposed, in strict keeping with this
character of phantasm. We pored together over such works
as the *Ververt* and *Chartreuse* of Gresset; the *Belphegor* of
Machiavelli; the *Heaven and Hell* of Swedenborg; the *Sub-
terranean Voyage of Nicholas Klimm* by Holberg; the *Chiro-
mancy* of Robert Flud, of Jean D'Indaginé, and of De la
Chambre; the *Journey into the Blue Distance* of Tieck; and
the *City of the Sun* of Campanella. One favorite volume
was a small octavo edition of the *Directorium Inquisito-
rum,* by the Dominican Eymeric de Gironne; and there
were passages in Pomponius Mela, about the old African
Satyrs and Ægipans, over which Usher would sit dreaming
for hours. His chief delight, however, was found in the
perusal of an exceedingly rare and curious book in quarto
Gothic—the manual of a forgotten church—the *Vigiliæ
Mortuorum secundum Chorum Ecclesiæ Maguntinæ.*

I could not help thinking of the wild ritual of this
work, and of its probable influence upon the hypochondriac, when, one evening, having informed me abruptly that
the lady Madeline was no more, he stated his intention
of preserving her corpse for a fortnight (previously to its
final interment) in one of the numerous vaults within the
main walls of the building. The worldly reason, however,
assigned for this singular proceeding, was one which I did

not feel at liberty to dispute. The brother had been led to his resolution, so he told me, by consideration of the unusual character of the malady of the deceased, of certain obtrusive and eager inquiries on the part of her medical men, and of the remote and exposed situation of the burial ground of the family. I will not deny that when I called to mind the sinister countenance of the person whom I met upon the staircase, on the day of my arrival at the house, I had no desire to oppose what I regarded as at best but a harmless, and by no means an unnatural, precaution.

At the request of Usher, I personally aided him in the arrangements for the temporary entombment. The body having been encoffined, we two alone bore it to its rest. The vault in which we placed it (and which had been so long unopened that our torches, half smothered in its oppressive atmosphere, gave us little opportunity for investigation) was small, damp, and entirely without means of admission for light; lying, at great depth, immediately beneath that portion of the building in which was my own sleeping apartment. It had been used, apparently, in remote feudal times, for the worst purposes of a donjon-keep, and in later days, as a place of deposit for powder, or some other highly combustible substance, as a portion of its floor, and the whole interior of a long archway through which we reached it, were carefully sheathed with copper. The door, of massive iron, had been also similarly protected. Its immense weight caused an unusually sharp grating sound, as it moved upon its hinges.

Having deposited our mournful burden upon tressels within this region of horror, we partially turned aside the yet unscrewed lid of the coffin, and looked upon the face of the tenant. A striking similitude between the brother and sister now first arrested my attention; and Usher, divining, perhaps, my thoughts, murmured out some few words from which I learned that the deceased and himself had been twins, and that sympathies of a scarcely intelligible nature had always existed between them. Our glances, however, rested not long upon the dead—for we could not regard her unawed. The disease which had thus entombed the lady in the maturity of youth, had left, as usual in all maladies of a strictly cataleptical character, the mockery of a faint blush upon the bosom and the face, and that suspiciously lingering smile upon the lip which is so terrible in death. We replaced and screwed down the lid, and having secured the door of iron, made our way, with toil, into the scarcely less gloomy apartments of the upper portion of the house.

And now, some days of bitter grief having elapsed, an observable change came over the features of the mental disorder of my friend. His ordinary manner had vanished. His ordinary occupations were neglected or forgotten. He roamed from chamber to chamber with hurried, unequal, and objectless step. The pallor of his countenance had assumed, if possible, a more ghastly hue—but the luminousness of his eye had utterly gone out. The once occasional huskiness of his tone was heard no more; and a tremulous quaver, as if of extreme terror, habitually characterized his utterance. There were times, indeed, when I thought his unceasingly agitated mind was laboring with some oppressive secret, to divulge which he struggled for the necessary courage. At times, again, I was obliged to resolve all into the mere inexplicable vagaries of madness; for I beheld him gazing upon vacancy for long hours, in an attitude of the profoundest attention, as if listening to some imaginary sound. It was no wonder that his condition terrified—that it infected me. I felt creeping upon me, by slow yet certain degrees, the wild influence of his own fantastic yet impressive superstitions.

It was, especially, upon retiring to bed late in the night of the seventh or eighth day after the placing of the lady

Madeline within the donjon, that I experienced the full power of such feelings. Sleep came not near my couch, while the hours waned and waned away. I struggled to reason off the nervousness which had dominion over me. I endeavored to believe that much, if not all of what I felt, was due to the bewildering influence of the gloomy furniture of the room—of the dark and tattered draperies, which, tortured into motion by the breath of a rising tempest, swayed fitfully to and fro upon the walls, and rustled uneasily about the decorations of the bed. But my efforts were fruitless. An irrepressible tremor gradually pervaded my frame; and, at length, there sat upon my very heart an incubus of utterly causeless alarm. Shaking this off with a gasp and a struggle, I uplifted myself upon the pillows, and peering earnestly within the intense darkness of the chamber, hearkened—I know not why, except that an instinctive spirit prompted me—to certain low and indefinite sounds which came, through the pauses of the storm, at long intervals, I knew not whence. Overpowered by an intense sentiment of horror, unaccountable yet unendurable, I threw on my clothes with haste (for I felt that I should sleep no more during the night), and endeavored to arouse myself from the pitiable condition into which I had fallen, by pacing rapidly to and fro through the apartment.

I had taken but few turns in this manner, when a light step on an adjoining staircase arrested my attention. I presently recognized it as that of Usher. In an instant afterward he rapped, with a gentle touch, at my door, and entered, bearing a lamp. His countenance was, as usual, cadaverously wan—but, moreover, there was a species of mad hilarity in his eyes—and evidently restrained hysteria in his whole demeanor. His air appalled me—but anything was preferable to the solitude which I had so long endured, and I even welcomed his presence as a relief.

"And you have not seen it?" he said abruptly, after having stared about him for some moments in silence—"You have not then seen it?—but stay! you shall." Thus speaking, and having carefully shaded his lamp, he hurried to one of the casements, and threw it freely open to the storm.

The impetuous fury of the entering gust nearly lifted us from our feet. It was, indeed, a tempestuous yet sternly beautiful night, and one wildly singular in its terror and its beauty. A whirlwind had apparently collected its force in our vicinity; for there were frequent and violent alterations in the direction of the wind; and the exceeding density of the clouds (which hung so low as to press upon the turrets of the house) did not prevent our perceiving the lifelike velocity with which they flew careering from all points against each other, without passing away into the distance. I say that even their exceeding density did not prevent our perceiving this—yet we had no glimpse of the moon or stars—nor was there any flashing forth of the lightning. But the under surfaces of the huge masses of agitated vapor, as well as all terrestrial objects immediately around us, were glowing in the unnatural light of a faintly luminous and distinctly visible gaseous exhalation which hung about and enshrouded the mansion.

"You must not—you shall not behold this!" said I, shudderingly, to Usher, as I led him, with a gentle violence, from the window to a seat. "These appearances, which bewilder you, are merely electrical phenomena not uncommon—or it may be that they have their ghastly origin in the rank miasma of the tarn. Let us close this casement—the air is chilling and dangerous to your frame. Here is one of your favorite romances. I will read and you shall listen;—and so we will pass away this terrible night together."

The antique volume which I had taken up was the "Mad Trist" of Sir Launcelot Canning; but I had called it a favorite of Usher's more in sad jest than in earnest; for, in truth, there is little in its uncouth and unimaginative prolixity which could have had interest for the lofty and spiritual ideality of my friend. It was, however, the only book immediately at hand; and I indulged a vague hope that the excitement which now agitated the hypochondriac, might find relief (for the history of mental disorder is full of similar anomalies) even in the extremeness of the folly which I should read. Could I have judged, indeed, by the wild, overstrained air of vivacity with which he hearkened, or apparently harkened, to the words of the tale, I might well have congratulated myself upon the success of my design.

I had arrived at that well-known portion of the story where Ethelred, the hero of the Trist, having sought in vain for peaceable admission into the dwelling of the hermit, proceeds to make good an entrance by force. Here, it will be remembered, the words of the narrative run thus:

"And Ethelred, who was by nature of a doughty heart, and who was now mighty withal, on account of the powerfulness of the wine which he had drunken, waited no longer to hold parley with the hermit, who, in sooth, was of an obstinate and maliceful turn; but, feeling the rain upon his shoulders, and fearing the rising of the tempest, uplifted his mace outright, and, with blows, made quickly room in the plankings of the door for his gauntleted hand; and now pulling therewith sturdily, he so cracked, and ripped, and tore all asunder, that the noise of the dry and hollow-sounding wood alarumed and reverberated throughout the forest."

At the termination of this sentence I started, and for a moment paused; for it appeared to me (although I at once concluded that my excited fancy had deceived me)—it appeared to me that, from some very remote portion of the mansion, there came, indistinctly, to my ears what might

have been, in its exact similarity of character, the echo
(but a stifled and dull one certainly) of the very cracking
and ripping sound which Sir Launcelot had so particularly
described. It was, beyond doubt, the coincidence alone
which had arrested my attention; for, amid the rattling of
the sashes of the casements, and the ordinary commingled
noises of the still increasing storm, the sound, in itself,
had nothing, surely, which should have interested or disturbed me. I continued the story:

"But the good champion Ethelred, now entering within the door, was sore enraged and amazed to perceive no
signal of the maliceful hermit; but, in the stead thereof, a
dragon of a scaly and prodigious demeanor, and of a fiery
tongue, which sate in guard before a palace of gold, with
a floor of silver; and upon the wall there hung a shield of
shining brass with this legend enwritten—

Who entereth herein, a conqueror hath bin;
Who slayeth the dragon, the shield he shall win;

And Ethelred uplifted his mace, and struck upon the
head of the dragon, which fell before him, and gave up his
pesty breath, with a shriek so horrid and harsh, and withal
so piercing, that Ethelred had fain to close his ears with
his hands against the dreadful noise of it, the like whereof
was never before heard."

Here again I paused abruptly, and now with a feeling
of wild amazement—for there could be no doubt whatever
that, in this instance, I did actually hear (although from
what direction it proceeded I found it impossible to say)
a low and apparently distant, but harsh, protracted, and
most unusual screaming or grating sound—the exact coun-
terpart of what my fancy had already conjured up for the
dragon's unnatural shriek as described by the romancer.

Oppressed, as I certainly was, upon the occurrence
of this second and most extraordinary coincidence, by
a thousand conflicting sensations, in which wonder and

extreme terror were predominant, I still retained sufficient presence of mind to avoid exciting, by any observation, the sensitive nervousness of my companion. I was by no means certain that he had noticed the sounds in question; although, assuredly, a strange alteration had, during the last few minutes, taken place in his demeanor. From a position fronting my own, he had gradually brought round his chair, so as to sit with his face to the door of the chamber; and thus I could but partially perceive his features, although I saw that his lips trembled as if he were murmuring inaudibly. His head had dropped upon his breast—yet I knew that he was not asleep, from the wide and rigid opening of the eye as I caught a glance of it in profile. The motion of his body, too, was at variance with this idea—for he rocked from side to side with a gentle yet constant and uniform sway. Having rapidly taken notice of all this, I resumed the narrative of Sir Launcelot, which thus proceeded:

"And now the champion, having escaped from the terrible fury of the dragon, bethinking himself of the brazen shield, and of the breaking up of the enchantment which was upon it, removed the carcass from out of the way before him, and approached valorously over the silver pavement of the castle to where the shield was upon the wall; which in sooth tarried not for his full coming, but fell down at his feet upon the silver floor, with a mighty great and terrible ringing sound."

No sooner had these syllables passed my lips, than—as if a shield of brass had indeed, at the moment, fallen heavily upon a floor of silver—I became aware of a distinct, hollow, metallic and clangorous, yet apparently muffled reverberation. Completely unnerved, I leaped to my feet; but the measured rocking movement of Usher was undisturbed. I rushed to the chair in which he sat. His eyes were bent fixedly before him, and throughout his whole countenance there reigned a stony rigidity. But, as I placed my

hand upon his shoulder, there came a strong shudder over
his whole person; a sickly smile quivered about his lips;
and I saw that he spoke in a low, hurried, and gibbering
murmur, as if unconscious of my presence. Bending closely over him, I at length drank in the hideous import of his
words.

"Not hear it?—yes, I hear it, and *have* heard it. Long—
long—long—many minutes, many hours, many days, have
I heard it—yet I dared not—oh, pity me, miserable wretch
that I am!—I dared not—I *dared* not speak! *We have put
her living in the tomb!* Said I not that my senses were
acute? I *now* tell you that I heard her first feeble movements in the hollow coffin. I heard them—many, many
days ago—yet I dared not—*I dared not speak!* And now—
to-night—Ethelred—ha! ha!—the breaking of the hermit's
door, and the death-cry of the dragon, and the clangor of
the shield!—say, rather, the rending of her coffin, and the
grating of the iron hinges of her prison, and her struggles
within the coppered archway of the vault! Oh, whither
shall I fly? Will she not be here anon? Is she not hurrying
to upbraid me for my haste? Have I not heard her footstep
on the stair? Do I not distinguish that heavy and horrible
beating of her heart? Madman!"—here he sprang furiously
to his feet, and shrieked out his syllables, as if in the effort
he were giving up his soul—*"Madman! I tell you that she
now stands without the door!"*

As if in the superhuman energy of his utterance there
had been found the potency of a spell—the huge antique
panels to which the speaker pointed threw slowly back,
upon the instant, their ponderous and ebony jaws. It was
the work of the rushing gust—but then without those doors
there did stand the lofty and enshrouded figure of the lady
Madeline of Usher. There was blood upon her white robes,
and the evidence of some bitter struggle upon every portion of her emaciated frame. For a moment she remained

trembling and reeling to and fro upon the threshold— then, with a low, moaning cry, fell heavily inward upon the person of her brother, and in her violent and now final death-agonies, bore him to the floor a corpse, and a victim to the terrors he had anticipated.

From that chamber, and from that mansion, I fled aghast. The storm was still abroad in all its wrath as I found myself crossing the old causeway. Suddenly there shot along the path a wild light, and I turned to see whence a gleam so unusual could have issued; for the vast house and its shadows were alone behind me. The radiance was that of the full, setting, and blood-red moon, which now shone vividly through that once barely discernible fissure, of which I have before spoken as extending from the roof of the building, in a zigzag direction, to the base. While I gazed, this fissure rapidly widened—there came a fierce breath of the whirlwind—the entire orb of the satellite burst at once upon my sight—my brain reeled as I saw the mighty walls rushing asunder—there was a long tumultuous shouting sound like the voice of a thousand waters— and the deep and dank tarn at my feet closed sullenly and silently over the fragments of the *"House of Usher."*

Germelshausen: or, A Strange Village

Friedrich Gerstäcker

(1860, transl. 1870)

Part the First

It was in the autumn of the year 184– that a young and active man, knapsack on back and stick in hand, was leisurely pursuing the broad highway that led from Maxisfeld to Wichselhausen.

It was easy to see that he was no wandering apprentice, seeking work from place to place, even had not the small neat portfolio strapped to his knapsack betrayed his calling. No one could mistake him for anything but an artist. The black, broad-brimmed hat, set jauntily on one side, the long fair hair and promising beard, bore testimony thereto, no less than the well-worn black velvet coat, which seemed rather too warm for the season. He had flung it open, displaying his white shirt—for he wore no waistcoat—carelessly held together at the throat by a knotted black silk handkerchief.

The clock struck when he was about a quarter of a mile from Maxisfeld, and he stood still, leaning on his stick, and listening attentively to the full deep chime, whose reverberations fell on his ear with almost a startling distinctness. Even when they ceased he still remained standing some time, dreamily gazing on the hilly country round him—thinking of those he had left behind in that happy village home by the Taunus mountains, of his mother, of his sisters, till his eyes almost filled. But the transient cloud passed from his joyous spirit as quickly as it had arisen. Lifting his hat from his head, he waved a gay fare-well in the direction of his home, and, grasping his stick firmly in his hand, went merrily on his way.

The sun was rather powerful in the exposed and sandy high-road, and many a time did our tourist glance right and left in quest of some more agreeable foot-path. Once, indeed, a road did appear to the right, but it seemed no improvement on the other, and led too much out of the way. He therefore held on to the other, until he came at last to a rocky stream, across which lay the ruins of an old stone bridge. Beyond this ran a green path leading into a valley, and having no particular object in travelling that way, except enriching his sketch-book with picturesque studies, he leaped across the stream upon the newly-mown grass, and went along the elastic turf under the shadow of thick bushes of alders, rejoicing in the change.

"Now," thought he to himself, "I may truly say, for once, that I do not know where I am going. No accom-modating finger-posts here, to tell you what the nearest place is called, and mislead you so invariably about the distance. I should just like to know how the folks measure their miles in these parts. It is uncommonly quiet here; certainly the country people have nothing to do out-of-doors on holidays, and after being all the week behind the plough or alongside of the cart, they do not care much for a holiday walk, but get their first nap in church and their second after dinner at the public-house. And talking of that, a glass of beer wouldn't be so far amiss this pip-ing hot day, but, till that is forthcoming, this clear brook must serve my turn." And with that he threw off his knap-sack and hat, flung himself down by the water, and drank to his heart's content.

Cooled and refreshed by the draught, he only paused a few minutes to take a hasty sketch of an old, curiously misshapen willow growing near, then resumed his knapsack and pursued his way, caring very little where it might lead.

It might have been an hour that he trudged along, sketching as he went, a rock here, an alder thicket or knotty oaken bough there, as fancy or taste dictated. The sun had meanwhile risen higher in the heavens, and he was just considering that he must make the best of his way, if he meant to be in time for the noon-day meal at the nearest village, when he saw in the valley before him, seated by the stream on an old stone, a peasant girl, earnestly watching the path on which he was walking. Concealed as he was by the alders, he saw her before she saw him; the instant, however, that, following the course of the brook, his form became visible among the trees, she started up with a cry of joy and hastened to meet him.

She was a lovely girl of seventeen, dressed in a somewhat remarkable but becoming costume, and Arnold, for such was the young artist's name, stood motionless with surprise and admiration as she flew towards him with outstretched arms of welcome. He knew, of course, that this joyous greeting was not meant for him; the maiden, indeed, no sooner discerned his features than she stopped short in dismay, turned first pale and then red, and faltered at last, with timid confusion at her mistake—"I beg your pardon, sir; I—I thought—"

"That it was somebody else, my pretty maid," said the student, smiling, "and now you are out of humour that another strange and indifferent face obtrudes itself in your way. Do not be angry with me for not being the right person."

"How can you speak so, sir? What right have I to be angry? but oh, if you only knew how glad I should have been!"

"He does not deserve that you should wait for him, whoever he may be," said Arnold, more and more struck with the grace and beauty of the simple peasant girl. "Were I in his place, you should not have waited for me a minute."

"Oh," she said, blushing, "if he could have come he would have been here by this time. Perhaps he is ill, or perhaps—dead; "and with a deep, heartfelt sigh she resumed her seat.

"Is it so long, then, since you heard from him?"

"Very, very long."

"Then he lives a long way off?"

"Oh, yes, a long way—in Bischofsroda."

"Bischofsroda? I have just spent a month there, and know every soul in it. What is his name?"

"Henry Vollgut," said she, timidly; "the son of the magistrate at Bischofsroda."

"H'm," returned Arnold. "I was in and out of the magistrate's house constantly, and his name was Bauerling, and I never met with any one called Vollgut in the whole place."

"There might be more people there than you were aware of," returned the girl, and a slight smile lighted up her fair face, still more winning than its previous touching melancholy.

"But Bischofsroda," persisted the student, "is not so far off that a man could not be here in a couple of hours, or three at the most."

"And yet he is not come," she said, sighing heavily again; "and he promised me so faithfully."

"If so he will come, depend upon it; a fellow must have a heart of stone who made you a promise and broke it, and that I am sure your Henry has not."

"No, indeed," she replied, earnestly, "but I must wait for him no longer, as I must be home by noon, or my father will be angry."

"And your home is—where?"

"Close by in the valley. Do you not hear the bell? It is ringing for service."

Arnold listened, and the slow peal of a bell at no great distance fell indeed on his ear, but instead of a deep, full sound it was singularly sharp and discordant. It struck him, too, as he looked in that direction, that a thick fog hung over that part of the valley, which he had not noticed before.

"Your bell is cracked," said he, smiling; "it rings falsely."

"Yes, I know it does," she replied, calmly, "and we should long ago have had it recast, but there is never money or time enough, as we have no bell-founders in the neighbourhood. After all, what does it matter? We all know it, and know what its striking means, so a cracked bell does as well as another."

"And what is the name of your village?"

"Germelshausen."

"Is it on the road to Wichselhausen?"

"Oh, yes; by the foot-path it is hardly half an hour's walk, less, perhaps, for you, if you are a good walker."

"Then I will go to your village with you, pretty one, and if you have a good tavern, take my dinner there."

"The tavern is only too good," she returned, with a sigh, giving one more backward glance, to see if the expected one were coming.

"Can a tavern be too good?"

"Yes, for the peasant," she said, seriously, as she walked on through the valley; "for there is plenty of work to do at home in the evening, which is neglected if he stays at the tavern late."

"But I am neglecting nothing to-day."

"Oh, with gentlemen it is otherwise. They do not work, and therefore they have not much to neglect; the peasantry earn their bread for them."

"Not exactly," said Arnold, rather amused; "we must earn it ourselves, and pretty hard, too, for what the peasant does he expects to be well paid for."

"But you do not work, sir?"

"Why shouldn't I?"

"Your hands do not look as if you did."

"Come here, I will show you what my work is. Sit down for a moment on that flat stone by the old lilac-bush."

"But what am I to do there?"

"Never mind, sit down," said the artist, eagerly flinging off his knapsack, and seizing sketch-book and pencil.

"But indeed I must go home."

"I shall have done in five minutes. I want to take into the world with me a remembrance of you, which even Henry himself could find no fault with."

"A remembrance of me? You are joking."

"I am going to take your likeness with me."

"You are a painter, then?"

"Yes."

"I am glad of it; then you can restore the pictures in the church at Germelshausen, for they are in a very bad condition now."

"What is your name, pretty maid?" asked the student, who was sketching away as if for his life.

"Gertrude."

"And what is your father?"

"He is the village magistrate. If you are an artist you must not go to the inn; you must go home with me, and after dinner you can talk everything over with my father."

"About the church pictures?"

"Yes," said she, gravely; "and then you will have to stay with us a long, long time, till our day comes round again."

"Your day? What do you mean?"

She looked full at him, but made no reply, and raised her eyes to the clouds gathering overhead with an indescribable expression of sorrow and dejection. So lovely did she appear at that moment that he forgot everything else in the interest he took in the completion of his work. There was not much time allowed him. The young girl rose suddenly, threw a handkerchief over her head to protect her from the sun, and said—"I must go; the day is short, and they are expecting me at home."

Arnold had finished his little sketch, and, dashing in the folds of the dress with a couple of bold strokes, said, as he showed her the drawing, "Have I hit you off?"

"That is myself!" cried Gertrude, almost terrified.

"Who else should it be?" said Arnold, laughing.

"And you will keep that face and take it away with you?" asked the maiden, anxiously.

"Certainly I shall," he replied; "and when I am a long, long way off I shall think of you very often."

"But will my father allow that?"

"Allow me to think of you? Can he help it?"

"No; but that you should take that away with you—out into the world."

"He can't prevent me, sweetheart," said Arnold, good-humouredly, "but would it be unpleasant to you to know that it is in my hands?"

"To me? No," said she, after a brief hesitation, "if only —I must ask my father first."

"Silly child," laughed the young painter, "even a Princess can make no objection to an artist making her features his own; no blame can attach to you. But don't run away so fast, little thing, I am going with you, unless you mean to leave me here without any dinner. Have you forgotten the church pictures?"

"Oh, yes! the pictures," said the maiden, stopping to wait for him.

Arnold, who had hastily fastened up his portfolio, was in a moment by her side, and both walked briskly towards the village. This lay much nearer than he had supposed by the sound of the cracked bell, for that which he had taken from a distance for a thicket of alders, appeared as they approached to be a hedge-row of fruit-trees, half hidden behind which lay the old village, with its unpretending church tower and its smoke-blackened houses, to the east and north-east bordered by open fields. Here they turned into a good road, planted on either side with fruit-trees. But over the village hung the gloomy fog, which Arnold had observed before, and broke the clear sunlight, which could only fall with a yellowish, unnatural glitter over the weather-beaten roofs. Arnold, however, had hardly a glance for all this, for Gertrude, who walked by his side, as soon as they came to the first houses, deliberately took his hand, and holding it in hers, stepped with him into the nearest street. A strange emotion thrilled the young student with the touch of this warm hand, and involuntarily his eye sought to meet that of the maiden. But Gertrude looked not towards him; her eyes modestly fastened on the ground, she led the guest to her father's house, and Arnold's attention was at last attracted by the inhabitants of the village whom they met, all of whom passed by without a greeting. This struck him at once, for in all the neighbouring villages it was the rule to greet a stranger at least by a "Good day," or "God greet thee." Here no one thought of doing it, and, as in a large town, the people went indifferently by, only stopping here and there, staring after him, but no one addressed him. None of them even greeted the maiden.

How strange looked the old houses, with their carved, pointed gables, and weather-worn thatched roofs! In spite of its being Sunday, not a window looked fresh and clean; the round panes, set in lead, looked dull and mouldy. Here and there, however, one opened as they passed, and the friendly face of a maiden or ancient dame looked out. Arnold was particularly struck with the remarkable costume of the people, which was very unlike that of the neighbouring villages. An indescribable stillness reigned over everything, and the young painter, to whom the silence became at last oppressive, said to his guide—"Do they keep *fête* days so strictly in your village that people, when they meet, do not even salute each other? If we did not hear now and then a dog bark, or a cock crow, one might imagine the place was dumb and dead."

"It is noontide," said Gertrude, calmly, "and people are not inclined to talk; you will find them merry enough this evening."

"Thank goodness," said Arnold, "here are some children playing in the street at any rate; everything was beginning to feel quite ghostly. We keep holiday differently in Bischofsroda."

"That is my father's house," said Gertrude, softly.

"But," said Arnold, laughing, "I have no business to walk in to dinner uninvited; I may be unwelcome. I only like to see friendly faces at table. Be kind enough to show me the inn, or let me find it for myself. Unless Germelshausen is an exception to other villages, it will be close to the church, and if you want the ale-house, you cannot do wrong in following the steeple."

"You are right, it is just there," said Gertrude, composedly; "but they are already expecting us at home, and you need not be afraid that you will not be welcomed."

"Expecting us? Ah, you mean your Henry! Yes, Gertrude, if you would take me to-day in his place, then I would stay with you till you yourself sent me away." He had spoken these last words with unconscious earnestness, gently pressing the hand that held his.

Gertrude stood suddenly still, looked him full in the face, and said, "Would you indeed?"

"Joyfully," replied the young man, now completely fascinated with the wonderful beauty of the maiden.

Gertrude said no more, but pursuing her way as if pon-
dering over the words of her companion, stopped at last
before a good-sized house, with a broad flight of stone
steps leading up to the door, and said again, with her former bashful timidity, "Here is where I live, sir, and if you
will be kind enough to come in with me to my father, he
will be proud to see you at his table."

Before Arnold could reply, the justice himself came out
on the steps, and a window opened above, at which appeared the good-natured face of an old woman.

"Why, Gertrude," said her father, "you have been away
very long this morning, and heyday! what a fine young
fellow you have brought home with you!"

"My good sir,—"

"There, don't stand upon the steps, come along; the
dumplings are ready, and they will be as hard as brickbats
presently."

"Yes, but that's not Henry," called out the old woman
from the window; "didn't I tell you he would never come
back?"

"All right, mother, all right," said the justice; "it's all
the same." And holding out his hand to the stranger, he
continued, "A hearty welcome to Germelshausen, young
gentleman, wherever my girl may have picked you up. Now
come to dinner, and fall to lustily; we can talk of other
things afterwards."

He allowed the young painter no more time for apology, shaking him heartily by the hand, which Gertrude
had let go as soon as he set foot on the stone step, drew
his arm in his, and led him into the family sitting-room.
Even in the house there prevailed a damp, earthy atmosphere, and accustomed as Arnold was to the habits of the
German peasant, who prefers to shut out all fresh air from
his room, and even in summer often lights the stove to
produce the roasting heat in which he delights, it struck

him as something unusual. The narrow entrance was by no
means inviting. The whitewash had fallen from the walls,
and appeared to have been only carelessly swept aside.
The solitary, dusky window at the back threw but scanty
light upon it, and the staircase leading to the upper floor
was old and decayed. Very little time, however, had he to
observe all this, for the next moment his host opened
the parlour-door, and Arnold found himself in a low, but
capacious, airy room, strewed with white sand, and in the
centre a table covered with a snowy linen cloth, an agreeable contrast to the somewhat repulsive effect of the rest
of the house.

Besides the old woman, who had now shut the window
and drawn her chair to the table, two rosy children sat
in the corner, and a buxom countrywoman—her costume
also unlike that of the adjacent villages—was admitting
a maid-servant bearing a large dish. And now the dumplings smoked upon the table, and all drew in their seats
for the welcome meal. No one, however, sat down, and
the children, as Arnold observed, looked with trembling
anxiety at their father. The latter approached his chair,
rested his arm upon it, and looked silently and gloomily
on the ground. Was he asking a blessing? Arnold saw that
his lips were tightly compressed, and his right hand hung
clenched by his side. There was no devotion in his features,
only rigid and yet irresolute defiance. Gertrude went softly up to him and laid her hand on his shoulder, and the
old woman stood speechless opposite, watching him with
anxious, imploring looks.

"Let us have our dinner," said the man abruptly, at last;
"it can't be helped."

He pushed a chair to his guest, and taking another himself, he seized the large ladle, and began to help the party.
At first it was anything but a cheerful meal. The whole
appearance of the man struck Arnold as unnatural, and the

evident depression of the others was not without its effect
on himself. The justice, however was not a man to spoil
his dinner with melancholy thoughts. As he rapped on the
table, the maid came in with glasses and bottles of rare old
wine, which soon infused new life into the party.

Through Arnold's veins the glorious liquor ran like
fire; never in his life had he tasted anything like it. Even
Gertrude drank of it, as well as the old woman, who sat at
her spinning-wheel in the corner, and murmured a little
song about the merry life in Germelshausen. The justice
was most changed of all. His manner was now as free and
joyous as it had been silent and serious before, and Arnold
himself could not resist the influence of that rare vintage.
Before he quite knew how it came about, the justice had
taken up a violin, and was playing a merry dance, and
Arnold, the fair Gertrude on his arm, whirled round the
room so wildly that he overturned the spinning-wheel and
the chairs, besides knocking up against the maid who was
trying to clear the table, and played such comical antics
that the whole party were in fits of laughter.

Suddenly all was still, and as Arnold looked with wonder at the justice, the latter pointed with his bow to the
window, and returned the instrument to the great wooden
chest from which it had been taken. Arnold turned to the
window, and saw that a coffin was being borne through the
streets. Six men in white linen carried it on their shoulders, and behind them walked an old man, holding by the
hand a little fair-haired girl. The old man walked on as if
wrapped up in his own thoughts, but the child, who could
not have been more than four years old, and knew nothing
of what lay in that dark coffin, nodded gaily to every familiar face she saw, and once laughed out merrily at the gam-
bols of a couple of dogs playing on the schoolhouse steps.

The silence lasted as long as the funeral was in sight;
and then Gertrude, approaching the young painter, said,

"Let us now be quiet for a little while. You have been wild enough; that strong wine got into your head. Fetch your hat, and we will have a short walk together; when we come back it will be time to go to the inn, for there is a dance to-night."

"Dance! that's right," replied Arnold, delighted; "I am come at the right time. And the first dance you are engaged to me."

"Certainly, if you wish it."

Arnold had already his hat and portfolio.

"What is that book for?" asked the justice.

"He draws, father," said Gertrude; "he has already taken my likeness."

The young man opened his portfolio, and showed the picture to the justice, who examined it for a short time in silence.

"And you want to take that home with you," he said at last; "and perhaps put it in a frame, and hang it up in your room?"

"And why not?" said Arnold.

"May he, father?" asked Gertrude.

"If he does not stay with us," replied the justice, jocosely, "I've no objection to his carrying it away with him, but there is one thing wanting."

"What?"

"The funeral that has just passed. Paint that into the picture, and you may take it away with you."

"Put the funeral by Gertrude's side!"

"There's room enough," said her father, doggedly; "and there it must be, or else I don't allow you to take my girl's portrait away with you. In such grave company, no one could think any harm of it."

Arnold shook his head, amused at the extraordinary notion of giving that fair girl a funeral as chaperone. The old man, however, seemed so strangely bent upon it, that to satisfy him he did as he wished. He could take the melancholy addition out again at his leisure. His skilful hand soon sketched from memory the figures he had seen pass, and the whole family pressed round him in undisguised astonishment at the rapid progress of the drawing.

"Have I done it right?" cried Arnold at last, as he sprung up, and held the picture at arm's length.

"Capitally," said the justice, nodding to him; "I could not have believed you could have done it so soon. Now you may have it if you like; and away with you for your walk to see the village, it may be long before you have such another opportunity. Only be back by five o'clock; we keep a feast to-night, and you must be there."

The atmosphere of the room had by this time become oppressive to Arnold, heated with the strong wine he had taken; he longed for the fresh air, and in a few minutes he and his fair companion were pursuing the road through the village. It was no longer quiet, as it had been before; children were playing in the street, the old people sitting at their doors watching them, and the whole place, with its curious old buildings, would have had a cheerful aspect could the sun have penetrated the thick brown smoke that hung like a cloud over the roofs.

"Is there a wood on fire in this neighbourhood?" he asked; "this smoke lies over no other village about here, and cannot be caused by the chimneys."

"It is fog," said Gertrude, calmly; "but have you never heard of Germelshausen?"

"Never."

"That is extraordinary, and the village so very, very old."

"The houses look so, at any rate, and the people have all such a remarkable appearance, and your dialect is unlike that of your neighbours; I suppose you go very little out of your village?"

"Very little," said Gertrude, shortly.

"And not a single swallow left! they can't have been long gone."

"For a long time," she answered, "they have not built their nests in Germelshausen. Perhaps they cannot bear the fog."

"But you don't always have it?"

"Always."

"That must be the reason that your fruit-trees do not bear, and yet at Maxisfeld they are obliged to support the branches, the produce this year is so abundant."

She made no answer, but walked silently by his side until they reached the extremity of the village. On the way she occasionally nodded and exchanged a word with one of the young girls, perhaps about the evening dance. And the girls, as they passed the young artist, looked at him with such compassionate glances, that he felt sadness stealing over him; but he could not trust himself to tell Gertrude the reason.

Part the Second

At last they had reached the further end, and lively as the village itself might be, everything here was still, solitary, and deathlike. The gardens looked as if they had not been trimmed for many years, grass grew in the pathways, and the young stranger noticed again that there was not a single apple or pear on any of the trees. Several people met them, among whom Arnold recognised the funeral procession on its way home. The mourners returned to the village as silently as they had left it. Arnold and his companion involuntarily bent their steps towards the cemetery. Wishing to cheer his guide, who had become very pensive, Arnold described other places he had visited, and how things went on in the outer world. She had never seen a railway, never even heard of one, and listened to his account with astonishment and attention. She knew nothing

of the telegraph, or of any other recent inventions; and
the young artist could not understand how it was possible
that people could be found living in Germany so completely shut out from the rest of the world.

During this conversation they reached "God's acre,"
and here he was equally struck by the antiquity of the
head-stones and monuments, simple as they all were.

"This is an old stone indeed," said he, as he bent over
the nearest, and with some difficulty deciphered the inscription: "Anna Maria Berthold, born Siegliz. Born December 1,
1181; died December 2, 1224."

"That is my mother," said Gertrude, gravely, as two large
bright tears filled her eyes, and rolled slowly down her cheeks.

"Your mother, dear Gertrude!" said Arnold, in amazement; "your ancestress you mean."

"No," she replied, "my own mother. My father married
again, and she you saw at home is my step-mother."

"But this stone says she died in 1224?"

"What matters the year?" she said, mournfully; "it is
sad enough to be parted from one's mother, and yet," she
added gently, and in a tone of deepest anguish, "perhaps it
was as well that God took her when He did."

Arnold shook his head, and stooped over the stone to
examine the inscription more closely, thinking, perhaps,
that the first 2 in the date of the year might really be an 8;
but the second 2 was exactly like the other, and 1884 was
impossible. It might have been a mistake of the stone-cut-
ter, and Gertrude appeared so absorbed in thoughts of the
departed that he did not like to disturb her with any more
questions. He left her for a time by the stone, on which
she had sunk down in prayer, and went to examine the
other monuments; but all, without exception, bore dates of
many hundred years back; no newer stone could be found,
although that burials still took place there, the last fresh
grave bore witness. From the low churchyard wall, there

was a very good view of the village, and Arnold seized the opportunity to make a sketch of it. But even over this spot hung the extraordinary smoke, while the sunshine was falling brightly over the distant hills and woods. At this moment, the old cracked bell struck the hour, and Gertrude, starting up in haste and dashing the tears from her eyes, invited the young man to follow her. Arnold was quickly by her side.

"Now," said she, smiling, "we must grieve no more; the church bell gives notice that it is time to dance. You have till now been under the impression that we of Germelshausen are melancholy folks; this evening you shall be convinced of the contrary."

"But those are surely the church doors, and I see nobody coming out."

"That is but natural," laughed the young girl, "because no one has been in, not even the Priest. Only the old sacristan allows himself no rest, and goes through the form of ringing the bells."

"And none of you go to church?"

"No, neither to Mass nor to confession," she replied, composedly; "we have a quarrel with the Pope, who lives among the Italians, and he won't allow it until we obey him again."

"Well, this is the first I have heard of it!"

"Ah!" said she, carelessly, "it was a long time ago. Look, there comes the sacristan out of the church alone, shutting the doors; he will not go this evening to the inn, but sit quietly at home."

"But the Priest comes?"

"Oh, that he does, and is the merriest of the party; he does not take it at all to heart."

"But when did all this happen?" asked Arnold, less interested in the facts themselves, than in her ingenuous manner of relating them.

"Ah," she said, "it is a long story, and the Priest has written it all out in a large, thick book. You can read it there, if it amuses you, and you understand Latin. But mind and say nothing about it when my father is by, for he hates the subject. Look! here come all the young people out of the houses. I must make haste home and dress, that I may not be the last."

"And the first dance, Gertrude?"

"Is yours, that I promise you."

Both quickly retraced their steps back to the village, which was animated with a very different spirit from that of the morning. Joyous groups of young people were collected everywhere, all dressed in their best; and at the inn to which they were flocking, garlands of flowers hung from the windows, and triumphant arches were raised at the doors. When Arnold saw everybody so smart, he felt that his travelling costume would never do; so he hastily pulled his best coat out of his knapsack, and had just completed a hurried toilet when Gertrude knocked at his door, and called him out. And strangely beautiful she looked in her simple, yet rich attire, as she cordially invited him to accompany her, leaving her father and mother to follow later.

"She doesn't take Henry's absence much to heart," he thought gaily, as he drew her arm in his, and hastened in the deepening twilight to the dancing-hall; but he took care not to express his thoughts on that subject, for the strange emotion that he had felt before thrilled his breast, and his heart beat higher in his bosom as he felt that fair girl hang on his arm.

"I must leave you to-morrow," sighed he, gently; almost involuntarily the words were whispered in the ear of his companion.

She replied, with a smile, "Do not trouble yourself about that; we shall be a long time together, longer, perhaps, than you will like."

"Should you like me then, Gertrude, to stay with you?"
he asked, the blood rushing to his temples as he spoke.

"Of course I should," was her naive reply; "you are so
good and kind, and my father likes you so much, and—
Henry is not yet come!" she added indignantly.

"And if he should come to-morrow?"

"To-morrow!" said Gertrude, fixing on him her large, dark
eyes, full of deep meaning. "A long, long night lies between.
To-morrow! you will know to-morrow what that word means.
But no more of that now"—breaking off in a more cheerful
tone—"this is our festival, to which we have been looking
forward so long, so very long; and we must not spoil it with
melancholy thoughts. Here we are at the inn. The company
will be surprised to see I have brought a new dancer with me."

Arnold would have questioned her further, but the
loud music which sounded from within quite drowned his
words. They were curious tunes that the musicians played;
he did not recognise one of them, and was at first quite
dazzled by the glare of the numerous lights. Gertrude led
him into the middle of the hall, where a crowd of young
peasant girls stood chattering together, and there left him
to himself that he might look about him before the dance
began, and become acquainted with the other young men.
The artist did not at first feel very comfortable amongst
so many strange faces; the remarkable costume and dialect
of the people perplexed him, and sweet as that unaccustomed accent might sound from Gertrude's lips, it seemed
very harsh when spoken by others. The young men seemed
disposed to be friendly, and one coming up, took him by
the hand, saying, "So you are going to stay with us, sir; we
lead a merry life, and the interval passes very fast."

"What interval?" asked Arnold, less astonished by the
expression than by the youth's appearing so convinced that
he intended to make the village his home. "You mean until
I return?"

"You mean to go?" asked the other, hastily.

"To-morrow, yes—or the day after to-morrow; but I am coming back."

"*To-morrow?*" laughed the young man. "Oh, that's all right. Yes, we can talk about that *to-morrow*. But come, that I may show you some of our amusements; because if you really mean to go away to-morrow, you may not have such another opportunity."

The bystanders laughed significantly together, and the young peasant, again taking Arnold's arm, led him right through the house, which was full of joyous guests. The first room they came to was occupied by card-players, each with a heap of gold before him. A second was devoted to the national game of ninepins, and a third to round games, and other sportive amusements; the young girls walking up and down, laughing and talking with their cavaliers, till a burst of music from the instruments, the signal for the dance, was given, and Gertrude stood by Arnold's side, and touched his arm.

"Come," she said, "we must not be the last, for as the justice's daughter, I must open the ball."

"What a strange melody that is," said Arnold; "how I shall dance to it, I cannot imagine."

"It will soon come," laughed Gertrude; "in five minutes you will feel at home in it, and I will help you through."

All now pressed gaily forward into the dancing-room, with the exception of the card-players, and in the bliss of holding that beautiful girl in his arms, Arnold forgot everything else. Again and again he danced with Gertrude, and though the other maidens made significant signs as they passed, no one attempted to dispute his right to his fair partner. One circumstance alone startled him. Close to the inn stood the old church, and from the hall could plainly be heard the shrill, discordant strokes of the old cracked bell. The effect of the first stroke was as if the wand of a magician had touched the assembly. The music broke off suddenly, and every one of the gay crowd stood motionless, silently counting the hour. With the last stroke, new life and merriment returned. This occurred at eight, at nine, and at ten o'clock, and when Arnold would have asked the reason, Gertrude put her finger on her lips, and looked so grave and sorrowful, that for the world he would not have vexed her by asking again.

At about ten o'clock there was a pause, and the musicians, whose lungs ought to have been of iron, preceded the young people into the supper-room. There all was merriment; the wine flowed freely, and Arnold, who could only do as others did, began to calculate the hole this wonderful evening would make in his travelling purse. But Gertrude sat close by him, and drank with him out of the same glass, and how could he dwell upon such sordid cares? And suppose Henry came to-morrow?

Eleven began to strike, and, as before, the revellers were silent, while there was the breathless counting of the slow, dull strokes. A strange horror came over Arnold, he knew not why; and he thought of his home and his mother. Slowly he raised his glass to his lips, and drank to the dear ones far away. The clock had struck, and the guests had sprung up from the table; the dance recommenced, and all hurried back to the hall.

"Whose health did you drink last?" asked Gertrude, as he drew her arm in his again.

He hesitated to answer. Would she laugh at him if he told her? No, she had prayed too tenderly that morning at her own mother's grave; and he answered in a low voice, "My mother's."

Gertrude said nothing as they ascended the stairs, but she laughed no more, and before beginning their dance, she asked him, "Do you love your mother so much?"

"Better than my life."

"And she loves you?"

"Does not a mother love her child?"

"And suppose you never went back to her?"

"Poor mother!" said Arnold, "her heart would break."

"The dance is beginning again," said she, hastily; "come, we must not lose a moment!"

And wilder than ever began the dance; so wildly, that Arnold began to wish himself out of it, and Gertrude also grew more grave and silent. Every moment the revel waxed higher and higher, and in a momentary pause, the old justice came up, patted the young man on the shoulder, and said, laughing, "That's right, young gentleman, shake your legs well to-night, you will have plenty of time to rest afterwards. Why, Trudchen, what are you looking so serious about? Is that a face for a dance? Be merry, I say! hear how they are going on! I must go and find my old lady, that we may have the last dance together. Keep it up! Those musicians are blowing their very breath out of their bodies." And humming a jolly chorus, he pressed through the crowd and disappeared.

Arnold was leading Gertrude to her place in the dance, but she suddenly drew back, seized his arm, and whispered, "Come!" He was allowed no time to ask where, for she glided from him, and escaped out of the hall.

"Where are you going, Trudchen?" asked one of her companions.

"I shall be back in a minute," was her brief answer, and in a few seconds she was standing with Arnold in the fresh night air.

"Where are you going, Gertrude?"

"Come!" Again she seized his arm, led him through the village to her father's house, into which she darted for a moment, and returned with a small bundle.

"What's that for?"

"Come!" was the sole reply, and she hurried him down the street, till the old walls of the village were left behind them. They had hitherto followed the broad highway, but now Gertrude struck off to the left, and up a small hillock, from which could be seen the illuminated doors and windows of the inn. Here she stood still, held out her hand to Arnold, and said earnestly—"Commend me to your mother. Farewell."

"Gertrude," he cried, in great agitation, "why do you send me from you like this in the middle of the night? Have I said one word to hurt you?"

"No, Arnold," she replied, for the first time calling him by name; "it is because I care for you that you must go."

"But I am not going to let you go back alone in the dark through the village," said Arnold, entreatingly. "You do not know how I love you, or the hold that you have taken on my heart in these few hours. You do not know—"

"Say no more," interrupted Gertrude, hastily; "we will not take leave of each other. When the clock has struck twelve—and it hardly wants ten minutes to it—then come back to the door of the inn. There I will wait for you."

"And till then—"

"Till then remain where you are. Promise me that you will not take a step, either to the right or to the left, till it has struck twelve."

"I promise, Gertrude; but then?"

"Then come," she said, held out her hand, and turned to go.

"Gertrude!" he cried, in the tone of the most bitter grief.

She hesitated one instant, then suddenly turned to him again, threw her arms round his neck, and he felt her icy lips pressed to his own. 'Twas but for one moment; the next she had tore herself away and fled to the village, and Arnold remained filled with wonder and excitement, but compelled by his promise to stay on the spot where she had left him.

Now, for the first time, he observed how the weather had changed in the last few hours. The wind howled in the trees, the heavens were covered with wild hurrying clouds, and several large raindrops gave warning of a coming storm. The lights from the inn shone brightly through the darkness, and occasional gusts of the wind brought the broken sound of the orchestra to his ears, but not for long. He had not been left alone many minutes before the old clock struck twelve.

In the same moment the music ceased, or was overpowered by the raging storm, which broke overhead so fiercely that Arnold was forced to crouch on the earth to avoid being blown off his feet. As he did so, he felt the bundle Gertrude had brought from the house. It was his knapsack and portfolio. He started up again in terror. The hour had struck, the wind howled as fiercely as ever, but not a light was any longer to be seen in the village. Even the dogs, which up to this time had been barking and howling, were now silent, and thick damp clouds rose up out of the valley.

"The time is up," muttered Arnold, as he threw his knapsack over his shoulder, "and I must see Gertrude once more, for I cannot part with her like this. The dance is over, and everybody must be going home; if the justice will not accommodate me for the night I must stay at the inn. I shall never find my way through the forest in the dark."

Carefully he descended the little eminence up which Gertrude had brought him, to return to the broad high-road which led into the village, but in vain did he grope among the bushes to find it. The ground had become soft and boggy, and in his thin boots he sank up to his ancles in mud, while a dense thicket of alders presented itself everywhere instead of the firm path. He could never have crossed it in the dark; he must find it if he went on, and, besides, he knew that the old wall of the village was just below, that he could not miss. But with all his pains he sought it in vain; the further he attempted to go the softer and more boggy became the ground, the bushes grew thicker, and so full of briars that his clothes were torn, and his hands streamed with blood. Coming from the village, had he taken the right or the left? He was afraid to bewilder himself still further, and having found a tolerably dry spot, he resolved to remain there until the clock had struck one. But it struck no more; not a dog howled, not a single human sound reached him, and with pain and difficulty, wet through, and shivering with cold, he struggled at last back to the hillock where Gertrude had left him. Twice from that spot he again attempted to pierce the thicket and find the village, but to no purpose. Completely exhausted, and filled with indescribable dread, he gave it up at last and sought the shelter of a tree, under which to pass the night.

Slowly, very slowly, passed the hours, for he was much too cold to hope for a moment's sleep. Every instant he was starting up to listen, fancying that he could hear the clang of the old bell again, but always finding himself mistaken. At length the first glimmer appeared in the east; the clouds had dispersed, the sky was clear and starry, the half-awakened birds chirped among the trees, and as the daylight increased he was able to recognise his position. But vain were his eager glances in search of the brown old church tower and the weather-worn roofs. Nothing but a thicket of alders, interspersed with a few stunted willows, extended on every side. Not a path was to be seen either right or left, nor any trace that a human dwelling was in the neighbourhood. The first rays of the sun now broke over the valley, and Arnold, determined to get at the bottom of the mystery, walked back a considerable part of the way he had come yesterday. He must, he thought, have missed his road, and have got gradually further from it in the dark, and, happen what may, he could find it now.

Presently he came to the stone where he had taken Gertrude's likeness—that spot he would have known among a thousand. He now knew exactly the way he had gone and the direction in which Germelshausen lay, and walked hastily back into the valley by the road which he had taken with Gertrude. Here he recognised the spot over which he had seen the thick smoke; nothing but an alder-bush concealed the first houses from him—it was all right now. He reached it, forced his way through, and found himself in the same boggy morass through which he had been struggling in the night. Hardly believing his own senses, he tried to force a passage, but so wet was the swamp that he was obliged to return to the dry land. The village had disappeared.

In this useless search many hours had passed, and his weary limbs failed him entirely. He could do no more, and he must rest; at the first village that he reached he could easily ask for a guide to Germelshausen, and take care not to miss his road again. Tired to death he threw himself under a tree—a deplorable object in his best clothes, it must be confessed, but that troubled him little. He took out his portfolio, and from it Gertrude's portrait, gazing sorrowfully on her beloved features. Of the deep impression they had made on his heart he was now for the first time aware. The boughs parted behind him, a dog sprang forward, and, as he hastily started up, he saw an old forester standing near, and looking at him with considerable curiosity.

"God greet you," cried Arnold, rejoiced to see a human face, and thrusting the drawing back into his portfolio. "I am very glad to see you, friend, for I believe I have lost my way."

"H'm," said the old man, "I think so too, if you have been all night among the bushes, and Dillstedt, with a good inn, not half a mile off. Bless my heart, you look as if you had been up to your neck among the thorns and bog."

"You know the forest well, then?" asked Arnold.

"Rather," laughed the other, as he struck a light for his pipe.

"What is the name of the next village?"

"Dillstedt—just out yonder. Go up that little hill, and you will see it lie just below you."

"And how far is it to Germelshausen?"

"*Where?*" asked the forester, taking his pipe from his mouth.

"To Germelshausen?"

"Upon my word," said the old man, looking keenly at him, "I know the forest well enough, but how many fathoms deep in the earth the 'Enchanted Village' lies, God only knows, and it does not concern us."

"The enchanted village!" cried Arnold.

"Germelshausen—yes, exactly," said the forester. "Where the bog is now, with the old willows and alders, it is said to have stood many hundred years ago, after which it sank down, nobody knows why or where; and the story goes, that every hundred years, on a certain day, it returns to the light, though no Christian would wish to come upon it by accident. But, I tell you what, this sleeping among the bushes does not seem to have agreed with you—you look as if you had seen a ghost. Take a pull at my flask, it will do you good. Down with it."

"Much obliged."

"Oh, that was not half enough. Try it again; it's the right sort of stuff, I can tell you. And now make haste on to your inn, and get into a warm bed."

"At Dillstedt?"

"Yes, of course; there is no nearer."

"And Germelshausen?"

"Do me the favour not to mention that place again just on this particular spot. Leave the dead in peace, and especially those who are said to have no peace, and may be standing invisibly between us now."

"But yesterday," said Arnold, who could command himself no longer, "yesterday the village stood here; I was in it—eat, drank, and danced there."

The forester looked at the young man from head to foot; then replied, with a smile—"Yes, but it had another name, hadn't it? There was a dance at Dillstedt yesterday, and mine host brews such strong beer that you might well lose your way."

For all reply, Arnold opened his portfolio, and took out the sketch he had made from the churchyard.

"Do you know that village?"

"No," said the forester, shaking his head; "there is no such town as that in the whole neighbourhood."

"That is Germelshausen. And do your young peasant girls dress like this girl?"

"H'm! no; I can't say they do. But what a strange funeral procession you have there."

Arnold made no answer; he returned the sketches to his portfolio, and heaved a deep sigh.

"You can't mistake the road to Dillstedt," said the forester, kindly, for a suspicion crossed his mind that the stranger was not quite right in his head, "but I will go with you if you like; it will not take me much out of my way."

"Thank you," replied Arnold, "I can easily find it myself. Then it is only once in a hundred years that the village reappears?"

"So people say," returned the forester. "Whether it is true or not is more than I can tell you."

Arnold resumed his knapsack. "God be with you," he said to the forester, holding out his hand.

"And with you," replied the other. "Where are you going now?"

"To Dillstedt."

"That's right. Just beyond that little hill you will come upon the broad road."

Arnold turned away, and walked slowly on till he reached the summit of the hill. There he could see the whole valley; he stopped short and looked back.

"Farewell, Gertrude," murmured he, softly, and went down the hill, the tears gushing from his eyes.

Mysterious Disappearances

Charles Bierce

(1888-1909)

The Difficulty of Crossing a Field

One morning in July, 1854, a planter named Williamson, living six miles from Selma, Alabama, was sitting with his wife and a child on the veranda of his dwelling. Immediately in front of the house was a lawn, perhaps fifty yards in extent between the house and public road, or, as it was called, the "pike." Beyond this road lay a close-cropped pasture of some ten acres, level and without a tree, rock, or any natural or artificial object on its surface. At the time there was not even a domestic animal in the field. In another field, beyond the pasture, a dozen slaves were at work under an overseer.

Throwing away the stump of a cigar, the planter rose, saying: "I forgot to tell Andrew about those horses." Andrew was the overseer.

Williamson strolled leisurely down the gravel walk, plucking a flower as he went, passed across the road and into the pasture, pausing a moment as he closed the gate leading into it, to greet a passing neighbor, Mr. Armour Wren, who lived on the adjoining plantation. Mr. Wren was in an open carriage with his son James, a lad of thirteen. When he had driven some two hundred yards from the point of meeting, Mr. Wren said to his son: "I forgot to tell Mr. Williamson about those horses."

Mr. Wren had sold to Mr. Williamson some horses, which were to have been sent for that day, but for some reason not now remembered it would be inconvenient to deliver them until the morrow. The coachman was directed to drive back, and as the vehicle turned Williamson was seen by all three, walking leisurely across the pasture. At that moment one of the coach horses stumbled and came near falling. It had no more than fairly recovered itself when James Wren cried: "Why, father, what has become of Mr. Williamson?"

It is not the purpose of this narrative to answer that question.

Mr. Wren's strange account of the matter, given under oath in the course of legal proceedings relating to the Williamson estate, here follows:

> "My son's exclamation caused me to look toward the spot where I had seen the deceased [*sic*] an instant before, but he was not there, nor was he anywhere visible. I cannot say that at the moment I was greatly startled, or realized the gravity of the occurrence, though I thought it singular. My son, however, was greatly astonished and kept repeating his question in different forms until we arrived at the gate. My black boy Sam was similarly affected, even in a greater degree, but I reckon more by my son's manner than by anything he had himself observed. [This sentence in the testimony was stricken out.] As we got out of the carriage at the gate of the field, and while Sam was hanging [*sic*] the team to the fence, Mrs. Williamson, with her child in her arms and followed by several servants, came running down the walk in great excitement,

crying: 'He is gone, he is gone! O God! what an awful thing!' and many other such exclamations, which I do not distinctly recollect. I got from them the impression that they related to something more than the mere disappearance of her husband, even if that had occurred before her eyes. Her manner was wild, but not more so, I think, than was natural under the circumstances. I have no reason to think she had at that time lost her mind. I have never since seen nor heard of Mr. Williamson."

This testimony, as might have been expected, was corroborated in almost every particular by the only other eye-witness (if that is a proper term), the lad James. Mrs. Williamson had lost her reason and the servants were, of course, not competent to testify. The boy James Wren had declared at first that he *saw* the disappearance, but there is nothing of this in his testimony given in court. None of the field hands working in the field to which Williamson was going had seen him at all, and the most rigorous search of the entire plantation and adjoining country failed to supply a clew. The most monstrous and grotesque fictions, originating with the blacks, were current in that part of the State for many years, and probably are to this day; but what has been here related is all that is certainly known of the matter. The courts decided that Williamson was dead, and his estate was distributed according to law.

An Unfinished Race

James Burne Worson was a shoemaker who lived in Leamington, Warwickshire, England. He had a little shop in one of the by-ways leading off the road to Warwick. In his humble sphere he was esteemed an honest man, although like many of his class in English towns he was somewhat addicted to drink. When in liquor he would make foolish wagers. On one of these too frequent occasions he was boasting of his prowess as a pedestrian and athlete, and the outcome was a match against nature. For a stake of one sovereign he undertook to run all the way to Coventry and back, a distance of something more than forty miles. This was on the 3d day of September in 1873. He set out at once, the man with whom he had made the bet—whose name is not recorded—accompanied by Barham Wise, a linen draper, and Hamerson Burns, a photographer, I think, following in a light cart or wagon.

For several miles Worson went on very well, at an easy gait, without apparent fatigue, for he had really great powers of endurance and was not sufficiently intoxicated to enfeeble them. The three men in the wagon kept a short distance in the rear, giving him occasional friendly "chaff" or encouragement, as the spirit moved them. Suddenly— in the very middle of the roadway, not a dozen yards from them, and with their eyes full upon him—the man seemed to stumble, pitched headlong forward, uttered a terrible cry and vanished. He did not fall to the earth—he vanished before touching it. No trace of him was ever discovered.

After remaining at and about the spot for some time, with aimless irresolution, the three men returned to Leamington, told their astonishing story and were afterward taken into custody. But they were of good standing, had always been considered truthful, were sober at the time of the occurrence, and nothing ever transpired to discredit their sworn account of their extraordinary adventure; concerning the truth of which, nevertheless, public opinion was divided, throughout the United Kingdom. If they had something to conceal, their choice of means is certainly one of the most amazing ever made by sane human beings.

Charles Ashmore's Trail

The family of Christian Ashmore consisted of his wife, his mother, two grown daughters, and a son of sixteen years. They lived in Troy, New York, were well-to-do, respectable persons, and had many friends, some of whom, reading these lines, will doubtless learn for the first time the extraordinary fate of the young man. From Troy the Ashmores moved in 1871 or 1872 to Richmond, Indiana, and a year or two later to the vicinity of Quincy, Illinois, where Mr. Ashmore bought a farm and lived on it. At some little distance from the farmhouse was a spring with a constant flow of clear, cold water, whence the family derived its supply for domestic use at all seasons.

On the evening of the 9th of November in 1878, at about nine o'clock, young Charles Ashmore left the family circle about the hearth, took a tin bucket and started toward the spring. As he did not return, the family became uneasy, and going to the door by which he had left the house, his father called without receiving an answer. He then lighted a lantern and with the eldest daughter, Martha, who insisted on accompanying him, went in search. A light snow had fallen, obliterating the path, but making the young man's trail conspicuous; each footprint was plainly defined. After going a little more than half-way—perhaps seventy-five yards—the father, who was in advance, halted, and elevating his lantern stood peering intently into the darkness ahead.

"What is the matter, father?" the girl asked.

This was the matter: the trail of the young man had abruptly ended, and all beyond was smooth, unbroken snow. The last footprints were as conspicuous as any in the line; the very nail-marks were distinctly visible. Mr. Ashmore looked upward, shading his eyes with his hat held between them and the lantern. The stars were shining; there was not a cloud in the sky; he was denied the explanation which had suggested itself, doubtful as it would have been—a new snowfall with a limit so plainly defined. Taking a wide circuit round the ultimate tracks, so as to leave them undisturbed for further examination, the man proceeded to the spring, the girl following, weak and terrified. Neither had spoken a word of what both had observed. The spring was covered with ice, hours old.

Returning to the house they noted the appearance of the snow on both sides of the trail its entire length. No tracks led away from it. The morning light showed nothing more. Smooth, spotless, unbroken, the shallow snow lay everywhere.

Four days later the grief-stricken mother herself went to the spring for water. She came back and related that in passing the spot where the footprints had ended she had heard the voice of her son and had been eagerly calling to him, wandering about the place, as she had fancied the voice to be now in one direction, now in another, until she was exhausted with fatigue and emotion. Questioned as to what the voice had said, she was unable to tell, yet averred that the words were perfectly distinct. In a moment the entire family was at the place, but nothing was heard, and the voice was believed to be an hallucination caused by the mother's great anxiety and her disordered nerves. But for months afterward, at irregular intervals of a few days, the voice was heard by the several members of the family, and by others. All declared it unmistakably the voice of Charles Ashmore; all agreed that it seemed to come from a great distance, faintly, yet with entire distinctness of articulation; yet none could determine its direction, nor repeat its words. The intervals of silence grew longer and longer, the voice fainter and farther, and by midsummer it was heard no more.

If anybody knows the fate of Charles Ashmore it is probably his mother. She is dead.

Science to the Front

In connection with this subject of "mysterious disappearance"—of which every memory is stored with abundant
example—it is pertinent to note the belief of Dr. Hern,
of Leipsic; not by way of explanation, unless the reader
may choose to take it so, but because of its intrinsic interest as a singular speculation. This distinguished scientist
has expounded his views in a book entitled "Verschwinden
und Seine Theorie," which has attracted some attention,
"particularly," says one writer, "among the followers of
Hegel, and mathematicians who hold to the actual existence of a so-called non-Euclidean space—that is to say,
of space which has more dimensions than length, breadth,
and thickness—space in which it would be possible to tie
a knot in an endless cord and to turn a rubber ball inside out without 'a solution of its continuity,' or in other
words, without breaking or cracking it."

Dr. Hern believes that in the visible world there are
void places—*vacua,* and something more—holes, as it
were, through which animate and inanimate objects may
fall into the invisible world and be seen and heard no
more. The theory is something like this: Space is pervaded
by luminiferous ether, which is a material thing—as much
a substance as air or water, though almost infinitely more
attenuated. All force, all forms of energy must be propagat-
ed in this; every process must take place in it which takes
place at all. But let us suppose that cavities exist in this
otherwise universal medium, as caverns exist in the earth,
or cells in a Swiss cheese. In such a cavity there would be
absolutely nothing. It would be such a vacuum as cannot
be artificially produced; for if we pump the air from a receiver there remains the luminiferous ether. Through one
of these cavities light could not pass, for there would be
nothing to bear it. Sound could not come from it; nothing
could be felt in it. It would not have a single one of the

conditions necessary to the action of any of our senses. In
such a void, in short, nothing whatever could occur. Now,
in the words of the writer before quoted—the learned doc-
tor himself nowhere puts it so concisely: "A man inclosed
in such a closet could neither see nor be seen; neither hear
nor be heard; neither feel nor be felt; neither live nor die,
for both life and death are processes which can take place
only where there is force, and in empty space no force
could exist." Are these the awful conditions (some will
ask) under which the friends of the lost are to think of
them as existing, and doomed forever to exist?

Baldly and imperfectly as here stated, Dr. Hern's theory,
in so far as it professes to be an adequate explanation
of "mysterious disappearances," is open to many obvious
objections; to fewer as he states it himself in the "spacious volubility" of his book. But even as expounded by its
author it does not explain, and in truth is incompatible
with some incidents of, the occurrences related in these
memoranda: for example, the sound of Charles Ashmore's
voice. It is not my duty to indue facts and theories with
affinity.

The Hall Bedroom

Mary E. Wilkins Freeman

(1903)

My name is Mrs. Elizabeth Jennings. I am a highly respectable woman. I may style myself a gentlewoman, for
in my youth I enjoyed advantages. I was well brought up,
and I graduated at a young ladies' seminary. I also married
well. My husband was that most genteel of all merchants,
an apothecary. His shop was on the corner of the main
street in Rockton, the town where I was born, and where I
lived until the death of my husband. My parents had died
when I had been married a short time, so I was left quite
alone in the world. I was not competent to carry on the
apothecary business by myself, for I had no knowledge of
drugs, and had a mortal terror of giving poisons instead
of medicines. Therefore I was obliged to sell at a considerable sacrifice, and the proceeds, some five thousand
dollars, were all I had in the world. The income was not
enough to support me in any kind of comfort, and I saw
that I must in some way earn money. I thought at first of
teaching, but I was no longer young, and methods had
changed since my school days. What I was able to teach,
nobody wished to know. I could think of only one thing to
do: take boarders. But the same objection to that business
as to teaching held good in Rockton. Nobody wished to
board. My husband had rented a house with a number of
bedrooms, and I advertised, but nobody applied. Finally

my cash was running very low, and I became desperate. I packed up my furniture, rented a large house in this town and moved here. It was a venture attended with many risks. In the first place the rent was exorbitant, in the next I was entirely unknown. However, I am a person of considerable ingenuity, and have inventive power, and much enterprise when the occasion presses. I advertised in a very original manner, although that actually took my last penny, that is, the last penny of my ready money, and I was forced to draw on my principal to purchase my first supplies, a thing which I had resolved never on any account to do. But the great risk met with a reward, for I had several applicants within two days after my advertisement appeared in the paper. Within two weeks my boarding-house was well established, I became very successful, and my success would have been uninterrupted had it not been for the mysterious and bewildering occurrences which I am about to relate. I am now forced to leave the house and rent another. Some of my old boarders accompany me, some, with the most unreasonable nervousness, refuse to be longer associated in any way, however indirectly, with the terrible and uncanny happenings which I have to relate. It remains to be seen whether my ill luck in this house will follow me into another, and whether my whole prosperity in life will be forever shadowed by the Mystery of the Hall Bedroom. Instead of telling the strange story myself in my own words, I shall present the journal of Mr. George H. Wheatcroft. I shall show you the portions beginning on January 18 of the present year, the date when he took up his residence with me. Here it is:

The Diary of an Ill-Fated Man

"January 18, 1883. Here I am established in my new boardinghouse. I have, as befits my humble means, the hall bedroom, even the hall bedroom on the third floor. I have heard all my life of hall bedrooms, I have seen hall bedrooms, I have been in them, but never until now, when I am actually established in one, did I comprehend what, at once, an ignominious and sternly uncompromising thing a hall bedroom is. It proves the ignominy of the dweller therein. No man at thirty-six (my age) would be domiciled in a hall bedroom, unless he were himself ignominious, at least comparatively speaking. I am proved by this means incontrovertibly to have been left far behind in the race. I see no reason why I should not live in this hall bedroom for the rest of my life, that is, if I have money enough to pay the landlady, and that seems probable, since my small funds are invested as safely as if I were an orphan-ward in charge of a pillar of a sanctuary. After the valuables have been stolen, I have most carefully locked the stable door. I have experienced the revulsion which comes sooner or later to the adventurous soul who experiences nothing but defeat and so-called ill luck. I have swung to the opposite extreme. I have lost in everything—I have lost in love, I have lost in money, I have lost in the struggle for preferment, I have lost in health and strength. I am now settled down in a hall bedroom to live upon my small income, and regain my health by mild potations of the mineral waters here, if possible; if not, to live here without my health— for mine is not a necessarily fatal malady—until Providence shall take me out of my hall bedroom. There is no one place more than another where I care to live. There is not sufficient motive to take me away, even if the mineral waters do not benefit me. So I am here and to stay in the hall bedroom. The landlady is civil, and even kind, as kind as a woman who has to keep her poor womanly eye upon the main chance can be. The struggle for money always injures the fine grain of a woman; she is too fine a thing to do it; she does not by nature belong with the gold grubbers, and it therefore lowers her; she steps from heights to claw and scrape and dig. But she can not help it often-times, poor thing, and her deterioration thereby is to be condoned. The landlady is all she can be, taking her strain of adverse circumstances into consideration, and the table is good, even conscientiously so. It looks to me as if she were foolish enough to strive to give the boarders their money's worth, with the due regard for the main chance which is inevitable. However, that is of minor importance to me, since my diet is restricted.

Diet and Psychology

"It is curious what an annoyance a restriction in diet can be even to a man who has considered himself somewhat indifferent to gastronomic delights. There was to-day a pudding for dinner, which I could not taste without pen-alty, but which I longed for. It was only because it looked unlike any other pudding that I had ever seen, and as-sumed a mental and spiritual significance. It seemed to me, whimsically no doubt, as if tasting it might give me a new sensation, and consequently a new outlook. Trivial things may lead to large results: why should I not get a new outlook by means of a pudding? Life here stretches before me most monotonously, and I feet like clutching at alleviations, though paradoxically, since I have settled down with the utmost acquiescence. Still one can not im-mediately overcome and change radically all one's nature. Now I look at myself critically and search for the keynote to my whole self, and my actions, I have always been con-scious of a reaching out, an overweening desire for the new, the untried, for the broadness of further horizons, the seas beyond seas, the thought beyond thought. This characteristic has been the primary cause of all my mis-fortunes. I have the soul of an explorer, and in nine out of ten cases this leads to destruction. If I had possessed capital and sufficient push, I should have been one of the searchers after the North Pole. I have been an eager student of astronomy. I have studied botany with avidity, and have dreamed of new flora in unexplored parts of the world, and the same with animal life and geology. I longed for riches in order to discover the power and sense of possession of the rich. I longed for love in order to discover the possibilities of the emotions. I longed for all that the mind of man could conceive as desirable for man, not so much for purely selfish ends, as from an insatiable thirst for knowledge of a universal trend. But I have limitations, I do not quite understand of what nature—for what mortal ever did quite understand his own limitations, since a knowledge of them would preclude their existence?—but they have prevented my progress to any extent. Therefore behold me in my hall bedroom, settled at last into a groove of fate so deep that I have lost the sight of even my horizons. Just at present, as I write here, my horizon on the left, that is my physical horizon, is a wall covered with cheap paper. The paper is an indeterminate pattern in white and gilt. There are a few photographs of my own hung about, and on the large wall space beside the bed there is a large oil painting which belongs to my landlady. It has a massive tarnished gold frame, and, curiously enough, the painting itself is rather good. I have no idea who the artist could have been. It is of the conventional landscape type in vogue some fifty years since, the type so fondly reproduced in chromos—the winding river with the little boat occupied by a pair of lovers, the cottage nestled among trees on the right shore, the gentle slope of the hills and the church spire in the background—but still it is well done. It gives me the impression of an artist without the slightest originality of design, but much of technique. But for some inexplicable reason the picture frets me. I find myself gazing at it when I do not wish to do so. It seems to compel my attention like some intent face in the room.

I shall ask Mrs. Jennings to have it removed. I will hang in its place some photographs which I have in a trunk.

"January 26. I do not write regularly in my journal. I never did. I see no reason why I should. I see no reason why anyone should have the slightest sense of duty in such a matter. Some days I have nothing which interests me sufficiently to write out, some days I feel either too ill or too indolent. For four days I have not written, from a mixture of all three reasons. Now, to-day I both feel like it and I have something to write. Also I am distinctly better than I have been. Perhaps the waters are benefiting me, or the change of air. Or possibly it is something else more subtle. Possibly my mind has seized upon something new, a discovery which causes it to react upon my failing body and serves as a stimulant. All I know is, I feel distinctly better, and am conscious of an acute interest in doing so, which is of late strange to me. I have been rather indifferent, and sometimes have wondered if that were not the cause rather than the result of my state of health. I have been so continually balked that I have settled into a state of inertia. I lean rather comfortably against my obstacles. After all, the worst of the pain always lies in the struggle. Give up and it is rather pleasant than otherwise. If one did not kick, the pricks would not in the least matter. However, for some reason, for the last few days, I seem to have awakened from my state of quiescence. It means future trouble for me, no doubt, but in the meantime I am not sorry. It began with the picture—the large oil painting. I went to Mrs. Jennings about it yesterday, and she, to my surprise—for I thought it a matter that could be easily arranged—objected to having it removed. Her reasons were two; both simple, both sufficient, especially since I, after all, had no very strong desire either way. It seems that the picture does not belong to her. It hung here when she rented the house. She says if it is removed, a very large and unsightly discoloration of the wall-paper will be exposed, and she does not like to ask for new paper. The owner, an old man, is traveling abroad, the agent is curt, and she has only been in the house a very short time. Then it would mean a sad upheaval of my room, which would disturb me. She also says that there is no place in the house where she can store the picture, and there is not a vacant space in another room for one so large. So I let the picture remain. It really, when I came to think of it, was very immaterial after all. But I got my photographs out of my trunk, and I hung them around the large picture. The wall is almost completely covered. I hung them yesterday afternoon, and last night I repeated a strange experience which I have had in some degree every night since I have been here, but was not sure whether it deserved the name of experience, but was not rather one of those dreams in which one dreams one is awake. But last night it came again, and now I know. There is something very singular about this room. I am very much interested. I will write down for future reference the events of last night. Concerning those of the preceding nights since I have slept in this room, I will simply say that they have been of a similar nature, but, as it were, only the preliminary stages, the prologue to what happened last night.

The Mystery of the First Night

"I am not depending upon the mineral waters here as the one remedy for my malady, which is sometimes of an acute nature, and indeed constantly threatens me with considerable suffering unless by medicine I can keep it in check. I will say that the medicine which I employ is not of the class commonly known as drugs. It is impossible that it can be held responsible for what I am about to transcribe. My mind last night and every night since I have slept in this room was in an absolutely normal state. I take this medicine, prescribed by the specialist in whose charge I was before coming here, regularly every four hours while awake. As I am never a good sleeper, it follows that I am enabled with no inconvenience to take any medicine during the night with the same regularity as during the day. It is my habit, therefore, to place my bottle and spoon where I can put my hand upon them easily without lighting the gas. Since I have been in this room, I have placed the bottle of medicine upon my dresser at the side of the room opposite the bed. I have done this rather than place it nearer, as once I jostled the bottle and spilled most of the contents, and it is not easy for me to replace it, as it is expensive. Therefore I placed it in security on the dresser, and, indeed, that is but three or four steps from my bed, the room being so small. Last night I wakened as usual, and I knew, since I had fallen asleep about eleven, that it must be in the neighborhood of three. I wake with almost clock-like regularity and it is never necessary for me to consult my watch.

"I had slept unusually well and without dreams, and I awoke fully at once, with a feeling of refreshment to which I am not accustomed. I immediately got out of bed and began stepping across the room in the direction of my dresser, on which I had set my medicine-bottle and spoon.

"To my utter amazement, the steps which had hitherto sufficed to take me across my room did not suffice to do so. I advanced several paces, and my outstretched hands touched nothing. I stopped and went on again. I was sure that I was moving in a straight direction, and even if I had not been I knew it was impossible to advance in any direction in my tiny apartment without coming into collision either with a wall or a piece of furniture. I continued to walk falteringly, as I have seen people on the stage: a step, then a long falter, then a sliding step. I kept my hands extended; they touched nothing. I stopped again. I had not the least sentiment of fear or consternation. It was rather the very stupefaction of surprise. 'How is this?' seemed thundering in my ears. 'What is this?'

"The room was perfectly dark. There was nowhere any glimmer, as is usually the case, even in a so-called dark room, from the walls, picture-frames, looking-glass or white objects. It was absolute gloom. The house stood in a quiet part of the town. There were many trees about; the electric street lights were extinguished at midnight; there was no moon and the sky was cloudy. I could not distinguish my one window, which I thought strange, even on such a dark night. Finally I changed my plan of motion and turned, as nearly as I could estimate, at right angles. Now, I thought, I must reach soon, if, I kept on, my writing-table underneath the window; or, if I am going in the opposite direction, the hall door. I reached neither. I am telling the unvarnished truth when I say that I began to count my steps and carefully measure my paces after that, and I traversed a space clear of furniture at least twenty feet by thirty—a very large apartment. And as I walked I was conscious that my naked feet were pressing something which gave rise to sensations the like of which I had never experienced before. As nearly as I can express it, it was as if my feet pressed something as elastic as air or water, which was in this case unyielding to my weight. It gave me a curious sensation of buoyancy and stimulation. At the same time this surface, if surface be the right name, which I trod, felt cool to my feet with the coolness of vapor or fluidity, seeming to overlap the soles. Finally I stood still; my surprise was at last merging into a measure of consternation. 'Where am I?' I thought. 'What am I going to do?' Stories that I had heard of travelers being taken from their beds and conveyed into strange and dangerous places, Middle Age stories of the Inquisition flashed through my brain. I knew all the time that for a man who had gone to bed in a commonplace hall bedroom in a very commonplace little town such surmises were highly ridiculous, but it is hard for the human mind to grasp anything but a human explanation of phenomena. Almost anything seemed then, and seems now, more rational than an explanation bordering upon the supernatural, as we understand the supernatural. At last I called, though rather softly, 'What does this mean?' I said quite aloud, 'Where am I? Who is here? Who is doing this? I tell you I will have no such nonsense. Speak, if there is anybody here.' But all was dead silence. Then suddenly a light flashed through the open transom of my door. Somebody had heard me—a man who rooms next door, a decent kind of man, also here for his health. He turned on the gas in the hall and called to me. 'What's the matter?' he asked, in an agitated, trembling voice. He is a nervous fellow.

The Startled Neighbor

"Directly, when the light flashed through my transom, I saw that I was in my familiar hall bedroom. I could see everything quite distinctly—my tumbled bed, my writing-table, my dresser, my chair, my little wash-stand, my clothes hanging on a row of pegs, the old picture on the wall. The picture gleamed out with singular distinctness in the light from the transom. The river seemed actually to run and ripple, and the boat to be gliding with the current. I gazed fascinated at it, as I replied to the anxious voice:

"'Nothing is the matter with me,' said I. 'Why?'

"'I thought I heard you speak,' said the man outside. 'I thought maybe you were sick.'

"'No,' I called back. 'I am all right. I am trying to find my medicine in the dark, that's all. I can see now you have lighted the gas.'

"'Nothing is the matter?'

"'No; sorry I disturbed you. Good-night.'

"'Good-night.' Then I heard the man's door shut after a minute's pause. He was evidently not quite satisfied. I took a pull at my medicine-bottle, and got into bed. He had left the hall-gas burning. I did not go to sleep again for some time. Just before I did so, some one, probably Mrs. Jennings, came out in the hall and extinguished the gas. This morning when I awoke everything was as usual in my room. I wonder if I shall have any such experience to-night.

"January 27. I shall write in my journal every day until this draws to some definite issue. Last night my strange experience deepened, as something tells me it will continue to do. I retired quite early, at half-past ten. I took the precaution, on retiring, to place beside my bed, on a chair, a box of safety matches, that I might not be in the dilemma of the night before. I took my medicine on retiring; that made me due to wake at half-past two. I had not fallen asleep directly, but had had certainly three hours of sound, dreamless slumber when I awoke. I lay a few minutes hesitating whether or not to strike a safety match and light my way to the dresser, whereon stood my medicine-bottle. I hesitated, not because I had the least sensation of fear, but because of the same shrinking from a nerve shock that leads one at times to dread the plunge into an icy bath. It seemed much easier to me to strike that match and cross my hall bedroom to my dresser, take my dose, then return quietly to my bed, than to risk the chance of floundering about in some unknown limbo either of fancy or reality.

Further Nocturnal Experiences

"At last, however, the spirit of adventure, which has always been such a ruling one for me, conquered. I rose. I took the box of safety matches in my hand, and started on, as

I conceived, the straight course for my dresser, about five feet across from my bed. As before, I traveled and traveled and did not reach it. I advanced with groping hands extended, setting one foot cautiously before the other, but I touched nothing except the indefinite, unnameable surface which my feet pressed. All of a sudden, though, I became aware of something. One of my senses was saluted, nay, more than that, hailed, with imperiousness, and that was, strangely enough, my sense of smell, but in a hitherto unknown fashion. It seemed as if the odor reached my mentality first. I reversed the usual process, which is, as I understand it, like this: the odor when encountered strikes first the olfactory nerve, which transmits the intelligence to the brain. It is as if, to put it rudely, my nose met a rose, and then the nerve belonging to the sense said to my brain, 'Here is a rose.' This time my brain said, 'Here is a rose,' and my sense then recognized it. I say rose, but it was not a rose, that is, not the fragrance of any rose which I had ever known. It was undoubtedly a flower-odor, and rose came perhaps the nearest to it. My mind realized it first with what seemed a leap of rapture. 'What is this delight?' I asked myself. And then the ravishing fragrance smote my sense. I breathed it in and it seemed to feed my thoughts, satisfying some hitherto unknown hunger. Then I took a step further and another fragrance appeared, which I liken to lilies for lack of something better, and then came violets, then mignonette. I can not describe the experience, but it was a sheer delight, a rapture of sublimated sense. I groped further and further, and always into new waves of fragrance. I seemed to be wading breast-high through flower-beds of Paradise, but all the time I touched nothing with my groping hands. At last a sudden giddiness as of surfeit overcame me. I realized that I might be in some unknown peril. I was distinctly afraid. I struck one of my safety matches, and I was in my hall bedroom, midway between my bed and my dresser. I took my dose of medicine and went to bed, and after a while fell asleep and did not wake till morning.

"January 28. Last night I did not take my usual dose of medicine. In these days of new remedies and mysterious results upon certain organizations, it occurred to me to wonder if possibly the drug might have, after all, something to do with my strange experience. I did not take my medicine. I put the bottle as usual on my dresser, since I feared if I interrupted further the customary sequence of affairs I might fail to wake. I placed my box of matches on the chair beside the bed. I fell asleep about quarter past eleven o'clock, and I waked when the clock was striking two—a little earlier than my wont. I did not hesitate this time. I rose at once, took my box of matches and proceeded as formerly. I walked what seemed a great space without coming into collision with anything. I kept sniffing for the wonderful fragrances of the night before, but they did not recur. Instead, I was suddenly aware that I was tasting something, some morsel of sweetness hitherto unknown, and, as in the case of the odor, the usual order seemed reversed, and it was as if I tasted it first in my mental consciousness. Then the sweetness rolled under my tongue. I thought involuntarily of 'Sweeter than honey or the honeycomb' of the Scripture. I thought of the Old Testament manna. An ineffable content as of satisfied hunger seized me. I stepped further, and a new savor was upon my palate. And so on. It was never cloying, though of such sharp sweetness that it fairly stung. It was the merging of a material sense into a spiritual one. I said to myself, 'I have lived my life and always have I gone hungry until now.' I could feel my brain act swiftly under the influence of this heavenly food as under a stimulant. Then suddenly I repeated the experience of the night before. I grew dizzy, and an indefinite fear and shrinking were upon me. I

struck my safety match and was back in my hall bedroom.
I returned to bed, and soon fell asleep. I did not take my
medicine. I am resolved not to do so longer. I am feeling
much better.

"January 29. Last night to bed as usual, matches in
place; fell asleep about eleven and waked at half-past one.
I heard the half-hour strike; I am waking earlier and earlier
every night. I had not taken my medicine, though it was
on the dresser as usual. I again took my match-box in hand
and started to cross the room, and, as always, traversed
strange spaces, but this night, as seems fated to be the
case every night, my experience was different. Last night I
neither smelled nor tasted, but I heard—my Lord, I heard!
The first sound of which I was conscious was one like the
constantly gathering and receding murmur of a river, and
it seemed to come from the wall behind my bed where the
old picture hangs. Nothing in nature except a river gives
that impression of at once advance and retreat. I could not
mistake it. On, ever on, came the swelling murmur of the
waves, past and ever past they died in the distance. Then I
heard above the murmur of the river a song in an unknown
tongue which I recognized as being unknown, yet which I
understood; but the understanding was in my brain, with
no words of interpretation. The song had to do with me,
but with me in unknown futures for which I had no images
of comparison in the past; yet a sort of ecstasy as of a
prophecy of bliss filled my whole consciousness. The song
never ceased, but as I moved on I came into new sound-
waves. There was the pealing of bells which might have been
made of crystal, and might have summoned to the gates of
heaven. There was music of strange instruments, great har-
monies pierced now and then by small whispers as of love,
and it all filled me with a certainty of a future of bliss.

"At last I seemed the centre of a mighty orchestra which
constantly deepened and increased until I seemed to feel

myself being lifted gently but mightily upon the waves of sound as upon the waves of a sea. Then again the terror and the impulse to flee to my own familiar scenes was upon me. I struck my match and was back in my hall bedroom. I do not see how I sleep at all after such wonders, but sleep I do. I slept dreamlessly until daylight this morning.

The Story of Strange Disappearances

"January 30. I heard yesterday something with regard to my hall bedroom which affected me strangely. I can not for the life of me say whether it intimidated me, filled me with the horror of the abnormal, or rather roused to a greater degree my spirit of adventure and discovery. I was down at the Cure, and was sitting on the veranda sipping idly my mineral water, when somebody spoke my name. 'Mr. Wheatcroft?' said the voice politely, interrogatively, somewhat apologetically, as if to provide for a possible mistake in my identity. I turned and saw a gentleman whom I recognized at once. I seldom forget names or faces. He was a Mr. Addison whom I had seen considerable of three years ago at a little summer hotel in the mountains. It was one of those passing acquaintances which signify little one way or the other. If never renewed, you have no regret; if renewed, you accept the renewal with no hesitation. It is in every way negative. But just now, in my feeble, friendless state, the sight of a face which beams with pleased remembrance is rather grateful. I felt distinctly glad to see the man. He sat down beside me. He also had a glass of the water. His health, while not as bad as mine, leaves much to be desired.

"Addison had often been in this town before. He had in fact lived here at one time. He had remained at the Cure three years, taking the waters daily. He therefore knows about all there is to be known about the town, which is not very large. He asked me where I was staying, and when

I told him the street, rather excitedly inquired the number. When I told him the number, which is 240, he gave a manifest start, and after one sharp glance at me sipped his water in silence for a moment. He had so evidently betrayed some ulterior knowledge with regard to my residence that I questioned him.

"'What do you know about 240 Pleasant Street?' said I.

"'Oh, nothing,' he replied, evasively, sipping his water.

"After a little while, however, he inquired, in what he evidently tried to render a casual tone, what room I occupied. 'I once lived a few weeks at 240 Pleasant Street myself,' he said. 'That house always was a boarding-house, I guess.'

"'It had stood vacant for a term of years before the present occupant rented it, I believe,' I remarked. Then I answered his question. 'I have the hall bedroom on the third floor,' said I. 'The quarters are pretty straitened, but comfortable enough as hall bedrooms go.'

Two Who Vanished

"But Mr. Addison had showed such unmistakable consternation at my reply that then I persisted in my questioning as to the cause, and at last he yielded and told me what he knew. He had hesitated both because he shrank from displaying what I might consider an unmanly superstition, and because he did not wish to influence me beyond what the facts of the case warranted. 'Well, I will tell you, Wheatcroft,' he said. 'Briefly all I know is this: When last I heard of 240 Pleasant Street it was not rented because of foul play which was supposed to have taken place there, though nothing was ever proved. There were two disappearances, and—in each case—of an occupant of the hall bedroom which you now have. The first disappearance was of a very beautiful girl who had come here for her health and was said to be the victim of a profound melancholy,

induced by a love disappointment. She obtained board at
240 and occupied the hall bedroom about two weeks; then
one morning she was gone, having seemingly vanished
into thin air. Her relatives were communicated with; she
had not many, nor friends either, poor girl, and a thor-
ough search was made, but the last I knew she had never
come to light. There were two or three arrests, but nothing ever came of them. Well, that was before my day here,
but the second disappearance took place when I was in the
house—a fine young fellow who had overworked in college. He had to pay his own way. He had taken cold, had
the grip, and that and the overwork about finished him,
and he came on here for a month's rest and recuperation.
He had been in that room about two weeks, a little less,
when one morning he wasn't there. Then there was a great
hullabaloo. It seems that he had let fall some hints to the
effect that there was something queer about the room,
but, of course, the police did not think much of that.
They made arrests right and left, but they never found
him, and the arrested were discharged, though some of
them are probably under a cloud of suspicion to this day.
Then the boarding-house was shut up. Six years ago nobody would have boarded there, much less occupied that
hall bedroom, but now I suppose new people have come in
and the story has died out. I dare say your landlady will
not thank me for reviving it.'

The Last Night

"I assured him that it would make no possible difference
to me. He looked at me sharply, and asked bluntly if I
had seen anything wrong or unusual about the room. I
replied, guarding myself from falsehood with a quibble,
that I had seen nothing in the least unusual about the
room, as indeed I had not, and have not now, but that may
come. I feel that that will come in due time. Last night

I neither saw, nor heard, nor smelled, nor tasted, but I felt. Last night, having started again on my exploration of, God knows what, I had not advanced a step before I touched something. My first sensation was one of disappointment. 'It is the dresser, and I am at the end of it now,' I thought. But I soon discovered that it was not the old painted dresser which I touched, but something carved, as nearly as I could discover with my unskilled finger-tips, with winged things. There were certainly long keen curves of wings which seemed to overlay an arabesque of fine leaf and flower work. I do not know what the object was that I touched. It may have been a chest. I may seem to be exaggerating when I say that it somehow failed or exceeded in some mysterious respect of being the shape of anything I had ever touched. I do not know what the material was. It was as smooth as ivory, but it did not feel like ivory; there was a singular warmth about it, as if it had stood long in hot sunlight. I continued, and I encountered other objects I am inclined to think were pieces of furniture of fashions and possibly of uses unknown to me, and about them all was the strange mystery as to shape. At last I came to what was evidently an open window of large area. I distinctly felt a soft, warm wind, yet with a crystal freshness, blow on my face. It was not the window of my hall bedroom, that I know. Looking out, I could see nothing. I only felt the wind blowing on my face.

"Then suddenly, without any warning, my groping hands to the right and left touched living beings, beings in the likeness of men and women, palpable creatures in palpable attire. I could feel the soft silken texture of their garments which swept around me, seeming to half infold me in clinging meshes like cobwebs. I was in a crowd of these people, whatever they were, and whoever they were, but, curiously enough, without seeing one of them I had a strong sense of recognition as I passed among them. Now and then a hand that I knew closed softly over mine; once an arm passed around me. Then I began to feel myself gently swept on and impelled by this softly moving throng; their floating garments seemed to fairly wind me about, and again a swift terror overcame me. I struck my match, and was back in my hall bedroom. I wonder if I had not better keep my gas burning to-night? I wonder if it be possible that this is going too far? I wonder what became of those other people, the man and the woman who occupied this room? I wonder if I had better not stop where I am?

"January 31. Last night I saw—I saw more than I can describe, more than is lawful to describe. Something which nature has rightly hidden has been revealed to me, but it is not for me to disclose too much of her secret. This much I will say, that doors and windows open into an out-of-doors to which the outdoors which we know is but a vestibule. And there is a river; there is something strange with respect to that picture. There is a river upon which one could sail away. It was flowing silently, for to-night I could only see. I saw that I was right in thinking I recognized some of the people whom I encountered the night before, though some were strange to me. It is true that the girl who disappeared from the hall bedroom was very beautiful. Everything which I saw last night was very beautiful to my one sense that could grasp it. I wonder what it would all be if all my senses together were to grasp it? I wonder if I had better not keep my gas burning to-night? I wonder—"

The Secret Chamber

This finishes the journal which Mr. Wheatcroft left in his hall bedroom. The morning after the last entry he was gone. His friend, Mr. Addison, came here, and a search was made. They even tore down the wall behind the picture, and they did find something rather queer for a house that had been used for boarders, where you would think no room would have been let run to waste. They found another room, a long narrow one, the length of the hall bedroom, but narrower, hardly more than a closet. There was no window, nor door, and all there was in it was a sheet of paper covered with figures, as if somebody had been doing sums. They made a lot of talk about those figures, and they tried to make out that the fifth dimension, whatever that is, was proved, but they said afterward they didn't prove anything. They tried to make out then that somebody had murdered poor Mr. Wheatcroft and hid the body, and they arrested poor Mr. Addison, but they couldn't make out anything against him. They proved he was in the Cure all that night and couldn't have done it. They don't know what became of Mr. Wheatcroft, and now they say two more disappeared from that same room before I rented the house.

The agent came and promised to put the new room they discovered into the hall bedroom and have everything new-papered and painted. He took away the picture; folks hinted there was something queer about that, I don't know what. It looked innocent enough, and I guess he burned it up. He said if I would stay he would arrange it with the owner, who everybody says is a very queer man, so I should not have to pay much if any rent. But I told him I couldn't stay if he was to give me the rent. That I wasn't afraid of anything myself, though I must say I wouldn't want to put anybody in that hall bedroom without telling him all about it; but my boarders would leave, and I knew I couldn't get any more. I told him I would rather have had a regular ghost than what seemed to be a way of going out of the house to nowhere and never coming back again. I moved, and, as I said before, it remains to be seen whether my ill luck follows me to this house or not. Anyway, it has no hall bedroom.

The Magic Shop
H. G. Wells
(1903)

I had seen the Magic Shop from afar several times; I had passed it once or twice, a shop window of alluring little objects, magic balls, magic hens, wonderful cones, ventriloquist dolls, the material of the basket trick, packs of cards that *looked* all right, and all that sort of thing, but never had I thought of going in until one day, almost without warning, Gip hauled me by my finger right up to the window, and so conducted himself that there was nothing for it but to take him in. I had not thought the place was there, to tell the truth—a modest-sized frontage in Regent Street, between the picture shop and the place where the chicks run about just out of patent incubators,—but there it was sure enough. I had fancied it was down nearer the Circus, or round the corner in Oxford Street, or even in Holbom; always over the way and a little inaccessible it had been, with something of the mirage in its position; but here it was now quite indisputably, and the fat end of Gip's pointing finger made a noise upon the glass.

"If I was rich," said Gip, dabbing a finger at the Disappearing Egg, "I'd buy myself that. And that"—which was The Crying Baby, Very Human—"and that," which was a mystery, and called, so a neat card asserted, "Buy One and Astonish Your Friends."

"Anything," said Gip, "will disappear under one of those cones. I have read about it in a book.

"And there, dadda, is the Vanishing Halfpenny—only they've put it this way up so's we can't see how it's done."

Gip, dear boy, inherits his mother's breeding, and he did not propose to enter the shop or worry in any way; only, you know, quite unconsciously he lugged my finger doorward, and he made his interest clear.

"That," he said, and pointed to the Magic Bottle.

"If you had that?" I said; at which promising inquiry he looked up with a sudden radiance.

"I could show it to Jessie," he said, thoughtful as ever of others.

"It's less than a hundred days to your birthday, Gibbles," I said, and laid my hand on the door handle.

Gip made no answer, but his grip tightened on my finger, and so we came into the shop.

It was no common shop this; it was a magic shop, and all the prancing precedence Gip would have taken in the matter of mere toys was wanting. He left the burthen of the conversation to me.

It was a little, narrow shop, not very well lit, and the door-bell pinged again with a plaintive note as we closed it behind us. For a moment or so we were alone and could glance about us. There was a tiger in *papier-mâché* on the glass case that covered the low counter—a grave, kind-eyed tiger that waggled his head in a methodical manner; there were several crystal spheres, a china hand holding magic cards, a stock of magic fish-bowls in various sizes, and an immodest magic hat that shamelessly displayed its springs. On the floor were magic mirrors; one to draw you out long and thin, one to swell your head and vanish your legs, and one to make you short and fat like a draught; and while we were laughing at these the shopman, as I suppose, came in.

At any rate, there he was behind the counter—a curious, sallow, dark man, with one ear larger than the other and a chin like the toe-cap of a boot.

"What can we have the pleasure?" he said, spreading his long, magic fingers on the glass case; and so with a start we were aware of him.

"I want," I said, "to buy my little boy a few simple tricks."

"Legerdemain?" he asked. "Mechanical? Domestic?"

"Anything amusing?" said I.

"Um!" said the shopman, and scratched his head for a moment as if thinking. Then, quite distinctly, he drew from his head a glass ball. "Something in this way?" he said, and held it out.

The action was unexpected. I had seen the trick done at entertainments endless times before—it's part of the common stock of conjurers—but I had not expected it here. "That's good," I said, with a laugh.

"Isn't it?" said the shopman.

Gip stretched out his disengaged hand to take this object and found merely a blank palm.

"It's in your pocket," said the shopman, and there it was!

"How much will that be?" I asked.

"We make no charge for glass balls," said the shopman politely. "We get them"—he picked one out of his elbow as he spoke—"free." He produced another from the back of his neck, and laid it beside its predecessor on the counter. Gip regarded his glass ball sagely, then directed a look of inquiry at the two on the counter, and finally brought his round-eyed scrutiny to the shopman, who smiled. "You may have those too," said the shopman, "and, if you *don't* mind one from my mouth— *So!*"

Gip counselled me mutely for a moment, and then in a profound silence put away the four balls, resumed my reassuring finger, and nerved himself for the next event.

"We get all our smaller tricks in that way," the shop-man remarked.

I laughed in the manner of one who subscribes to a jest. "Instead of going to the wholesale shop," I said. "Of course, it's cheaper."

"In a way," the shopman said. "Though we pay in the end. But not so heavily—as people suppose. . . . Our larger tricks, and our daily provisions and all the other things we want, we get out of that hat. . . . And you know, sir, if you'll excuse my saying it, there *isn't* a wholesale shop, not for Genuine Magic goods, sir. I don't know if you no-ticed our inscription—the Genuine Magic shop." He drew a business-card from his cheek and handed it to me. "Gen-uine," he said, with his finger on the word, and added, "There is absolutely no deception, sir."

He seemed to be carrying out the joke pretty thorough-ly, I thought.

He turned to Gip with a smile of remarkable affability. "You, you know, are the Right Sort of Boy."

I was surprised at his knowing that, because, in the interests of discipline, we keep it rather a secret even at home; but Gip received it in unflinching silence, keeping a steadfast eye on him.

"It's only the Right Sort of Boy gets through that door-way."

And, as if by way of illustration, there came a rattling at the door, and a squeaking little voice could be faintly heard. "Nyar! I warn 'a go in there, dadda, I *warn* 'a go in there. Ny-a-a-ah!" and then the accents of a down-trod-den parent, urging consolations and propitiations. "It's locked, Edward," he said.

"But it isn't," said I.

"It is, sir," said the shopman, "always—for that sort of child," and as he spoke we had a glimpse of the other youngster, a little, white face, pallid from sweet-eating

and over-sapid food, and distorted by evil passions, a ruthless little egotist, pawing at the enchanted pane. "It's no
good, sir," said the shopman, as I moved, with my natural
helpfulness, doorward, and presently the spoilt child was
carried off howling.

"How do you manage that?" I said, breathing a little
more freely.

"Magic!" said the shopman, with a careless wave of the
hand, and behold! sparks of coloured fire flew out of his
fingers and vanished into the shadows of the shop.

"You were saying," he said, addressing himself to Gip,
"before you came in, that you would like one of our 'Buy
One and Astonish your Friends' boxes?"

Gip, after a gallant effort, said "Yes."

"It's in your pocket."

And leaning over the counter—he really had an extraor-
dinarily long body—this amazing person produced the
article in the customary conjurer's manner. "Paper," he
said, and took a sheet out of the empty hat with the
springs; "string," and behold his mouth was a string-box,
from which he drew an unending thread, which when he
had tied his parcel he bit off—and, it seemed to me, swallowed the ball of string. And then he lit a candle at the
nose of one of the ventriloquist's dummies, stuck one of
his fingers (which had become sealing-wax red) into the
flame, and so sealed the parcel. "Then there was the Disappearing Egg," he remarked, and produced one from within
my coat-breast and packed it, and also The Crying Baby,
Very Human. I handed each parcel to Gip as it was ready,
and he clasped them to his chest.

He said very little, but his eyes were eloquent; the
clutch of his arms was eloquent. He was the playground of
unspeakable emotions. These, you know, were *real* Magics.

Then, with a start, I discovered something moving
about in my hat—something soft and jumpy. I whipped

it off, and a ruffled pigeon—no doubt a confederate—
dropped out and ran on the counter, and went, I fancy,
into a cardboard box behind the *papier-mâché* tiger.

"Tut, tut!" said the shopman, dexterously relieving me
of my headdress; "careless bird, and—as I live—nesting!"

He shook my hat, and shook out into his extended hand
two or three eggs, a large marble, a watch, about half-a-
dozen of the inevitable glass balls, and then crumpled,
crinkled paper, more and more and more, talking all the
time of the way in which people neglect to brush their hats
inside as well as out, politely, of course, but with a certain
personal application. "All sorts of things accumulate, sir. . . .
Not *you,* of course, in particular. . . . Nearly every customer.
. . . Astonishing what they carry about with them. . . ." The
crumpled paper rose and billowed on the counter more
and more and more, until he was nearly hidden from us,
until he was altogether hidden, and still his voice went on
and on. "We none of us know what the fair semblance of
a human being may conceal, sir. Are we all then no better
than brushed exteriors, whited sepulchres—"

His voice stopped—exactly like when you hit a neighbour's gramophone with a well-aimed brick, the same instant silence, and the rustle of the paper stopped, and
everything was still. . . .

"Have you done with my hat?" I said, after an interval.

There was no answer.

I stared at Gip, and Gip stared at me, and there were
our distortions in the magic mirrors, looking very rum,
and grave, and quiet. . . .

"I think we'll go now," I said. "Will you tell me how
much all this comes to? . . . .

"I say," I said, on a rather louder note, "I want the bill;
and my hat, please."

It might have been a sniff from behind the paper pile. . . .

"Let's look behind the counter, Gip," I said. "He's making fun of us."

I led Gip round the head-wagging tiger, and what do you think there was behind the counter? No one at all! Only my hat on the floor, and a common conjurer's lopeared white rabbit lost in meditation, and looking as stupid and crumpled as only a conjurer's rabbit can do. I resumed my hat, and the rabbit lolloped a lollop or so out of my way.

"Dadda!" said Gip, in a guilty whisper.

"What is it, Gip?" said I.

"I *do* like this shop, dadda."

"So should I," I said to myself, "if the counter wouldn't suddenly extend itself to shut one off from the door." But I didn't call Gip's attention to that. "Pussy!" he said, with a hand out to the rabbit as it came lolloping past us; "Pussy, do Gip a magic!" and his eyes followed it as it squeezed through a door I had certainly not remarked a moment before. Then this door opened wider, and the man with one ear larger than the other appeared again. He was smiling still, but his eye met mine with something between amusement and defiance. "You'd like to see our show-room, sir," he said, with an innocent suavity. Gip tugged my finger forward. I glanced at the counter and met the shopman's eye again. I was beginning to think the magic just a little too genuine. "We haven't *very* much time," I said. But somehow we were inside the show-room before I could finish that.

"All goods of the same quality," said the shopman, rubbing his flexible hands together, "and that is the Best. Nothing in the place that isn't genuine Magic, and warranted thoroughly rum. Excuse me, sir!"

I felt him pull at something that clung to my coatsleeve, and then I saw he held a little, wriggling red demon by the tail—the little creature bit and fought and tried to get at his hand—and in a moment he tossed it carelessly behind a counter. No doubt the thing was only an image of twisted india-rubber, but for the moment—! And his gesture was exactly that of a man who handles some petty biting bit of vermin. I glanced at Gip, but Gip was looking at a magic rocking-horse. I was glad he hadn't seen the thing. "I say," I said, in an undertone, and indicating Gip and the red demon with my eyes, "you haven't many things like that about, have you?"

"None of ours! Probably brought it with you," said the shopman—also in an undertone, and with a more dazzling smile than ever. "Astonishing what people *will* carry about with them unawares!" And then to Gip, "Do you see anything you fancy here?"

There were many things that Gip fancied there.

He turned to this astonishing tradesman with mingled confidence and respect. "Is that a Magic Sword?" he said.

"A Magic Toy Sword. It neither bends, breaks, nor cuts the fingers. It renders the bearer invincible in battle against any one under eighteen. Half-a-crown to seven and sixpence, according to size. These panoplies on cards are for juvenile knights-errant and very useful—shield of safety, sandals of swiftness, helmet of invisibility."

"Oh, daddy!" gasped Gip.

I tried to find out what they cost, but the shopman did not heed me. He had got Gip now; he had got him away from my finger; he had embarked upon the exposition of all his confounded stock, and nothing was going to stop him. Presently I saw with a qualm of distrust and something very like jealousy that Gip had hold of this person's finger as usually he has hold of mine. No doubt the fellow was interesting, I thought, and had an interestingly faked lot of stuff, really *good* faked stuff, still—

I wandered after them, saying very little, but keeping an eye on this prestidigital fellow. After all, Gip was enjoying it. And no doubt when the time came to go we should be able to go quite easily.

It was a long, rambling place, that show-room, a gallery broken up by stands and stalls and pillars, with archways leading off to other departments, in which the queerest-looking assistants loafed and stared at one, and with perplexing mirrors and curtains. So perplexing, indeed, were these that I was presently unable to make out the door by which we had come.

The shopman showed Gip magic trains that ran without steam or clockwork, just as you set the signals, and then some very, very valuable boxes of soldiers that all came alive directly you took off the lid and said— I myself haven't a very quick ear and it was a tongue-twisting sound, but Gip—he has his mother's ear—got it in no time. "Bravo!" said the shopman, putting the men back into the box unceremoniously and handing it to Gip. "Now," said the shopman, and in a moment Gip had made them all alive again.

"You'll take that box?" asked the shopman.

"We'll take that box," said I, "unless you charge its full value. In which case it would need a Trust Magnate—"

"Dear heart! *No!*" and the shopman swept the little men back again, shut the lid, waved the box in the air, and there it was, in brown paper, tied up and—*with Gip's full name and address on the paper!*

The shopman laughed at my amazement.

"This is the genuine magic," he said. "The real thing."

"It's a little too genuine for my taste," I said again.

After that he fell to showing Gip tricks, odd tricks, and still odder the way they were done. He explained them, he turned them inside out, and there was the dear little chap nodding his busy bit of a head in the sagest manner.

I did not attend as well as I might. "Hey, presto!" said the Magic Shopman, and then would come the clear, small "Hey, presto!" of the boy. But I was distracted by other things. It was being borne in upon me just how tremendously rum this place was; it was, so to speak, inundated by a sense of rumness. There was something a little rum about the fixtures even, about the ceiling, about the floor, about the casually distributed chairs. I had a queer feeling that whenever I wasn't looking at them straight they went askew, and moved about, and played a noiseless puss-in-the-corner behind my back. And the cornice had a serpentine design with masks—masks altogether too expressive for proper plaster.

Then abruptly my attention was caught by one of the odd-looking assistants. He was some way off and evidently unaware of my presence—I saw a sort of three-quarter length of him over a pile of toys and through an arch—and, you know, he was leaning against a pillar in an idle sort of way doing the most horrid things with his features! The particular horrid thing he did was with his nose. He did it just as though he was idle and wanted to amuse himself. First of all it was a short, blobby nose, and then suddenly he shot it out like a telescope, and then out it flew and became thinner and thinner until it was like a long, red, flexible whip. Like a thing in a nightmare it was! He flourished it about and flung it forth as a fly-fisher flings his line.

My instant thought was that Gip mustn't see him. I turned about, and there was Gip quite preoccupied with the shopman, and thinking no evil. They were whispering together and looking at me. Gip was standing on a little stool, and the shopman was holding a sort of big drum in his hand.

"Hide and seek, dadda!" cried Gip. "You're He!"

And before I could do anything to prevent it, the shopman had clapped the big drum over him.

I saw what was up directly. "Take that off," I cried, "this instant! You'll frighten the boy. Take it off!"

The shopman with the unequal ears did so without a word, and held the big cylinder towards me to show its emptiness. And the little stool was vacant! In that instant my boy had utterly disappeared? . . .

You know, perhaps, that sinister something that comes like a hand out of the unseen and grips your heart about. You know it takes your common self away and leaves you tense and deliberate, neither slow nor hasty, neither angry nor afraid. So it was with me.

I came up to this grinning shopman and kicked his stool aside.

"Stop this folly!" I said. "Where is my boy?"

"You see," he said, still displaying the drum's interior, "there is no deception—"

I put out my hand to grip him, and he eluded me by a dexterous movement. I snatched again, and he turned from me and pushed open a door to escape. "Stop!" I said, and he laughed, receding. I leapt after him—into utter darkness.

Thud!

"Lor' bless my 'eart! I didn't see you coming, sir!"

I was in Regent Street, and I had collided with a decent-looking working man; and a yard away, perhaps, and looking a little perplexed with himself, was Gip. There was some sort of apology, and then Gip had turned and come to me with a bright little smile, as though for a moment he had missed me.

And he was carrying four parcels in his arm!

He secured immediate possession of my finger.

For the second I was rather at a loss. I stared round to see the door of the magic shop, and, behold, it was not there! There was no door, no shop, nothing, only the common pilaster between the shop where they sell pictures and the window with the chicks! . . .

I did the only thing possible in that mental tumult; I walked straight to the kerbstone and held up my umbrella for a cab.

"'Ansoms," said Gip, in a note of culminating exultation.

I helped him in, recalled my address with an effort, and got in also. Something unusual proclaimed itself in my tail-coat pocket, and I felt and discovered a glass ball. With a petulant expression I flung it into the street.

Gip said nothing.

For a space neither of us spoke.

"Dadda!" said Gip, at last, "that *was* a proper shop!"

I came round with that to the problem of just how the whole thing had seemed to him. He looked completely undamaged—so far, good; he was neither scared nor unhinged, he was simply tremendously satisfied with the afternoon's entertainment, and there in his arms were the four parcels.

Confound it! what could be in them?

"Um!" I said. "Little boys can't go to shops like that every day."

He received this with his usual stoicism, and for a moment I was sorry I was his father and not his mother, and so couldn't suddenly there, *coram publico,* in our hansom, kiss him. After all, I thought, the thing wasn't so very bad.

But it was only when we opened the parcels that I really began to be reassured. Three of them contained boxes of soldiers, quite ordinary lead soldiers, but of so good a quality as to make Gip altogether forget that originally these parcels had been Magic Tricks of the only genuine sort, and the fourth contained a kitten, a little living white kitten, in excellent health and appetite and temper.

I saw this unpacking with a sort of provisional relief. I hung about in the nursery for quite an unconscionable time. . . .

That happened six months ago. And now I am beginning to believe it is all right. The kitten had only the magic natural to all kittens, and the soldiers seem as steady a company as any colonel could desire. And Gip?

The intelligent parent will understand that I have to go cautiously with Gip.

But I went so far as this one day. I said, "How would you like your soldiers to come alive, Gip, and march about by themselves?"

"Mine do," said Gip. "I just have to say a word I know before I open the lid."

"Then they march about alone?"

"Oh, *quite,* dadda. I shouldn't like them if they didn't do that."

I displayed no unbecoming surprise, and since then I have taken occasion to drop in upon him once or twice, unannounced, when the soldiers were about, but so far I have never discovered them performing in anything like a magical manner. . . .

It's so difficult to tell.

There's also a question of finance. I have an incurable habit of paying bills. I have been up and down Regent Street several times, looking for that shop. I am inclined to think, indeed, that in that matter honour is satisfied, and that, since Gip's name and address are known to them, I may very well leave it to these people, whoever they may be, to send in their bill in their own time.

Number 13

M. R. James

(1904)

Among the towns of Jutland, Viborg justly holds a high place. It is the seat of a bishopric; it has a handsome but almost entirely new cathedral, a charming garden, a lake of great beauty, and many storks. Near it is Hald, accounted one of the prettiest things in Denmark; and hard by is Finderup, where Marsk Stig murdered King Erik Clipping on St. Cecilia's Day, in the year 1286. Fifty-six blows of square-headed iron maces were traced on Erik's skull when his tomb was opened in the seventeenth century. But I am not writing a guide-book.

There are good hotels in Viborg—Preisler's and the Phœnix are all that can be desired. But my cousin, whose experiences I have to tell you now, went to the Golden Lion the first time that he visited Viborg. He has not been there since, and the following pages will perhaps explain the reason of his abstention.

The Golden Lion is one of the very few houses in the town that were not destroyed in the great fire of 1726, which practically demolished the cathedral, the Sognekirke, the Raadhuus, and so much else that was old and interesting. It is a great red-brick house—that is, the front is of brick, with corbie steps on the gables and a text over the door; but the courtyard into which the omnibus drives is of black and white wood and plaster.

The sun was declining in the heavens when my cousin walked up to the door, and the light smote full upon the imposing façade of the house. He was delighted with the old-fashioned aspect of the place, and promised himself a thoroughly satisfactory and amusing stay in an inn so typical of old Jutland.

It was not business in the ordinary sense of the word that had brought Mr. Anderson to Viborg. He was engaged upon some researches into the Church history of Denmark, and it had come to his knowledge that in the Kigsarkiv of Viborg there were papers, saved from the fire, relating to the last days of Roman Catholicism in the country. He proposed, therefore, to spend a considerable time—perhaps as much as a fortnight or three weeks—in examining and copying these, and he hoped that the Golden Lion would be able to give him a room of sufficient size to serve alike as a bedroom and a study. His wishes were explained to the landlord, and, after a certain amount of thought, the latter suggested that perhaps it might be the best way for the gentleman to look at one or two of the larger rooms and pick one for himself. It seemed a good idea.

The top floor was soon rejected as entailing too much getting upstairs after the day's work; the second floor contained no room of exactly the dimensions required; but on the first floor there was a choice of two or three rooms which would, so far as size went, suit admirably.

The landlord was strongly in favour of Number 17, but Mr. Anderson pointed out that its windows commanded only the blank wall of the next house, and that it would be very dark in the afternoon. Either Number 12 or Number 14 would be better, for both of them looked on the street, and the bright evening light and the pretty view would more than compensate him for the additional amount of noise.

Eventually Number 12 was selected. Like its neighbours, it had three windows, all on one side of the room; it
was fairly high and unusually long. There was, of course,
no fireplace, but the stove was handsome and rather old—
a cast-iron erection, on the side of which was a represen-
tation of Abraham sacrificing Isaac, and the inscription,
'1 Bog Mose, Cap. 22,' above. Nothing else in the room
was remarkable; the only interesting picture was an old
coloured print of the town, date about 1820.

Supper-time was approaching, but when Anderson, refreshed by the ordinary ablutions, descended the staircase,
there were still a few minutes before the bell rang. He devoted them to examining the list of his fellow-lodgers. As
is usual in Denmark, their names were displayed on a large
blackboard, divided into columns and lines, the numbers
of the rooms being painted in at the beginning of each
line. The list was not exciting. There was an advocate,
or Sagförer, a German, and some bagmen from Copenha-
gen. The one and only point which suggested any food for
thought was the absence of any Number 13 from the tale
of the rooms, and even this was a thing which Anderson
had already noticed half a dozen times in his experience of
Danish hotels. He could not help wondering whether the
objection to that particular number, common as it is, was
so widespread and so strong as to make it difficult to let
a room so ticketed, and he resolved to ask the landlord if
he and his colleagues in the profession had actually met
with many clients who refused to be accommodated in the
thirteenth room.

He had nothing to tell me (I am giving the story as I
heard it from him) about what passed at supper, and the
evening, which was spent in unpacking and arranging his
clothes, books, and papers, was not more eventful. Towards
eleven o'clock he resolved to go to bed, but with him,
as with a good many other people nowadays, an almost

necessary preliminary to bed, if he meant to sleep, was the
reading of a few pages of print, and he now remembered
that the particular book which he had been reading in the
train, and which alone would satisfy him at that present
moment, was in the pocket of his great-coat, then hanging
on a peg outside the dining-room.

To run down and secure it was the work of a moment,
and, as the passages were by no means dark, it was not
difficult for him to find his way back to his own door.
So, at least, he thought; but when he arrived there, and
turned the handle, the door entirely refused to open, and
he caught the sound of a hasty movement towards it from
within. He had tried the wrong door, of course. Was his
own room to the right or to the left? He glanced at the
number: it was 13. His room would be on the left; and so
it was. And not before he had been in bed for some minutes, had read his wonted three or four pages of his book,
blown out his light, and turned over to go to sleep, did it
occur to him that, whereas on the blackboard of the hotel
there had been no Number 13, there was undoubtedly a
room numbered 13 in the hotel. He felt rather sorry he
had not chosen it for his own. Perhaps he might have done
the landlord a little service by occupying it, and given him
the chance of saying that a well-born English gentleman
had lived in it for three weeks and liked it very much.
But probably it was used as a servant's room or something
of the kind. After all, it was most likely not so large or
good a room as his own. And he looked drowsily about
the room, which was fairly perceptible in the half-light
from the street-lamp. It was a curious effect, he thought.
Rooms usually look larger in a dim light than a full one,
but this seemed to have contracted in length and grown
proportionately higher. Well, well! sleep was more important than these vague ruminations—and to sleep he went.

On the day after his arrival Anderson attacked the Rig-sarkiv of Viborg. He was, as one might expect in Denmark, kindly received, and access to all that he wished to see was made as easy for him as possible. The documents laid before him were far more numerous and interesting than he had at all anticipated. Besides official papers, there was a large bundle of correspondence relating to Bishop Jörgen Friis, the last Roman Catholic who held the see, and in these there cropped up many amusing and what are called 'intimate' details of private life and individual character. There was much talk of a house owned by the Bishop, but not inhabited by him, in the town. Its tenant was apparently somewhat of a scandal and a stumbling-block to the reforming party. He was a disgrace, they wrote, to the city; he practised secret and wicked arts, and had sold his soul to the enemy. It was of a piece with the gross corruption and superstition of the Babylonish Church that such a viper and blood-sucking *Troldmand* should be patronized and harboured by the Bishop. The Bishop met these reproaches boldly; he protested his own abhorrence of all such things as secret arts, and required his antagonists to bring the matter before the proper court—of course, the spiritual court—and sift it to the bottom. No one could be more ready and willing than himself to condemn Mag. Nicolas Francken if the evidence showed him to have been guilty of any of the crimes informally alleged against him.

Anderson had not time to do more than glance at the next letter of the Protestant leader, Rasmus Nielsen, before the record office was closed for the day, but he gathered its general tenor, which was to the effect that Christian men were now no longer bound by the decisions of Bishops of Rome, and that the Bishop's Court was not, and could not be, a fit or competent tribunal to judge so grave and weighty a cause.

On leaving the office, Mr. Anderson was accompanied
by the old gentleman who presided over it, and, as they
walked, the conversation very naturally turned to the papers of which I have just been speaking.

Herr Scavenius, the Archivist of Viborg, though very
well informed as to the general run of the documents under his charge, was not a specialist in those of the Reformation period. He was much interested in what Anderson
had to tell him about them. He looked forward with great
pleasure, he said, to seeing the publication in which Mr.
Anderson spoke of embodying their contents. "This house
of the Bishop Friis," he added, "it is a great puzzle to me
where it can have stood. I have studied carefully the topo-
graphy of old Viborg, but it is most unlucky—of the old
terrier of the Bishop's property which was made in 1560,
and of which we have the greater part in the Arkiv, just
the piece which had the list of the town property is missing. Never mind. Perhaps I shall some day succeed to find
him."

After taking some exercise—I forget exactly how or
where—Anderson went back to the Golden Lion, his supper, his game of patience, and his bed. On the way to
his room it occurred to him that he had forgotten to talk
to the landlord about the omission of Number 13 from the
hotel board, and also that he might as well make sure that
Number 13 did actually exist before he made any reference
to the matter.

The decision was not difficult to arrive at. There was
the door with its number as plain as could be, and work
of some kind was evidently going on inside it, for as he
neared the door he could hear footsteps and voices, or a
voice, within. During the few seconds in which he halted
to make sure of the number, the footsteps ceased, seemingly very near the door, and he was a little startled at
hearing a quick hissing breathing as of a person in strong

excitement. He went on to his own room, and again he was
surprised to find how much smaller it seemed now than it
had when he selected it. It was a slight disappointment,
but only slight. If he found it really not large enough,
he could very easily shift to another. In the meantime he
wanted something—as far as I remember it was a pocket-
handkerchief—out of his portmanteau, which had been
placed by the porter on a very inadequate trestle or stool
against the wall at the furthest end of the room from his
bed. Here was a very curious thing: the portmanteau was
not to be seen. It had been moved by officious servants;
doubtless the contents had been put in the wardrobe. No,
none of them were there. This was vexatious. The idea of
a theft he dismissed at once. Such things rarely happen in
Denmark, but some piece of stupidity had certainly been
performed (which is not so uncommon), and the *stuepige* must be severely spoken to. Whatever it was that he
wanted, it was not so necessary to his comfort that he
could not wait till the morning for it, and he therefore
settled not to ring the bell and disturb the servants. He
went to the window—the right-hand window it was—and
looked out on the quiet street. There was a tall building
opposite, with large spaces of dead wall; no passers by; a
dark night; and very little to be seen of any kind.

The light was behind him, and he could see his own
shadow clearly cast on the wall opposite. Also the shadow
of the bearded man in Number 11 on the left, who passed
to and fro in shirtsleeves once or twice, and was seen first
brushing his hair, and later on in a nightgown. Also the
shadow of the occupant of Number 13 on the right. This
might be more interesting. Number 13 was, like himself,
leaning on his elbows on the window-sill looking out into
the street. He seemed to be a tall thin man—or was it
by any chance a woman?—at least, it was someone who
covered his or her head with some kind of drapery before

going to bed, and, he thought, must be possessed of a red lamp-shade—and the lamp must be flickering very much. There was a distinct playing up and down of a dull red light on the opposite wall. He craned out a little to see if he could make any more of the figure, but beyond a fold of some light, perhaps white, material on the window-sill he could see nothing.

Now came a distant step in the street, and its approach seemed to recall Number 13 to a sense of his exposed position, for very swiftly and suddenly he swept aside from the window, and his red light went out. Anderson, who had been smoking a cigarette, laid the end of it on the window-sill and went to bed.

Next morning he was woke by the *stuepige* with hot water, etc. He roused himself, and after thinking out the correct Danish words, said as distinctly as he could:

"You must not move my portmanteau. Where is it?"

As is not uncommon, the maid laughed, and went away without making any distinct answer.

Anderson, rather irritated, sat up in bed, intending to call her back, but he remained sitting up, staring straight in front of him. There was his portmanteau on its trestle, exactly where he had seen the porter put it when he first arrived. This was a rude shock for a man who prided himself on his accuracy of observation. How it could possibly have escaped him the night before he did, not pretend to understand; at any rate, there it was now.

The daylight showed more than the portmanteau; it let the true proportions of the room with its three windows appear, and satisfied its tenant that his choice after all had not been a bad one. When he was almost dressed he walked to the middle one of the three windows to look out at the weather. Another shock awaited him. Strangely unobservant he must have been last night. He could have sworn

ten times over that he had been smoking at the right-hand
window the last thing before he went to bed, and here was
his cigarette-end on the sill of the middle window.

He started to go down to breakfast. Rather late, but
Number 13 was later: here were his boots still outside
his door—a gentleman's boots. So then Number 13 was
a man, not a woman. Just then he caught sight of the
number on the door. It was 14. He thought he must have
passed Number 13 without noticing it. Three stupid
mistakes in twelve hours were too much for a methodical, accurate-minded man, so he turned back to make sure.
The next number to 14 was number 12, his own room.
There was no Number 13 at all.

After some minutes devoted to a careful consideration
of everything he had had to eat and drink during the last
twenty-four hours, Anderson decided to give the question
up. If his eyes or his brain were giving way he would have
plenty of opportunities for ascertaining that fact; if not,
then he was evidently being treated to a very interesting
experience. In either case the development of events would
certainly be worth watching.

During the day he continued his examination of the
episcopal correspondence which I have already summa-
rized. To his disappointment, it was incomplete. Only one
other letter could be found which referred to the affair
of Mag. Nicolas Francken. It was from the Bishop Jörgen
Friis to Rasmus Nielsen. He said:

"Although we are not in the least degree inclined to assent to your judgment concerning our court, and shall be
prepared if need be to withstand you to the uttermost in
that behalf, yet forasmuch as our trusty and well-beloved
Mag. Nicolas Francken, against whom you have dared
to allege certain false and malicious charges, hath been
suddenly removed from among us, it is apparent that the

question for this term falls. But forasmuch as you further allege that the Apostle and Evangelist St. John in his heavenly Apocalypse describes the Holy Roman Church under the guise and symbol of the Scarlet Woman, be it known to you," etc.

Search as he would, Anderson could find no sequel to this letter nor any clue to the cause or manner of the 'removal' of the *casus belli*. He could only suppose that Francken had died suddenly; and as there were only two days between the date of Nielsen's last letter—when Francken was evidently still in being—and that of the Bishop's letter, the death must have been completely unexpected.

In the afternoon he paid a short visit to Hald, and took his tea at Baekkelund; nor could he notice, though he was in a somewhat nervous frame of mind, that there was any indication of such a failure of eye or brain as his experiences of the morning had led him to fear.

At supper he found himself next to the landlord.

"What," he asked him, after some indifferent conversation, "is the reason why in most of the hotels one visits in this country the number thirteen is left out of the list of rooms? I see you have none here."

The landlord seemed amused.

"To think that you should have noticed a thing like that! I've thought about it once or twice myself, to tell the truth. An educated man, I've said, has no business with these superstitious notions. I was brought up myself here in the high school of Viborg, and our old master was always a man to set his face against anything of that kind. He's been dead now this many years—a fine upstanding man he was, and ready with his hands as well as his head. I recollect us boys, one snowy day—"

Here he plunged into reminiscence.

"Then you don't think there is any particular objection to having a Number 13?" said Anderson.

"Ah! to be sure. Well, you understand, I was brought up to the business by my poor old father. He kept an hotel in Aarhuus first, and then, when we were born, he moved to Viborg here, which was his native place, and had the Phœnix here until he died. That was in 1876. Then I started business in Silkeborg, and only the year before last I moved into this house."

Then followed more details as to the state of the house and business when first taken over.

"And when you came here, was there a Number 13?"

"No, no. I was going to tell you about that. You see, in a place like this, the commercial class—the travellers—are what we have to provide for in general. And put them in Number 13? Why, they'd as soon sleep in the street, or sooner. As far as I'm concerned myself, it wouldn't make a penny difference to me what the number of my room was, and so I've often said to them; but they stick to it that it brings them bad luck. Quantities of stories they have among them of men that have slept in a Number 13 and never been the same again, or lost their best customers, or—one thing and another," said the landlord, after searching for a more graphic phrase.

"Then, what do you use your Number 13 for?" said Anderson, conscious as he said the words of a curious anxiety quite disproportionate to the importance of the question.

"My Number 13? Why, don't I tell you that there isn't such a thing in the house? I thought you might have noticed that. If there was it would be next door to your own room."

"Well, yes; only I happened to think—that is, I fancied last night that I had seen a door numbered thirteen in that passage; and, really, I am almost certain I must have been right, for I saw it the night before as well."

Of course, Herr Kristensen laughed this notion to scorn, as Anderson had expected, and emphasized with much iteration the fact that no Number 13 existed or had existed before him in that hotel.

Anderson was in some ways relieved by his certainty, but still puzzled, and he began to think that the best way to make sure whether he had indeed been subject to an illusion or not was to invite the landlord to his room to smoke a cigar later on in the evening. Some photographs of English towns which he had with him formed a sufficiently good excuse.

Herr Kristensen was flattered by the invitation, and most willingly accepted it. At about ten o'clock he was to make his appearance, but before that Anderson had some letters to write, and retired for the purpose of writing them. He almost blushed to himself at confessing it, but he could not deny that it was the fact that he was becoming quite nervous about the question of the existence of Number 13; so much so that he approached his room by way of Number 11, in order that he might not be obliged to pass the door, or the place where the door ought to be. He looked quickly and suspiciously about the room when entered it, but there was nothing, beyond that indefinable air of being smaller than usual, to warrant any misgivings. There was no question of the presence or absence of his portmanteau to-night. He had himself emptied it of its contents and lodged it under his bed. With a certain effort he dismissed the thought of Number 13 from his mind, and sat down to his writing.

His neighbours were quiet enough. Occasionally a door opened in the passage and pair of boots was thrown out, or a bagman walked past humming to himself, and outside, from time to time a cart thundered over the atrocious cobble-stones, or a quick step hurried along the flags.

Anderson finished his letters, ordered whisky and soda, and then went to the window and studied the dead wall opposite and the shadows upon it.

As far as he could remember, Number 14 had been occupied by the lawyer, a staid man, who said little at meals, being generally engaged in studying a small bundle of papers beside his plate. Apparently, however, he was in the habit of giving vent to his animal spirits when alone. Why else should he be dancing? The shadow from the next room evidently showed that he was. Again and again his thin form crossed the window, his arms waved, and a gaunt leg was kicked up with surprising agility. He seemed to be barefooted, and the floor must be well laid, for no sound betrayed his movements. Sagförer Herr Anders Jensen, dancing at ten o'clock at night in a hotel bedroom, seemed a fitting subject for a historical painting in the grand style; and Anderson's thoughts, like those of Emily in the 'Mysteries of Udolpho,' began to 'arrange themselves in the following lines':

'When I return to my hotel.
   At ten o'clock p.m.,
The waiters think I am unwell;
   I do not care for them.
But when I've locked my chamber door,
   And put my boots outside,
I dance all night upon the floor.
   And even if my neighbours swore,
I'd go on dancing all the more.
   For I'm acquainted with the law.
And in despite of all their jaw.
   Their protests I deride.'

Had not the landlord at this moment knocked at the door, it is probable that quite a long poem might have been laid before the reader. To judge from his look of surprise when he found himself in the room, Herr Kristensen was struck, as Anderson had been, by something unusual in its aspect. But he made no remark. Anderson's photographs interested him mightily, and formed the text of many autobiographical discourses. Nor is it quite clear how the conversation could have been diverted into the desired channel of Number 13, had not the lawyer at this moment begun to sing, and to sing in a manner which could leave no doubt in anyone's mind that he was either exceedingly drunk or raving mad. It was a high, thin voice that they heard, and it seemed dry, as if from long disuse. Of words or tune there was no question. It went sailing up to a surprising height, and was carried down with a despairing moan as of a winter wind in a hollow chimney, or an organ whose wind fails suddenly. It was a really horrible sound, and Anderson felt that if he had been alone he must have fled for refuge and society to some neighbour bagman's room.

The landlord sat open-mouthed.

"I don't understand it," he said at last, wiping his forehead. "It is dreadful. I have heard it once before, but I made sure it was a cat."

"Is he mad?" said Anderson.

"He must be; and what a sad thing! Such a good customer, too, and so successful in his business, by what I hear, and a young family to bring up."

Just then came an impatient knock at the door, and the knocker entered, without waiting to be asked. It was the lawyer, in deshabille and very rough-haired; and very angry he looked.

"I beg pardon, sir," he said, "but I should be much obliged if you would kindly desist—"

Here he stopped, for it was evident that neither of the persons before him was responsible for the disturbance; and after a moment's lull it swelled forth again more wildly than before.

"But what in the name of Heaven does it mean?" broke out the lawyer. "Where is it? Who is it? Am I going out of my mind?"

"Surely, Herr Jensen, it comes from your room next door? Isn't there a cat or something stuck in the chimney?"

This was the best that occurred to Anderson to say, and he realized its futility as he spoke; but anything was better than to stand and listen to that horrible voice, and look at the broad, white face of the landlord, all perspiring and quivering as he clutched the arms of his chair.

"Impossible," said the lawyer, "impossible. There is no chimney. I came here because I was convinced the noise was going on here. It was certainly in the next room to mine."

"Was there no door between yours and mine?" said Anderson eagerly.

"No, sir," said Herr Jensen, rather sharply. "At least, not this morning."

"Ah!" said Anderson. "Nor to-night?"

"I am not sure," said the lawyer with some hesitation.

Suddenly the crying or singing voice in the next room died away, and the singer was heard seemingly to laugh to himself in a crooning manner. The three men actually shivered at the sound. Then there was a silence.

"Come," said the lawyer, "what have you to say, Herr Kristensen? What does this mean?"

"Good Heaven!" said Kristensen. "How should I tell! I know no more than you, gentlemen. I pray I may never hear such a noise again."

"So do I," said Herr Jensen, and he added something under his breath. Anderson thought it sounded like the last words of the Psalter, *'omnis spiritus laudet Dominum,'* but he could not be sure.

"But we must do something," said Anderson—"the three of us. Shall we go and investigate in the next room?"

"But that is Herr Jensen's room," wailed the landlord. "It is no use; he has come from there himself."

"I am not so sure," said Jensen. "I think this gentleman is right: we must go and see."

The only weapons of defence that could be mustered on the spot were a stick and umbrella. The expedition went out into the passage, not without quakings. There was a deadly quiet outside, but a light shone from under the next door. Anderson and Jensen approached it. The latter turned the handle, and gave a sudden vigorous push. No use. The door stood fast.

"Herr Kristensen," said Jensen, "will you go and fetch the strongest servant you have in the place? We must see this through."

The landlord nodded, and hurried off, glad to be away from the scene of action. Jensen and Anderson remained outside looking at the door.

"It *is* Number 13, you see," said the latter.

"Yes; there is your door, and there is mine," said Jensen.

"My room has three windows in the daytime," said Anderson, with difficulty suppressing a nervous laugh.

"By George, so has mine!" said the lawyer, turning and looking at Anderson. His back was now to the door. In that moment the door opened, and an arm came out and clawed at his shoulder. It was clad in ragged, yellowish linen, and the bare skin, where it could be seen, had long gray hair upon it.

Anderson was just in time to pull Jensen out of its reach with a cry of disgust and fright, when the door shut again, and a low laugh was heard.

Jensen had seen nothing, but when Anderson hurriedly told him what a risk he had run, he fell into a great state of agitation, and suggested that they should retire from the enterprise and lock themselves up in one or other of their rooms.

However, while he was developing this plan, the landlord and two able-bodied men arrived on the scene, all looking rather serious and alarmed. Jensen met them with a torrent of description and explanation, which did not at all tend to encourage them for the fray.

The men dropped the crowbars they brought, and said flatly that they were going to risk their throats in that devil's den. The landlord was miserably nervous and decided, conscious that if the danger were not faced his hotel was ruined, and very loath to face it himself. Luckily Anderson hit upon a way of rallying the demoralized force.

"Is this," he said, "the Danish courage I heard so much of? It isn't a German in there, and if it was, we are five to one."

The two servants and Jensen were stung action by this, and made a dash at the door.

"Stop!" said Anderson. "Don't lose your heads. You stay out here with the light, landlord, and one of you two men break the door, and don't go in when it gives way."

The men nodded, and the younger stepped forward, raised his crowbar, and dealt tremendous blow on the upper panel. The result was not in the least what any of them anticipated. There was no cracking or rending of wood— only a dull sound, as if the solid wall had been struck. The man dropped his tool with a shout, and began rubbing his elbow. His cry drew their eyes upon him for a moment; then Anderson looked at the door again. It was gone; the plaster wall of the passage stared him in the face, with a considerable gash in it where the crowbar had struck it. Number 13 had passed out of existence.

For a brief space they stood perfectly still, gazing at the blank wall. An early cock in the yard beneath was heard to crow; and as Anderson glanced in the direction of the sound, he saw through the window at the end of the long passage that the eastern sky was paling to the dawn.

* * *

"Perhaps," said the landlord, with hesitation, "you gentlemen would like another room for to-night—a double-bed-
ded one?"

Neither Jensen nor Anderson was averse to the suggestion. They felt inclined to hunt in couples after their late
experience. It was found convenient, when each of them
went to his room to collect the articles he wanted for the
night, that the other should go with him and hold the
candle. They noticed that both Number 12 and Number
14 had *three* windows.

Next morning the same party re-assembled in Number
12. The landlord was naturally anxious to avoid engaging
outside help, and yet it was imperative that the mystery
attaching to that part of the house should be cleared up.
Accordingly the two servants had been induced to take
upon them the function of carpenters. The furniture was
cleared away, and, at the cost of a good many irretrievably
damaged planks, that portion of the floor was taken up
which lay nearest to Number 14.

You will naturally suppose that a skeleton—say that
of Mag. Nicolas Francken—was discovered. That was not
so. What they did find lying between the beams which
supported the flooring was a small copper box. In it was
a neatly-folded vellum document, with about twenty lines
of writing. Both Anderson and Jensen (who proved to
be something of a palæographer) were much excited by
this discovery, which promised to afford the key to these
extraordinary phenomena.

* * *

I possess a copy of an astrological work which I have never read. It has, by way of frontispiece, a woodcut by Hans Sebald Beham, representing a number of sages seated round a table. This detail may enable connoisseurs to identify the book. I cannot myself recollect its title, and it is not at this moment within reach; but the fly-leaves of it are covered with writing, and, during the ten years in which I have owned the volume, I have not been able to determine which way up this writing ought to be read, much less in what language it is. Not dissimilar was the position of Anderson and Jensen after the protracted examination to which they submitted the document in the copper box.

After two days' contemplation of it, Jensen, who was the bolder spirit of the two, hazarded the conjecture that the language was either Latin or Old Danish.

Anderson ventured upon no surmises, and was very willing to surrender the box and the parchment to the Historical Society of Viborg to be placed in their museum.

I had the whole story from him a few months later, as we sat in a wood near Upsala, after a visit to the library there, where we—or, rather, I—had laughed over the contract by which Daniel Salthenius (in later life Professor of Hebrew at Königsberg) sold himself to Satan. Anderson was not really amused.

"Young idiot!" he said, meaning Salthenius, who was only an undergraduate when he committed that indiscretion, "how did he know what company he was courting?"

And when I suggested the usual considerations he only grunted. That same afternoon he told me what you have read; but he refused to draw any inferences from it, and to assent to any that I drew for him.

A Somewhat Improbable Story

G. K. Chesterton

(1909)

I cannot remember whether this tale is true or not. If I
read it through very carefully I have a suspicion that I
should come to the conclusion that it is not. But, unfor-
tunately, I cannot read it through very carefully, because,
you see, it is not written yet. The image and the idea of
it clung to me through a great part of my boyhood; I may
have dreamt it before I could talk; or told it to myself before I could read; or read it before I could remember. On
the whole, however, I am certain that I did not read it, for
children have very clear memories about things like that;
and of the books which I was really fond I can still remember, not only the shape and bulk and binding, but even the
position of the printed words on many of the pages. On
the whole, I incline to the opinion that it happened to me
before I was born.

* * *

At any rate, let us tell the story now with all the advantages
of the atmosphere that has clung to it. You may suppose
me, for the sake of argument, sitting at lunch in one of
those quick-lunch restaurants in the City where men take
their food so fast that it has none of the quality of food,
and take their half-hour's vacation so fast that it has none

of the qualities of leisure; to hurry through one's leisure
is the most unbusiness-like of actions. They all wore tall
shiny hats as if they could not lose an instant even to hang
them on a peg, and they all had one eye a little off, hypno-
tised by the huge eye of the clock. In short, they were the
slaves of the modern bondage, you could hear their fetters
clanking. Each was, in fact, bound by a chain; the heaviest
chain ever tied to a man—it is called a watch-chain.

Now, among these there entered and sat down opposite
to me a man who almost immediately opened an uninterrupted monologue. He was like all the other men in dress,
yet he was startlingly opposite to them in all manner. He
wore a high shiny hat and a long frock coat, but he wore
them as such solemn things were meant to be worn; he
wore the silk hat as if it were a mitre, and the frock coat
as if it were the ephod of a high priest. He not only hung
his hat up on the peg, but he seemed (such was his stateli-
ness) almost to ask permission of the hat for doing so, and
to apologise to the peg for making use of it. When he had
sat down on a wooden chair with the air of one considering its feelings and given a sort of slight stoop or bow to
the wooden table itself, as if it were an altar, I could not
help some comment springing to my lips. For the man was
a big, sanguine-faced, prosperous-looking man, and yet
he treated everything with a care that almost amounted to
nervousness.

For the sake of saying something to express my interest
I said, "This furniture is fairly solid; but, of course, people do treat it much too carelessly."

As I looked up doubtfully my eye caught his, and
was fixed as his was fixed in an apocalyptic stare. I had
thought him ordinary as he entered, save for his strange,
cautious manner; but if the other people had seen him
then they would have screamed and emptied the room.
They did not see him, and they went on making a clatter

with their forks, and a murmur with their conversation. But the man's face was the face of a maniac.

"Did you mean anything particular by that remark?" he asked at last, and the blood crawled back slowly into his face.

"Nothing whatever," I answered. "One does not mean anything here; it spoils people's digestions."

He limped back and wiped his broad forehead with a big handkerchief; and yet there seemed to be a sort of regret in his relief.

"I thought perhaps," he said in a low voice, "that another of them had gone wrong."

"If you mean another digestion gone wrong," I said, "I never heard of one here that went right. This is the heart of the Empire, and the other organs are in an equally bad way."

"No, I mean another street gone wrong," and he said heavily and quietly, "but as I suppose that doesn't explain much to you, I think I shall have to tell you the story. I do so with all the less responsibility, because I know you won't believe it. For forty years of my life I invariably left my office, which is in Leadenhall Street, at half-past five in the afternoon, taking with me an umbrella in the right hand and a bag in the left hand. For forty years two months and four days I passed out of the side office door, walked down the street on the left-hand side, took the first turning to the left and the third to the right, from where I bought an evening paper, followed the road on the right-hand side round two obtuse angles, and came out just outside a Metropolitan station, where I took a train home. For forty years two months and four days I fulfilled this course by accumulated habit: it was not a long street that I traversed, and it took me about four and a half minutes to do it. After forty years two months and four days, on the fifth day I went out in the same manner, with my umbrella in the right hand and my bag in the left, and I

began to notice that walking along the familiar street tired
me somewhat more than usual; and when I turned it I was
convinced that I had turned down the wrong one. For now
the street shot up quite a steep slant, such as one only sees
in the hilly parts of London, and in this part there were no
hills at all. Yet it was not the wrong street; the name written on it was the same; the shuttered shops were the same;
the lamp-posts and the whole look of the perspective was
the same; only it was tilted upwards like a lid. Forgetting
any trouble about breathlessness or fatigue I ran furiously
forward, and reached the second of my accustomed turn-
ings, which ought to bring me almost within sight of the
station. And as I turned that corner I nearly fell on the
pavement. For now the street went up straight in front
of my face like a steep staircase or the side of a pyramid.
There was not for miles round that place so much as a
slope like that of Ludgate Hill. And this was a slope like
that of the Matterhorn. The whole street had lifted itself
like a single wave, and yet every speck and detail of it was
the same, and I saw in the high distance, as at the top of
an Alpine pass, picked out in pink letters the name over
my paper shop.

"I ran on and on blindly now, passing all the shops and
coming to a part of the road where there was a long grey
row of private houses. I had, I know not why, an irrational
feeling that I was a long iron bridge in empty space. An
impulse seized me, and I pulled up the iron trap of a coal-
hole. Looking down through it I saw empty space and the
stairs.

"When I looked up again a man was standing in his
front garden, having apparently come out of his house; he
was leaning over the railings and gazing at me. We were all
alone on that nightmare road; his face was in shadow; his
dress was dark and ordinary; but when I saw him standing
so perfectly still I knew somehow that he was not of this

world. And the stars behind his head were larger and fiercer than ought to be endured by the eyes of men.

"'If you are a kind angel,' I said, 'or a wise devil, or have anything in common with mankind, tell me what is this street possessed of devils.'

"After a long silence he said, 'What do you say that it is?'

"'It is Bumpton Street, of course,' I snapped. 'It goes to Oldgate Station.'

"'Yes,' he admitted gravely; 'it goes there sometimes. Just now, however, it is going to heaven.'

"'To heaven?' I said. 'Why?'

"'It is going to heaven for justice,' he replied. 'You must have treated it badly. Remember always that there is one thing that cannot be endured by anybody or anything. That one unendurable thing is to be overworked and also neglected. For instance, you can overwork women—everybody does. But you can't neglect women—I defy you to. At the same time, you can neglect tramps and gypsies and all the apparent refuse of the State so long as you do not overwork it. But no beast of the field, no horse, no dog can endure long to be asked to do more than his work and yet have less than his honour. It is the same with streets. You have worked this street to death, and yet you have never remembered its existence. If you had a healthy democracy, even of pagans, they would have hung this street with garlands and given it the name of a god. Then it would have gone quietly. But at last the street has grown tired of your tireless insolence; and it is bucking and rearing its head to heaven. Have you never sat on a bucking horse?'

"I looked at the long grey street, and for a moment it seemed to me to be exactly like the long grey neck of a horse flung up to heaven. But in a moment my sanity returned, and I said, 'But this is all nonsense. Streets go to the place they have to go. A street must always go to its end.'

"'Why do you think so of a street?' he asked, standing very still.

"'Because I have always seen it do the same thing,' I replied, in reasonable anger. 'Day after day, year after year, it has always gone to Oldgate Station; day after . . .'

"I stopped, for he had flung up his head with the fury of the road in revolt.

"'And you?' he cried terribly. 'What do you think the road thinks of you? Does the road think you are alive? Are you alive? Day after day, year after year, you have gone to Oldgate Station . . .' Since then I have respected the things called inanimate."

And bowing slightly to the mustard-pot, the man in the restaurant withdrew.

The Door in the Wall

H. G. Wells

(1909)

I

One confidential evening, not three months ago, Lionel Wallace told me this story of the Door in the Wall. And at the time I thought that so far as he was concerned it was a true story.

He told it me with such a direct simplicity of conviction that I could not do otherwise than believe in him. But in the morning, in my own flat, I woke to a different atmosphere, and as I lay in bed and recalled the things he had told me, stripped of the glamour of his earnest slow voice, denuded of the focused, shaded table light, the shadowy atmosphere that wrapped about him and me, and the pleasant bright things, the dessert and glasses and napery of the dinner we had shared, making them for the time a bright little world quite cut off from everyday realities, I saw it all as frankly incredible. "He was mystifying!" I said, and then: "How well he did it! . . . It isn't quite the thing I should have expected him, of all people, to do well."

Afterwards as I sat up in bed and sipped my morning tea, I found myself trying to account for the flavour of reality that perplexed me in his impossible reminiscences, by supposing they did in some way suggest, present, convey—I hardly know which word to use—experiences it was otherwise impossible to tell.

Well, I don't resort to that explanation now. I have got over my intervening doubts. I believe now, as I believed at the moment of telling, that Wallace did to the very best of his ability strip the truth of his secret for me. But whether he himself saw, or only thought he saw, whether he himself was the possessor of an inestimable privilege or the victim of a fantastic dream, I cannot pretend to guess. Even the facts of his death, which ended my doubts for ever, throw no light on that.

That much the reader must judge for himself.

I forget now what chance comment or criticism of mine moved so reticent a man to confide in me. He was, I think, defending himself against an imputation of slackness and unreliability I had made in relation to a great public move-ment, in which he had disappointed me. But he plunged suddenly. "I have," he said, "a preoccupation—

"I know," he went on, after a pause, "I have been negli-gent. The fact is—it isn't a case of ghosts or apparitions—but—it's an odd thing to tell of, Redmond—I am haunted. I am haunted by something—that rather takes the light out of things, that fills me with longings . . ."

He paused, checked by that English shyness that so often overcomes us when we would speak of moving or grave or beautiful things. "You were at Saint Æthelstan's all through," he said, and for a moment that seemed to me quite irrelevant. "Well"—and he paused. Then very halt-ingly at first, but afterwards more easily, he began to tell of the thing that was hidden in his life, the haunting mem-ory of a beauty and a happiness that filled his heart with insatiable longings, that made all the interests and specta-cle of worldly life seem dull and tedious and vain to him.

Now that I have the clue to it, the thing seems written visibly in his face. I have a photograph in which that look of detachment has been caught and intensified. It reminds me of what a woman once said of him—a woman who had loved him greatly. "Suddenly," she said, "the interest goes out of him. He forgets you. He doesn't care a rap for you— under his very nose . . ."

Yet the interest was not always out of him, and when he was holding his attention to a thing Wallace could contrive to be an extremely successful man. His career, indeed, is set with successes. He left me behind him long ago: he soared up over my head, and cut a figure in the world that I couldn't cut—anyhow. He was still a year short of forty, and they say now that he would have been in office and very probably in the new Cabinet if he had lived. At school he always beat me without effort—as it were by nature. We were at school together at Saint Æthelstan's College in West Kensington for almost all our school-time. He came into the school as my coequal, but he left far above me, in a blaze of scholarships and brilliant performance. Yet I think I made a fair average running. And it was at school I heard first of the "Door in the Wall"—that I was to hear of a second time only a month before his death.

To him at least the Door in the Wall was a real door, leading through a real wall to immortal realities. Of that I am now quite assured.

And it came into his life quite early, when he was a little fellow between five and six. I remember how, as he sat making his confession to me with a slow gravity, he reasoned and reckoned the date of it. "There was," he said, "a crimson Virginia creeper in it—all one bright uniform crimson, in a clear amber sunshine against a white wall. That came into the impression somehow, though I don't clearly remember how, and there were horse-chestnut leaves upon the clean pavement outside the green door. They were blotched yellow and green, you know, not brown nor dirty, so that they must have been new fallen. I take it that means October. I look out for horse-chestnut leaves every year and I ought to know.

"If I'm right in that, I was about five years and four months old."

He was, he said, rather a precocious little boy—he learnt to talk at an abnormally early age, and he was so sane and "old-fashioned," as people say, that he was permitted an amount of initiative that most children scarcely attain by seven or eight. His mother died when he was two, and he was under the less vigilant and authoritative care of a nursery governess. His father was a stern, preoccupied lawyer, who gave him little attention, and expected great things of him. For all his brightness he found life a little grey and dull, I think. And one day he wandered.

He could not recall the particular neglect that enabled him to get away, nor the course he took among the West Kensington roads. All that had faded among the incurable blurs of memory. But the white wall and the green door stood out quite distinctly.

As his memory of that childish experience ran, he did at the very first sight of that door experience a peculiar emotion, an attraction, a desire to get to the door and open it and walk in. And at the same time he had the clearest conviction that either it was unwise or it was wrong of him—he could not tell which—to yield to this attraction. He insisted upon it as a curious thing that he knew from the very beginning—unless memory has played him the queerest trick—that the door was unfastened, and that he could go in as he chose.

I seem to see the figure of that little boy, drawn and repelled. And it was very clear in his mind, too, though why it should be so was never explained, that his father would be very angry if he went in through that door.

Wallace described all these moments of hesitation to me with the utmost particularity. He went right past the door, and then, with his hands in his pockets and making an infantile attempt to whistle, strolled right along beyond the end of the wall. There he recalls a number of mean dirty shops, and particularly that of a plumber and decorator with a dusty disorder of earthenware pipes, sheet lead, ball taps, pattern books of wall paper, and tins of enamel. He stood pretending to examine these things, and coveting, passionately desiring, the green door.

Then, he said, he had a gust of emotion. He made a run for it, lest hesitation should grip him again; he went plump with outstretched hand through the green door and let it slam behind him. And so, in a trice, he came into the garden that has haunted all his life.

It was very difficult for Wallace to give me his full sense of that garden into which he came.

There was something in the very air of it that exhilarated, that gave one a sense of lightness and good happening and well-being; there was something in the sight of it that made all its colour clean and perfect and subtly luminous. In the instant of coming into it one was exquisitely glad— as only in rare moments, and when one is young and joyful one can be glad in this world. And everything was beautiful there. . . .

Wallace mused before he went on telling me. "You see," he said, with the doubtful inflection of a man who pauses at incredible things, "there were two great panthers there. . . . Yes, spotted panthers. And I was not afraid. There was a long wide path with marble-edged flower borders on either side, and these two huge velvety beasts were playing there with a ball. One looked up and came towards me, a little curious as it seemed. It came right up to me, rubbed its soft round ear very gently against the small hand I held out, and purred. It was, I tell you, an enchanted garden. I know. And the size? Oh! it stretched far and wide, this way and that. I believe there were hills far away. Heaven knows where West Kensington had suddenly got to. And somehow it was just like coming home.

"You know, in the very moment the door swung to behind me, I forgot the road with its fallen chestnut leaves,
its cabs and tradesmen's carts, I forgot the sort of gravita-
tional pull back to the discipline and obedience of home, I
forgot all hesitations and fear, forgot discretion, forgot all
the intimate realities of this life. I became in a moment a
very glad and wonder-happy little boy—in another world.
It was a world with a different quality, a warmer, more
penetrating and mellower light, with a faint clear gladness
in its air, and wisps of sun-touched cloud in the blueness
of its sky. And before me ran this long wide path, invit-
ingly, with weedless beds on either side, rich with untend-
ed flowers, and these two great panthers. I put my little
hands fearlessly on their soft fur, and caressed their round
ears and the sensitive corners under their ears, and played
with them, and it was as though they welcomed me home.
There was a keen sense of home-coming in my mind, and
when presently a tall, fair girl appeared in the pathway
and came to meet me, smiling, and said 'Well?' to me, and
lifted me, and kissed me, and put me down, and led me by
the hand, there was no amazement, but only an impression
of delightful rightness, of being reminded of happy things
that had in some strange way been overlooked. There were
broad red steps, I remember, that came into view between
spikes of delphinium, and up these we went to a great
avenue between very old and shady dark trees. All down
this avenue, you know, between the red chapped stems,
were marble seats of honour and statuary, and very tame
and friendly white doves. . . .

"Along this cool avenue my girl-friend led me, looking down—I recall the pleasant lines, the finely-modelled
chin of her sweet kind face—asking me questions in a soft,
agreeable voice, and telling me things, pleasant things I
know, though what they were I was never able to recall.
. . . Presently a little Capuchin monkey, very clean, with

a fur of ruddy brown and kindly hazel eyes, came down a tree to us and ran beside me, looking up at me and grinning, and presently leapt to my shoulder. So we two went on our way in great happiness."

He paused.

"Go on," I said.

"I remember little things. We passed an old man musing among laurels, I remember, and a place gay with paroquets, and came through a broad shaded colonnade to a spacious cool palace, full of pleasant fountains, full of beautiful things, full of the quality and promise of heart's desire. And there were many things and many people, some that still seem to stand out clearly and some that are a little vague; but all these people were beautiful and kind. In some way—I don't know how—it was conveyed to me that they all were kind to me, glad to have me there, and filling me with gladness by their gestures, by the touch of their hands, by the welcome and love in their eyes. Yes—"

He mused for a while. "Playmates I found there. That was very much to me, because I was a lonely little boy. They played delightful games in a grass-covered court where there was a sun-dial set about with flowers. And as one played one loved. . . .

"But—it's odd—there's a gap in my memory. I don't remember the games we played. I never remembered. Afterwards, as a child, I spent long hours trying, even with tears, to recall the form of that happiness. I wanted to play it all over again—in my nursery—by myself. No! All I remember is the happiness and two dear playfellows who were most with me. . . . Then presently came a sombre dark woman, with a grave, pale face and dreamy eyes, a sombre woman, wearing a soft long robe of pale purple, who carried a book, and beckoned and took me aside with her into a gallery above a hall—though my playmates were loth to have me go, and ceased their game and stood watching as I was carried away. 'Come back to us!' they cried. 'Come back to us soon!' I looked up at her face, but she heeded them not at all. Her face was very gentle and grave. She took me to a seat in the gallery, and I stood beside her, ready to look at her book as she opened it upon her knee. The pages fell open. She pointed, and I looked, marveling, for in the living pages of that book I saw myself; it was a story about myself, and in it were all the things that had happened to me since ever I was born. . . .

"It was wonderful to me, because the pages of that book were not pictures, you understand, but realities."

Wallace paused gravely—looked at me doubtfully.

"Go on," I said. "I understand."

"They were realities—yes, they must have been; people moved and things came and went in them; my dear mother, whom I had near forgotten; then my father, stern and upright, the servants, the nursery, all the familiar things of home. Then the front door and the busy streets, with traffic to and fro. I looked and marveled, and looked half doubtfully again into the woman's face and turned the pages over, skipping this and that, to see more of this book and more, and so at last I came to myself hovering and hesitating outside the green door in the long white wall, and felt again the conflict and the fear.

"'And next?' I cried, and would have turned on, but the cool hand of the grave woman delayed me.

"'Next?' I insisted, and struggled gently with her hand, pulling up her fingers with all my childish strength, and as she yielded and the page came over she bent down upon me like a shadow and kissed my brow.

"But the page did not show the enchanted garden, nor the panthers, nor the girl who had led me by the hand, nor the playfellows who had been so loth to let me go. It showed a long grey street in West Kensington, in that chill hour of afternoon before the lamps are lit, and I was there, a wretched little figure, weeping aloud, for all that I could do to restrain myself, and I was weeping because I could not return to my dear playfellows who had called after me, 'Come back to us! Come back to us soon!' I was there. This was no page in a book, but harsh reality; that enchanted place and the restraining hand of the grave mother at whose knee I stood had gone—whither had they gone?"

He halted again, and remained for a time staring into the fire.

"Oh! the woefulness of that return!" he murmured.

"Well?" I said, after a minute or so.

"Poor little wretch I was!—brought back to this grey world again! As I realised the fulness of what had happened to me, I gave way to quite ungovernable grief. And the shame and humiliation of that public weeping and my disgraceful home-coming remain with me still. I see again the benevolent-looking old gentleman in gold spectacles who stopped and spoke to me—prodding me first with his umbrella. 'Poor little chap,' said he; 'and are you lost then?'—and me a London boy of five and more! And he must needs bring in a kindly young policeman and make a crowd of me, and so march me home. Sobbing, conspicuous, and frightened, I came back from the enchanted garden to the steps of my father's house.

"That is as well as I can remember my vision of that garden—the garden that haunts me still. Of course, I can convey nothing of that indescribable quality of translucent unreality, that difference from the common things of experience that hung about it all; but that—that is what happened. If it was a dream, I am sure it was a day-time and altogether extraordinary dream. . . . H'm!—naturally there followed a terrible questioning, by my aunt, my father, the nurse, the governess—everyone. . . .

"I tried to tell them, and my father gave me my first thrashing for telling lies. When afterwards I tried to tell my aunt, she punished me again for my wicked persistence. Then, as I said, everyone was forbidden to listen to me, to hear a word about it. Even my fairytale books were taken away from me for a time—because I was too 'imaginative.' Eh? Yes, they did that! My father belonged to the old school. . . . And my story was driven back upon myself. I whispered it to my pillow—my pillow that was often damp and salt to my whispering lips with childish tears. And I added always to my official and less fervent prayers this one heartfelt request: 'Please God I may dream of the garden. Oh! take me back to my garden!' Take me back to my garden! I dreamt often of the garden. I may have added to it, I may have changed it; I do not know. . . . All this, you understand, is an attempt to reconstruct from fragmentary memories a very early experience. Between that and the other consecutive memories of my boyhood there is a gulf. A time came when it seemed impossible I should ever speak of that wonder glimpse again."

I asked an obvious question.

"No," he said. "I don't remember that I ever attempted to find my way back to the garden in those early years. This seems odd to me now, but I think that very probably a closer watch was kept on my movements after this misadventure to prevent my going astray. No, it wasn't till you knew me that I tried for the garden again. And I believe there was a period—incredible as it seems now—when I forgot the garden altogether—when I was about eight or nine it may have been. Do you remember me as a kid at Saint Æthelstan's?"

"Rather!"

"I didn't show any signs, did I, in those days of having a secret dream?"

II

He looked up with a sudden smile.

"Did you ever play North-West Passage with me? . . . No, of course you didn't come my way!"

"It was the sort of game," he went on, "that every imaginative child plays all day. The idea was the discovery of a North-West Passage to school. The way to school was plain enough; the game consisted in finding some way that wasn't plain, starting off ten minutes early in some almost hopeless direction, and working my way round through unaccustomed streets to my goal. And one day I got entangled among some rather low-class streets on the other side of Campden Hill, and I began to think that for once the game would be against me and that I should get to school late. I tried rather desperately a street that seemed a cul-de-sac, and found a passage at the end. I hurried through that with renewed hope. 'I shall do it yet,' I said, and passed a row of frowsy little shops that were inexplicably familiar to me, and behold! there was my long white wall and the green door that led to the enchanted garden!

"The thing whacked upon me suddenly. Then, after all, that garden, that wonderful garden, wasn't a dream!"

He paused.

"I suppose my second experience with the green door marks the world of difference there is between the busy life of a schoolboy and the infinite leisure of a child. Anyhow, this second time I didn't for a moment think of going in straight away. You see— For one thing, my mind was full of the idea of getting to school in time—set on not breaking my record for punctuality. I must surely have felt some little desire at least to try the door—yes. I must have felt that. . . . But I seem to remember the attraction of the door mainly as another obstacle to my overmastering determination to get to school. I was immensely interested by this discovery I had made, of course—I went on with my mind full of it—but I went on. It didn't check me. I ran past, tugging out my watch, found I had ten minutes still to spare, and then I was going downhill into familiar surroundings. I got to school, breathless, it is true, and wet with perspiration, but in time. I can remember hanging up my coat and hat. . . . Went right by it and left it behind me. Odd, eh?"

He looked at me thoughtfully, "Of course I didn't know then that it wouldn't always be there. Schoolboys have limited imaginations. I suppose I thought it was an awfully jolly thing to have it there, to know my way back to it, but there was the school tugging at me. I expect I was a good deal distraught and inattentive that morning, recalling what I could of the beautiful strange people I should presently see again. Oddly enough I had no doubt in my mind that they would be glad to see me. . . . Yes, I must have thought of the garden that morning just as a jolly sort of place to which one might resort in the interludes of a strenuous scholastic career.

"I didn't go that day at all. The next day was a half holiday, and that may have weighed with me. Perhaps, too, my state of inattention brought down impositions upon me, and docked the margin of time necessary for the detour. I don't know. What I do know is that in the meantime the enchanted garden was so much upon my mind that I could not keep it to myself.

"I told. What was his name?—a ferrety-looking youngster we used to call Squiff."

"Young Hopkins," said I.

"Hopkins it was. I did not like telling him. I had a feeling that in some way it was against the rules to tell him, but I did. He was walking part of the way home with me; he was talkative, and if we had not talked about the enchanted garden we should have talked of something else,

and it was intolerable to me to think about any other subject. So I blabbed.

"Well, he told my secret. The next day in the play interval I found myself surrounded by half a dozen bigger
boys, half teasing, and wholly curious to hear more of
the enchanted garden. There was that big Fawcett—you
remember him?—and Carnaby and Morley Reynolds. You
weren't there by any chance? No, I think I should have remembered if you were. . . .

"A boy is a creature of odd feelings. I was, I really believe, in spite of my secret self-disgust, a little flattered
to have the attention of these big fellows. I remember
particularly a moment of pleasure caused by the praise
of Crawshaw—you remember Crawshaw major, the son of
Crawshaw the composer?—who said it was the best lie he
had ever heard. But at the same time there was a really
painful undertow of shame at telling what I felt was indeed a sacred secret. That beast Fawcett made a joke about
the girl in green—"

Wallace's voice sank with the keen memory of that shame.
"I pretended not to hear," he said. "Well, then Carnaby
suddenly called me a young liar, and disputed with me
when I said the thing was true. I said I knew where to find
the green door, could lead them all there in ten minutes.
Carnaby became outrageously virtuous, and said I'd have
to—and bear out my words or suffer. Did you ever have
Carnaby twist your arm? Then perhaps you'll understand
how it went with me. I swore my story was true. There
was nobody in the school then to save a chap from Carnaby, though Crawshaw put in a word or so. Carnaby had
got his game. I grew excited and red-eared, and a little
frightened. I behaved altogether like a silly little chap,
and the outcome of it all was that instead of starting alone
for my enchanted garden, I led the way presently—cheeks

flushed, ears hot, eyes smarting, and my soul one burning misery and shame—for a party of six mocking, curious, and threatening schoolfellows.

"We never found the white wall and the green door. . . ."

"You mean—?"

"I mean I couldn't find it. I would have found it if I could.

"And afterwards when I could go alone I couldn't find it. I never found it. I seem now to have been always looking for it through my school-boy days, but I never came upon it—never."

"Did the fellows—make it disagreeable?"

"Beastly. . . . Carnaby held a council over me for wanton lying. I remember how I sneaked home and upstairs to hide the marks of my blubbering. But when I cried myself to sleep at last it wasn't for Carnaby, but for the garden, for the beautiful afternoon I had hoped for, for the sweet friendly women and the waiting playfellows, and the game I had hoped to learn again, that beautiful forgotten game. . . .

"I believed firmly that if I had not told— I had bad times after that—crying at night and wool-gathering by day. For two terms I slackened and had bad reports. Do you remember? Of course you would! It was you—your beating me in mathematics that brought me back to the grind again."

III

For a time my friend stared silently into the red heart of the fire. Then he said: "I never saw it again until I was seventeen.

"It leapt upon me for the third time—as I was driving to Paddington on my way to Oxford and a scholarship. I had just one momentary glimpse. I was leaning over the apron of my hansom smoking a cigarette, and no doubt thinking myself no end of a man of the world, and suddenly there was the door, the wall, the dear sense of unforgettable and still attainable things.

"We clattered by—I too taken by surprise to stop my cab until we were well past and round a corner. Then I had a queer moment, a double and divergent movement of my will: I tapped the little door in the roof of the cab, and brought my arm down to pull out my watch. 'Yes, sir!' said the cabman, smartly. 'Er—well—it's nothing,' I cried. *'My* mistake! We haven't much time! Go on!' And he went on. . . .

"I got my scholarship. And the night after I was told of that I sat over my fire in my little upper room, my study, in my father's house, with his praise—his rare praise—and his sound counsels ringing in my ears, and I smoked my favourite pipe—the formidable bulldog of adolescence— and thought of that door in the long white wall. 'If I had stopped,' I thought, 'I should have missed my scholarship, I should have missed Oxford—muddled all the fine career before me! I begin to see things better!' I fell musing deeply, but I did not doubt then this career of mine was a thing that merited sacrifice.

"Those dear friends and that clear atmosphere seemed very sweet to me, very fine but remote. My grip was fixing now upon the world. I saw another door opening—the door of my career."

He stared again into the fire. Its red light picked out a stubborn strength in his face for just one flickering moment, and then it vanished again.

"Well," he said and sighed, "I have served that career. I have done—much work, much hard work. But I have dreamt of the enchanted garden a thousand dreams, and seen its door, or at least glimpsed its door, four times since then. Yes—four times. For a while this world was so bright and interesting, seemed so full of meaning and opportunity, that the half-effaced charm of the garden was

by comparison gentle and remote. Who wants to pat panthers on the way to dinner with pretty women and distinguished men? I came down to London from Oxford, a man
of bold promise that I have done something to redeem.
Something—and yet there have been disappointments. . . .

"Twice I have been in love—I will not dwell on that—
but once, as I went to someone who, I knew, doubted
whether I dared to come, I took a short cut at a venture
through an unfrequented road near Earl's Court, and so
happened on a white wall and a familiar green door. 'Odd!'
said I to myself, 'but I thought this place was on Campden Hill. It's the place I never could find somehow—like
counting Stonehenge—the place of that queer daydream of
mine.' And I went by it intent upon my purpose. It had no
appeal to me that afternoon.

"I had just a moment's impulse to try the door, three
steps aside were needed at the most—though I was sure
enough in my heart that it would open to me—and then I
thought that doing so might delay me on the way to that
appointment in which I thought my honour was involved.
Afterwards I was sorry for my punctuality—might at least
have peeped in, I thought, and waved a hand to those panthers, but I knew enough by this time not to seek again
belatedly that which is not found by seeking. Yes, that
time made me very sorry. . . .

"Years of hard work after that, and never a sight of the
door. It's only recently it has come back to me. With it
there has come a sense as though some thin tarnish had
spread itself over my world. I began to think of it as a sorrowful and bitter thing that I should never see that door
again. Perhaps I was suffering a little from overwork—
perhaps it was what I've heard spoken of as the feeling
of forty. I don't know. But certainly the keen brightness
that makes effort easy has gone out of things recently, and
that just at a time—with all these new political develop-
ments—when I ought to be working. Odd, isn't it? But I

do begin to find life toilsome, its rewards, as I come near them, cheap. I began a little while ago to want the garden quite badly. Yes—and I've seen it three times."

"The garden?"

"No—the door! And I haven't gone in!"

He leant over the table to me, with an enormous sorrow in his voice as he spoke. "Thrice I have had my chance—thrice! If ever that door offers itself to me again, I swore, I will go in, out of this dust and heat, out of this dry glitter of vanity, out of these toilsome futilities. I will go and never return. This time I will stay . . . I swore it, and when the time came—*I didn't go.*

"Three times in one year have I passed that door and failed to enter. Three times in the last year.

"The first time was on the night of the snatch division on the Tenants' Redemption Bill, on which the Government was saved by a majority of three. You remember? No one on our side—perhaps very few on the opposite side—expected the end that night. Then the debate collapsed like eggshells. I and Hotchkiss were dining with his cousin at Brentford; we were both unpaired, and we were called up by telephone, and set off at once in his cousin's motor. We got in barely in time, and on the way we passed my wall and door—livid in the moonlight, blotched with hot yellow as the glare of our lamps lit it, but unmistakable. 'My God!' cried I. 'What?' said Hotchkiss. 'Nothing!' I answered, and the moment passed.

"'I've made a great sacrifice,' I told the whip as I got in. 'They all have,' he said, and hurried by.

"I do not see how I could have done otherwise then. And the next occasion was as I rushed to my father's bedside to bid that stern old man farewell. Then, too, the claims of life were imperative. But the third time was different; it happened a week ago. It fills me with hot remorse to recall it. I was with Gurker and Ralphs—it's no secret now, you know, that I've had my talk with Gurker. We had

been dining at Frobisher's, and the talk had become intimate between us. The question of my place in the recon-
structed Ministry lay always just over the boundary of the
discussion. Yes—yes. That's all settled. It needn't be talked
about yet, but there's no reason to keep a secret from you.
. . . Yes—thanks! thanks! But let me tell you my story.

"Then, on that night things were very much in the air.
My position was a very delicate one. I was keenly anxious
to get some definite word from Gurker, but was hampered
by Ralphs' presence. I was using the best power of my
brain to keep that light and careless talk not too obviously
directed to the point that concerned me. I had to. Ralphs'
behaviour since has more than justified my caution. . . .
Ralphs, I knew, would leave us beyond the Kensington
High Street, and then I could surprise Gurker by a sudden
frankness. One has sometimes to resort to these little de-
vices. . . . And then it was that in the margin of my field
of vision I became aware once more of the white wall, the
green door before us down the road.

"We passed it talking. I passed it. I can still see the
shadow of Gurker's marked profile, his opera hat tilted
forward over his prominent nose, the many folds of his
neck wrap going before my shadow and Ralphs' as we
sauntered past.

"I passed within twenty inches of the door. 'If I say
good-night to them, and go in,' I asked myself, 'what will
happen?' And I was all a-tingle for that word with Gurker.

"I could not answer that question in the tangle of my
other problems. 'They will think me mad,' I thought.
'And suppose I vanish now!—Amazing disappearance of a
prominent politician!' That weighed with me. A thousand
inconceivably petty worldlinesses weighed with me in that
crisis."

Then he turned on me with a sorrowful smile, and,
speaking slowly, "Here I am!" he said.

"Here I am!" he repeated, "and my chance has gone from me. Three times in one year the door has been offered me—the door that goes into peace, into delight, into a beauty beyond dreaming, a kindness no man on earth can know. And I have rejected it, Redmond, and it has gone—"

"How do you know?"

"I know. I know. I am left now to work it out, to stick to the tasks that held me so strongly when my moments came. You say I have success—this vulgar, tawdry, irksome, envied thing. I have it." He had a walnut in his big hand. "If that was my success," he said, and crushed it, and held it out for me to see.

"Let me tell you something, Redmond. This loss is destroying me. For two months, for ten weeks nearly now, I have done no work at all, except the most necessary and urgent duties. My soul is full of inappeasable regrets. At nights—when it is less likely I shall be recognised—I go out. I wander. Yes. I wonder what people would think of that if they knew. A Cabinet Minister, the responsible head of that most vital of all departments, wandering alone—grieving—sometimes near audibly lamenting—for a door, for a garden!"

IV

I can see now his rather pallid face, and the unfamiliar sombre fire that had come into his eyes. I see him very vividly to-night. I sit recalling his words, his tones, and last evening's Westminster Gazette still lies on my sofa, containing the notice of his death. At lunch to-day the club was busy with his death. We talked of nothing else.

They found his body very early yesterday morning in a deep excavation near East Kensington Station. It is one of two shafts that have been made in connection with an extension of the railway southward. It is protected from

the intrusion of the public by a hoarding upon the high
road, in which a small doorway has been cut for the con-
venience of some of the workmen who live in that direction. The doorway was left unfastened through a misun-
derstanding between two gangers, and through it he made
his way. . . .

My mind is darkened with questions and riddles.

It would seem he walked all the way from the House
that night—he has frequently walked home during the
past Session—and so it is I figure his dark form coming
along the late and empty streets, wrapped up, intent. And
then did the pale electric lights near the station cheat the
rough planking into a semblance of white? Did that fatal
unfastened door awaken some memory?

Was there, after all, ever any green door in the wall at
all?

I do not know. I have told his story as he told it to
me. There are times when I believe that Wallace was no
more than the victim of the coincidence between a rare
but not unprecedented type of hallucination and a careless
trap, but that indeed is not my profoundest belief. You
may think me superstitious, if you will, and foolish; but,
indeed, I am more than half convinced that he had, in
truth, an abnormal gift, and a sense, something—I know
not what—that in the guise of wall and door offered him
an outlet, a secret and peculiar passage of escape into another and altogether more beautiful world. At any rate,
you will say, it betrayed him in the end. But did it betray
him? There you touch the inmost mystery of these dream-
ers, these men of vision and the imagination. We see our
world fair and common, the hoarding and the pit. By our
daylight standard he walked out of security into darkness,
danger, and death.

But did he see like that?

The Madness of Andelsprutz
Lord Dunsany
(1910)

I first saw the city of Andelsprutz on an afternoon in spring. The day was full of sunshine as I came by the way of the fields, and all that morning I had said, "There will be sunlight on it when I see for the first time the beautiful conquered city whose fame has so often made for me lovely dreams." Suddenly I saw its fortifications lifting out of the fields, and behind them stood its belfries. I went in by a gate and saw its houses and streets, and a great disappointment came upon me. For there is an air about a city, and it has a way with it, whereby a man may recognized one from another at once. There are cities full of happiness and cities full of pleasure, and cities full of gloom. There are cities with their faces to heaven, and some with their faces to earth; some have a way of looking at the past and others look at the future; some notice you if you come among them, others glance at you, others let you go by. Some love the cities that are their neighbours, others are dear to the plains and to the heath; some cities are bare to the wind, others have purple cloaks and others brown cloaks, and some are clad in white. Some tell the old tale of their infancy, with others it is secret; some cities sing and some mutter, some are angry, and some have broken hearts, and each city has her way of greeting Time.

I had said: "I will see Andelsprutz arrogant with her beauty," and I had said: "I will see her weeping over her conquest."

I had said: "She will sing songs to me," and "she will be reticent," "she will be all robed," and "she will be bare but splendid."

But the windows of Andelsprutz in her houses looked vacantly over the plains like the eyes of a dead madman. At the hour her chimes sounded unlovely and discordant, some of them were out of tune, and the bells of some were cracked, her roofs were bald and without moss. At evening no pleasant rumour arose in her streets. When the lamps were lit in the houses no mystical flood of light stole out into the dusk, you merely saw that there were lighted lamps; Andelsprutz had no way with her and no air about her. When the night fell and the blinds were all drawn down, then I perceived what I had not thought in the daylight. I knew then that Andelsprutz was dead.

I saw a fair-haired man who drank beer in a café, and I said to him:

"Why is the city of Andelsprutz quite dead, and her soul gone hence?"

He answered: "Cities do not have souls and there is never any life in bricks."

And I said to him: "Sir, you have spoken truly."

And I asked the same question of another man, and he gave me the same answer, and I thanked him for his courtesy. And I saw a man of a more slender build, who had black hair, and channels in his cheeks for tears to run in, and I said to him:

"Why is Andelsprutz quite dead, and when did her soul go hence?"

And he answered: "Andelsprutz hoped too much. For thirty years would she stretch out her arms toward the land of Akla every night, to Mother Akla from whom she had been stolen. Every night she would be hoping and sighing, and stretching out her arms to Mother Akla. At midnight, once a year, on the anniversary of the terrible day, Akla would send spies to lay a wreath against the walls of Andelsprutz. She could do no more. And on this night, once in every year, I used to weep, for weeping was the mood of the city that nursed me. Every night while other cities slept did Andelsprutz sit brooding here and hoping, till thirty wreaths lay mouldering by her walls, and still the armies of Akla could not come.

"But after she had hoped so long, and on the night that faithful spies had brought her thirtieth wreath, Andelsprutz went suddenly mad. All the bells clanged hideously in the belfries, horses bolted in the streets, the dogs all howled, the stolid conquerors awoke and turned in their beds and slept again; and I saw the grey shadowy form of Andelsprutz rise up, decking her hair with the phantasms of cathedrals, and stride away from her city. And the great shadowy form that was the soul of Andelsprutz went away muttering to the mountains, and there I followed her—for had she not been my nurse? Yes, I went away alone into the mountains, and for three days, wrapped in a cloak, I slept in their misty solitudes. I had no food to eat, and to drink I had only the water of the mountain streams. By day no living thing was near to me, and I heard nothing but the noise of the wind, and the mountain streams roaring. But for three nights I heard all round me on the mountain the sounds of a great city: I saw the lights of tall cathedral windows flash momentarily on the peaks, and at times the glimmering lantern of some fortress patrol. And I saw the huge misty outline of the soul of Andelsprutz sitting decked with her ghostly cathedrals, speaking to herself, with her eyes fixed before her in a mad stare, telling of ancient wars. And her confused speech for all those nights upon the mountain was sometimes the voice of traffic, and then of church bells, and then of bugles, but oftenest it was the voice of red war; and it was all incoherent, and she was quite mad.

"The third night it rained heavily all night long, but I stayed up there to watch the soul of my native city. And she still sat staring straight before her, raving; but here voice was gentler now, there were more chimes in it, and occasional song. Midnight passed, and the rain still swept down on me, and still the solitudes of the mountain were full of the mutterings of the poor mad city. And the hours after midnight came, the cold hours wherein sick men die.

"Suddenly I was aware of great shapes moving in the rain, and heard the sound of voices that were not of my city nor yet of any that I ever knew. And presently I discerned, though faintly, the souls of a great concourse of cities, all bending over Andelsprutz and comforting her, and the ravines of the mountains roared that night with the voices of cities that had lain still for centuries. For there came the soul of Camelot that had so long ago forsaken Usk; and there was Ilion, all girt with towers, still cursing the sweet face of ruinous Helen; I saw there Babylon and Persepolis, and the bearded face of bull-like Nineveh, and Athens mourning her immortal gods.

"All these souls if cities that were dead spoke that night on the mountain to my city and soothed her, until at last she muttered of war no longer, and her eyes stared wildly no more, but she hid her face in her hands and for some while wept softly. At last she arose, and walking slowly and with bended head, and leaning upon Ilion and Carthage, went mournfully eastwards; and the dust of her highways swirled behind her as she went, a ghostly dust that never turned to mud in all that drenching rain. And so the souls of the cities led her away, and gradually they disappeared from the mountain, and the ancient voices died away in the distance.

"Now since then have I seen my city alive; but once I met with a traveler who said that somewhere in the midst of a great desert are gathered together the souls of all dead cities. He said that he was lost once in a place where there was no water, and he heard their voices speaking all the night."

But I said: "I was once without water in a desert and heard a city speaking to me, but knew not whether it really spoke to me or not, for on that day I heard so many terrible things, and only some of them were true."

And the man with the black hair said: "I believe it to be true, though whither she went I know not. I only know that a shepherd found me in the morning faint with hunger and cold, and carried me down here; and when I came to Andelsprutz it was, as you have perceived it, dead."

Space

John Buchan

(1911)

"Est impossibile? Certum est. "—Tertullian.

Leithen told me this story one evening in early September as we sat beside the pony track which gropes its way from Glenavelin up the Correi na Sidhe. I had arrived that afternoon from the south, while he had been taking an off-day from a week's stalking, so we had walked up the glen together after tea to get the news of the forest. A rifle was out on the Correi na Sidhe beat, and a thin spire of smoke had risen from the top of Sgurr Dearg to show that a stag had been killed at the burn-head. The lumpish hill pony with its deer-saddle had gone up the Correi in a gillie's charge while we followed at leisure, picking our way among the loose granite rocks and the patches of wet bogland. The track climbed high on one of the ridges of Sgurr Dearg, till it hung over a caldron of green glen with the Alt-na-Sidhe churning in its linn a thousand feet below. It was a breathless evening, I remember, with a pale-blue sky just clearing from the haze of the day. West-wind weather may make the North, even in September, no bad imitation of the Tropics, and I sincerely pitied the man who all these stifling hours had been toiling on the screes of Sgurr Dearg. By-and-by we sat down on a bank of heather, and idly watched the trough swimming at our feet.

The clatter of the pony's hoofs grew fainter, the drone of bees had gone, even the midges seemed to have forgotten their calling. No place on earth can be so deathly still as a deer-forest early in the season before the stags have begun roaring, for there are no sheep with their homely noises, and only the rare croak of a raven breaks the silence. The hillside was far from sheer—one could have walked down with a little care—but something in the shape of the hollow and the remote gleam of white water gave it an extraordinary depth and space. There was a shimmer left from the day's heat, which invested bracken and rock and scree with a curious airy unreality. One could almost have believed that the eye had tricked the mind, that all was mirage, that five yards from the path the solid earth fell away into nothingness. I have a bad head, and instinctively I drew farther back into the heather. Leithen's eyes were looking vacantly before him.

"Did you ever know Hollond?" he asked.

Then he laughed shortly. "I don't know why I asked that, but somehow this place reminded me of Hollond. That glimmering hollow looks as if it were the beginning of eternity. It must be eerie to live with the feeling always on one."

Leithen seemed disinclined for further exercise. He lit a pipe and smoked quietly for a little. "Odd that you didn't know Hollond. You must have heard his name. I thought you amused yourself with metaphysics."

Then I remembered. There had been an erratic genius who had written some articles in *Mind* on that dreary subject, the mathematical conception of infinity. Men had praised them to me, but I confess I never quite understood their argument. "Wasn't he some sort of mathematical professor?" I asked.

"He was, and, in his own way, a tremendous swell. He wrote a book on Number which has translations in every

European language. He is dead now, and the Royal Society founded a medal in his honour. But I wasn't thinking of that side of him."

It was the time and place for a story, for the pony would not be back for an hour. So I asked Leithen about the other side of Hollond which was recalled to him by Correi na Sidhe. He seemed a little unwilling to speak . . .

"I wonder if you will understand it. You ought to, of course, better than me, for you know something of philosophy. But it took me a long time to get the hang of it, and I can't give you any kind of explanation. He was my fag at Eton, and when I began to get on at the Bar I was able to advise him on one or two private matters, so that he rather fancied my legal ability. He came to me with his story because he had to tell someone, and he wouldn't trust a colleague. He said he didn't want a scientist to know, for scientists were either pledged to their own theories and wouldn't understand, or, if they understood, would get ahead of him in his researches. He wanted a lawyer, he said, who was accustomed to weighing evidence. That was good sense, for evidence must always be judged by the same laws, and I suppose in the long-run the most abstruse business comes down to a fairly simple deduction from certain data. Anyhow, that was the way he used to talk, and I listened to him, for I liked the man, and had an enormous respect for his brains. At Eton he sluiced down all the mathematics they could give him, and he was an astonishing swell at Cambridge. He was a simple fellow, too, and talked no more jargon than he could help. I used to climb with him in the Alps now and then, and you would never have guessed that he had any thoughts beyond getting up steep rocks.

"It was at Chamonix, I remember, that I first got a hint of the matter that was filling his mind. We had been taking an off-day, and were sitting in the hotel garden, watching

the Aiguilles getting purple in the twilight. Chamonix
always makes me choke a little—it is so crushed in by
those great snow masses. I said something about it—said
I liked the open spaces like the Gornergrat or the Bel Alp
better. He asked me why: if it was the difference of the air,
or merely the wider horizon? I said it was the sense of not
being crowded, of living in an empty world. He repeated
the word 'empty' and laughed.

"'By "empty" you mean,' he said, 'where things don't
knock up against you?'

"I told him No. I mean just empty, void, nothing but
blank aether.

"'You don't knock up against things here, and the air is
as good as you want. It can't be the lack of ordinary emptiness you feel.'

"I agreed that the word needed explaining. 'I suppose
it is mental restlessness,' I said. 'I like to feel that for a
tremendous distance there is nothing round me. Why, I
don't know. Some men are built the other way and have a
terror of space.'

"He said that that was better. 'It is a personal fancy,
and depends on your *knowing* that there is nothing between you and the top of the Dent Blanche. And you know
because your eyes tell you there is nothing. Even if you
were blind, you might have a sort of sense about adjacent
matter. Blind men often have it. But in any case, whether
got from instinct or sight, the *knowledge* is what matters.'

"Hollond was embarking on a Socratic dialogue in which
I could see little point. I told him so, and he laughed.

"'I am not sure that I am very clear myself. But yes—
there *is* a point. Supposing you knew—not by sight or by
instinct, but by sheer intellectual knowledge, as I know
the truth of a mathematical proposition—that what we
call empty space was full, crammed. Not with lumps of
what we call matter like hills and houses, but with things
as real—as real to the mind. Would you still feel crowded?'

"'No,' I said, 'I don't think so. It is only what we call matter that signifies. It would be just as well not to feel crowded by the other thing, for there would be no escape from it. But what are you getting at? Do you mean atoms or electric currents or what?'

"He said he wasn't thinking about that sort of thing, and began to talk of another subject.

"Next night, when we were pigging it at the Géant *cabane*, he started again on the same tack. He asked me how I accounted for the fact that animals could find their way back over great tracts of unknown country. I said I supposed it was the homing instinct.

"'Rubbish, man,' he said. 'That's only another name for the puzzle, not an explanation. There must be some reason for it. They must *know* something that we cannot understand. Tie a cat in a bag and take it fifty miles by train and it will make its way home. That cat has some clue that we haven't.'

"I was tired and sleepy, and told him that I did not care a rush about the psychology of cats. But he was not to be snubbed, and went on talking.

"'How if Space is really full of things we cannot see and as yet do not know? How if all animals and some savages have a cell in their brain or a nerve which responds to the invisible world? How if all Space be full of these landmarks, not material in our sense, but quite real? A dog barks at nothing, a wild beast makes an aimless circuit. Why? Perhaps because Space is made up of corridors and alleys, ways to travel and things to shun? For all we know, to a greater intelligence than ours the top of Mont Blanc may be as crowded as Piccadilly Circus.'

"But at that point I fell asleep and left Hollond to repeat his questions to a guide who knew no English and a snoring porter.

"Six months later, one foggy January afternoon, Hollond rang me up at the Temple and proposed to come to see me that night after dinner. I thought he wanted to talk Alpine shop, but he turned up in Duke Street about nine with a kit-bag full of papers. He was an odd fellow to look at—a yellowish face with the skin stretched tight on the cheek-bones, clean-shaven, a sharp chin which he kept poking forward, and deep-set, greyish eyes. He was a hard fellow, too, always in pretty good condition, which was remarkable considering how he slaved for nine months out of the twelve. He had a quiet, slow-spoken manner, but that night I saw that he was considerably excited.

"He said that he had come to me because we were old friends. He proposed to tell me a tremendous secret. 'I must get another mind to work on it or I'll go crazy. I don't want a scientist. I want a plain man.'

"Then he fixed me with a look like a tragic actor's. 'Do you remember that talk we had in August at Chamonix—about Space? I daresay you thought I was playing the fool. So I was in a sense, but I was feeling my way towards something which has been in my mind for ten years. Now I have got it, and you must hear about it. You may take my word that it's a pretty startling discovery.'

"I lit a pipe and told him to go ahead, warning him that I knew about as much science as the dustman.

"I am bound to say that it took me a long time to understand what he meant. He began by saying that everybody thought of Space as an 'empty homogeneous medium.' 'Never mind at present what the ultimate constituents of that medium are. We take it as a finished product, and we think of it as mere extension, something without any quality at all. That is the view of civilised man. You will find all the philosophers taking it for granted. Yes, but every living thing does not take that view. An animal, for instance. It feels a kind of quality in Space. It can find its way over new country, because it perceives certain landmarks, not necessarily material, but perceptible, or if you like intelligible. Take an Australian savage. He has the same power, and, I believe, for the same reason. He is conscious of intelligible landmarks.'

"'You mean what people call a sense of direction,' I put in.

"'Yes, but what in Heaven's name is a sense of direction? The phrase explains nothing. However incoherent the mind of the animal or the savage may be, it is there somewhere, working on some data. I've been all through the psychological and anthropological side of the business, and after you eliminate the clues from sight and hearing and smell and half-conscious memory there remains a solid lump of the inexplicable.'

"Hollond's eye had kindled, and he sat doubled up in his chair, dominating me with a finger.

"'Here, then is a power which man is civilising himself out of. Call it anything you like, but you must admit that it is a power. Don't you see that it is a perception of another kind of reality that we are leaving behind us? . . . Well, you know the way nature works. The wheel comes full circle, and what we think we have lost we regain in a higher form. So for a long time I have been wondering whether the civilised mind could not recreate for itself this lost gift, the gift of seeing the quality of Space. I mean that I wondered whether the scientific modern brain could not get to the stage of realising that Space is not an empty homogeneous medium, but full of intricate differences, intelligible and real, though not with our common reality.'

"I found all this very puzzling and he had to repeat it several times before I got a glimpse of what he was talking about.

"'I've wondered for a long time,' he went on, 'but now quite suddenly, I have begun to know.' He stopped and asked me abruptly if I knew much about mathematics.

"'It's a pity,' he said, 'but the main point is not technical, though I wish you could appreciate the beauty of some of my proofs.' Then he began to tell me about his last six months' work. I should have mentioned that he was a brilliant physicist besides other things. All Hollond's tastes were on the borderlands of sciences, where mathematics fades into metaphysics and physics merges in the abstrusest kind of mathematics. Well, it seems he had been working for years at the ultimate problem of matter, and especially of that rarefied matter we call aether or space. I forget what his view was—atoms or molecules or electric waves. If he ever told me I have forgotten, but I'm not certain that I ever knew. However, the point was that these ultimate constituents were dynamic and mobile, not a mere passive medium but a medium in constant movement and change. He claimed to have discovered—by ordinary inductive experiment—that the constituents of aether possessed certain functions, and moved in certain figures obedient to certain mathematical laws. Space, I gathered, was perpetually 'forming fours' in some fancy way.

"Here he left his physics and became the mathematician. Among his mathematical discoveries had been certain curves or figures or something whose behaviour involved a new dimension. I gathered that this wasn't the ordinary Fourth Dimension that people talk of, but that fourth-dimensional inwardness or involution was part of it. The explanation lay in the pile of manuscripts he left with me, but though I tried honestly I couldn't get the hang of it. My mathematics stopped with desperate finality just as he got into his subject.

"His point was that the constituents of Space moved according to these new mathematical figures of his. They were always changing, but the principles of their change were as fixed as the law of gravitation. Therefore, if you once grasped these principles you knew the contents of the void. What do you make of that?"

I said that it seemed to me a reasonable enough argument, but that it got one very little way forward. "A man," I said, "might know the contents of Space and the laws of their arrangement and yet be unable to see anything more than his fellows. It is a purely academic knowledge. His mind knows it as the result of many deductions, but his senses perceive nothing."

Leithen laughed. "Just what I said to Hollond. He asked the opinion of my legal mind. I said I could not pronounce on his argument but that I could point out that he had established no *trait d'union* between the intellect which understood and the senses which perceived. It was like a blind man with immense knowledge but no eyes, and therefore no peg to hang his knowledge on and make it useful. He had not explained his savage or his cat. 'Hang it, man,' I said, 'before you can appreciate the existence of your Spacial forms you have to go through elaborate experiments and deductions. You can't be doing that every minute. Therefore you don't get any nearer to the *use* of the sense you say that man once possessed, though you can explain it a bit.'"

"What did he say?" I asked.

"The funny thing was that he never seemed to see my difficulty. When I kept bringing him back to it he shied off with a new wild theory of perception. He argued that the mind can live in a world of realities without any sensuous stimulus to connect them with the world of our ordinary life. Of course that wasn't my point. I supposed that this world of Space was real enough to him, but I wanted to know how he got there. He never answered me. He was the typical Cambridge man, you know—dogmatic about uncertainties, but curiously diffident about the obvious. He laboured to get me to understand the notion of his mathematical forms, which I was quite willing to take on trust from him. Some queer things he said, too. He took our feeling about Left and Right as an example of our instinct for the quality of Space. But when I objected that Left and Right varied with each object, and only existed in connection with some definite material thing, he said that that was exactly what he meant. It was an example of the mobility of the Spacial forms. Do you see any sense in that?"

I shook my head. It seemed to me pure craziness.

"And then he tried to show me what he called the 'involution of Space,' by taking two points on a piece of paper. The points were a foot away when the paper was flat, they coincided when it was doubled up. He said that there were no gaps between the figures, for the medium was continuous, and he took as an illustration the loops on a cord. You are to think of a cord always looping and unlooping itself according to certain mathematical laws. Oh, I tell you, I gave up trying to follow him. And he was so desperately in earnest all the time. By his account Space was a sort of mathematical pandemonium."

Leithen stopped to refill his pipe, and I mused upon the ironic fate which had compelled a mathematical genius to make his sole confidant of a philistine lawyer, and induced that lawyer to repeat it confusedly to an ignoramus at twilight on a Scotch hill. As told by Leithen it was a very halting tale.

"But there was one thing I could see very clearly," Leithen went on, "and that was Hollond's own case. This crowded world of Space was perfectly real to him. How he had got to it I do not know. Perhaps his mind, dwelling constantly on the problem, had unsealed some atrophied cell and restored the old instinct. Anyhow, he was living his daily life with a foot in each world.

"He often came to see me, and after the first hectic discussions he didn't talk much. There was no noticeable change in him—a little more abstracted perhaps. He would walk in the street or come into a room with a quick look round him, and sometimes for no earthly reason he would swerve. Did you ever watch a cat crossing a room? It sidles along by the furniture and walks over an open space of carpet as if it were picking its way among obstacles. Well, Hollond behaved like that, but he had always been counted a little odd, and nobody noticed it but me.

"I knew better than to chaff him, and had stopped argument, so there wasn't much to be said. But sometimes he would give me news about his experiences. The whole thing was perfectly clear and scientific and above board, and nothing creepy about it. You know how I hate the washy supernatural stuff they give us nowadays. Hollond was well and fit, with an appetite like a hunter. But as he talked, sometimes—well, you know I haven't much in the way of nerves or imagination—but I used to get a little eerie. Used to feel the solid earth dissolving round me. It was the opposite of vertigo, if you understand me—a sense of airy realities crowding in on you,—crowding the mind, that is, not the body.

"I gathered from Hollond that he was always conscious of corridors and halls and alleys in Space, shifting, but shifting according to inexorable laws. I never could get quite clear as to what this consciousness was like. When I asked he used to look puzzled and worried and helpless. I made out from him that one landmark involved a sequence, and once given a bearing from an object you could keep the direction without a mistake. He told me he could easily, if he wanted, go in a dirigible from the top of Mont Blanc to the top of Snowdon in the thickest fog and without a compass, if he were given the proper angle to start from. I confess I didn't follow that myself. Material

objects had nothing to do with the Spacial forms, for a
table or a bed in our world might be placed across a cor-
ridor of Space. The forms played their game independent
of our kind of reality. But the worst of it was, that if you
kept your mind too much in one world you were apt to
forget about the other and Hollond was always barking his
shins on stones and chairs and things.

"He told me all this quite simply and frankly. Remember his mind and no other part of him lived in his
new world. He said it gave him an odd sense of detachment to sit in a room among people, and to know that
nothing there but himself had any relation at all to the
infinite strange world of Space that flowed around them.
He would listen, he said, to a great man talking, with one
eye on the cat on the rug, thinking to himself how much
more the cat knew than the man."

"How long was it before he went mad?" I asked.

It was a foolish question, and made Leithen cross. "He
never went mad in your sense. My dear fellow, you're very
much wrong if you think there was anything pathological
about him—then. The man was brilliantly sane. His mind
was as keen is a keen sword. I couldn't understand him,
but I could judge of his sanity right enough."

I asked if it made him happy or miserable.

"At first I think it made him uncomfortable. He was
restless because he knew too much and too little. The unknown pressed in on his mind as bad air weighs on the
lungs. Then it lightened and he accepted the new world
in the same sober practical way that he took other things.
I think that the free exercise of his mind in a pure medium gave him a feeling of extraordinary power and ease.
His eyes used to sparkle when he talked. And another odd
thing he told me. He was a keen rock-climber, but, curiously enough, he had never a very good head. Dizzy heights
always worried him, though he managed to keep hold on

himself. But now all that had gone. The sense of the fulness of Space made him as happy—happier I believe—with his legs dangling into eternity, as sitting before his own study fire.

"I remember saying that it was all rather like the mediaeval wizards who made their spells by means of numbers and figures.

"He caught me up at once. 'Not numbers,' he said. "Number has no place in Nature. It is an invention of the human mind to atone for a bad memory. But figures are a different matter. All the mysteries of the world are in them, and the old magicians knew that at least, if they knew no more.'

"He had only one grievance. He complained that it was terribly lonely. 'It is the Desolation,' he would quote, 'spoken of by Daniel the prophet.' He would spend hours travelling those eerie shifting corridors of Space with no hint of another human soul. How could there be? It was a world of pure reason, where human personality had no place. What puzzled me was why he should feel the absence of this. One wouldn't, you know, in an intricate problem of geometry or a game of chess. I asked him, but he didn't understand the question. I puzzled over it a good deal, for it seemed to me that if Hollond felt lonely, there must be more in this world of his than we imagined. I began to wonder if there was any truth in fads like psychical research. Also, I was not so sure that he was as normal as I had thought: it looked as if his nerves might be going bad.

"Oddly enough, Hollond was getting on the same track himself. He had discovered, so he said, that in sleep everybody now and then lived in this new world of his. You know how one dreams of triangular railway platforms with trains running simultaneously down all three sides and not colliding. Well, this sort of cantrip was 'common form,' as we say at the Bar, in Hollond's Space, and he was very

curious about the why and wherefore of Sleep. He began
to haunt psychological laboratories, where they experiment with the charwoman and the odd man, and he
used to go up to Cambridge for *séances*. It was a foreign
atmosphere to him, and I don't think he was very happy
in it. He found so many charlatans that he used to get
angry, and declare he would be better employed at Mother's Meetings!"

From far up the Glen came the sound of the pony's hoofs.
The stag had been loaded up and the gillies were returning. Leithen looked at his watch. "We'd better wait and see
the beast," he said.

. . . "Well, nothing happened for more than a year.
Then one evening in May he burst into my rooms in high
excitement. You understand quite clearly that there was no
suspicion of horror or fright or anything unpleasant about
this world he had discovered. It was simply a series of
interesting and difficult problems. All this time Hollond
had been rather extra well and cheery. But when he came
in I thought I noticed a different look in his eyes, something puzzled and diffident and apprehensive.

"'There's a queer performance going on in the other
world,' he said. 'It's unbelievable. I never dreamed of such
a thing. I—I don't quite know how to put it, and I don't
know how to explain it, but—but I am becoming aware
that there are other beings—other minds—moving in
Space besides mine.'

"I suppose I ought to have realised then that things
were beginning to go wrong. But it was very difficult, he
was so rational and anxious to make it all clear. I asked him
how he knew. There could, of course, on his own showing
be no *change* in that world, for the forms of Space moved
and existed under inexorable laws. He said he found his
own mind failing him at points. There would come over

him a sense of fear—intellectual fear—and weakness, a sense of something else, quite alien to Space, thwarting him. Of course he could only describe his impressions very lamely, for they were purely of the mind, and he had no material peg to hang them on, so that I could realise them. But the gist of it was that he had been gradually becoming conscious of what he called 'Presences' in his world. They had no effect on Space—did not leave footprints in its corridors, for instance—but they affected his mind. There was some mysterious contact established between him and them. I asked him if the affection was unpleasant and he said 'No, not exactly.' But I could see a hint of fear in his eyes.

"Think of it. Try to realise what intellectual fear is. I can't, but it is conceivable. To you and me fear implies pain to ourselves or some other, and such pain is always in the last resort pain of the flesh. Consider it carefully and you will see that it is so. But imagine fear so sublimated and transmuted as to be the tension of pure spirit. I can't realise it, but I think it possible. I don't pretend to understand how Hollond got to know about these Presences. But there was no doubt about the fact. He was positive, and he wasn't in the least mad—not in our sense. In that very month he published his book on Number, and gave a German professor who attacked it a most tremendous public trouncing.

"I know what you are going to say,—that the fancy was a weakening of the mind from within. I admit I should have thought of that but he looked so confoundedly sane and able that it seemed ridiculous. He kept asking me my opinion, as a lawyer, on the facts he offered. It was the oddest case ever put before me, but I did my best for him. I dropped all my own views of sense and nonsense. I told him that, taking all that he had told me as fact, the Presences might be either ordinary minds traversing Space in

sleep; or minds such as his which had independently cap-
tured the sense of Space's quality; or, finally, the spirits of
just men made perfect, behaving as psychical researchers
think they do. It was a ridiculous task to set a prosaic
man, and I wasn't quite serious. But Holland was serious
enough.

"He admitted that all three explanations were conceivable, but he was very doubtful about the first. The projec-
tion of the spirit into Space during sleep, he thought, was
a faint and feeble thing, and these were powerful Presences.
With the second and the third he was rather impressed. I
suppose I should have seen what was happening and tried
to stop it; at least, looking back that seems to have been my
duty. But it was difficult to think that anything was wrong
with Hollond; indeed the odd thing is that all this time the
idea of madness never entered my head. I rather backed him
up. Somehow the thing took my fancy, though I thought
it moonshine at the bottom of my heart. I enlarged on the
pioneering before him. 'Think,' I told him, 'what may be
waiting for you. You may discover the meaning of Spirit.
You may open up a new world, as rich as the old one, but
imperishable. You may prove to mankind their immortality
and deliver them for ever from the fear of death. Why, man,
you are picking at the lock of all the world's mysteries.'

"But Hollond did not cheer up. He seemed strangely
languid and dispirited. 'That is all true enough,' he said,
'if you are right, if your alternatives are exhaustive. But
suppose they are something else, something . . .' What
that 'something' might be he had apparently no idea, and
very soon he went away.

"He said another thing before he left. We asked me if
I ever read poetry, and I said, not often. Nor did he: but
he had picked up a little book somewhere and found a
man who knew about the Presences. I think his name was
Traherne, one of the seventeenth-century fellows. He

quoted a verse which stuck to my fly-paper memory. It ran something like

"'Within the region of the air,
   Compassed about with Heavens fair,
   Great tracts of lands there may be found,
     Where many numerous hosts,
     In those far distant coasts,
   For other great and glorious ends
   Inhabit, my yet unknown friends.'

Hollond was positive he did not mean angels or anything of the sort. I told him that Traherne evidently took a cheerful view of them. He admitted that, but added: 'He had religion, you see. He believed that everything was for the best. I am not a man of faith, and can only take comfort from what I understand. I'm in the dark, I tell you . . .'

"Next week I was busy with the Chilian Arbitration case, and saw nobody for a couple of months. Then one evening I ran against Hollond on the Embankment, and thought him looking horribly ill. He walked back with me to my rooms, and hardly uttered one word all the way. I gave him a stiff whisky-and-soda, which he gulped down absent-mindedly. There was that strained, hunted look in his eyes that you see in a frightened animal's. He was always lean, but now he had fallen away to skin and bone.

"'I can't stay long,' he told me, 'for I'm off to the Alps to-morrow and I have a lot to do.' Before then he used to plunge readily into his story, but now he seemed shy about beginning. Indeed I had to ask him a question.

"'Things are difficult,' he said hesitatingly, and rather distressing. 'Do you know, Leithen, I think you were wrong about—about what I spoke to you of. You said there must be one of three explanations. I am beginning to think that there is a fourth. . . .'

"He stopped for a second or two, then suddenly leaned forward and gripped my knee so fiercely that I cried out. 'That world is the Desolation,' he said in a choking voice, 'and perhaps I am getting near the Abomination of the Desolation that the old prophet spoke of. I tell you, man, I am on the edge of a terror, a terror,' he almost screamed, 'that no mortal can think of and live.'

"You can imagine that I was considerably startled. It was lightning out of a clear sky. How the devil could one associate horror with mathematics? I don't see it yet . . . At any rate, I— You may be sure I cursed my folly for ever pretending to take him seriously. The only way would have been to have laughed him out of it at the start. And yet I couldn't, you know—it was too real and reasonable. Anyhow, I tried a firm tone now, and told him the whole thing was arrant raving bosh. I bade him be a man and pull himself together. I made him dine with me, and took him home, and got him into a better state of mind before he went to bed. Next morning I saw him off at Charing Cross, very haggard still, but better. He promised to write to me pretty often. . . ."

The pony, with a great eleven-pointer lurching athwart its back, was abreast of us, and from the autumn mist came the sound of soft Highland voices. Leithen and I got up to go, when we heard that the rifle had made direct for the Lodge by a short cut past the Sanctuary. In the wake of the gillies we descended the Correi road into a glen all swimming with dim purple shadows. The pony minced and boggled; the stag's antlers stood out sharp on the rise against a patch of sky, looking like a skeleton tree. Then we dropped into a covert of birches and emerged on the white glen highway.

Leithen's story had bored and puzzled me at the start, but now it had somehow gripped my fancy. Space a domain of endless corridors and Presences moving in them! The world was not quite the same as an hour ago. It was the hour, as the French say, "between dog and wolf," when the mind is disposed to marvels. I thought of my stalking on the morrow, and was miserably conscious that I would miss my stag. Those airy forms would get in the way. Confound Leithen and his yarns!

"I want to hear the end of your story," I told him, as the lights of the Lodge showed half a mile distant.

"The end was a tragedy," he said slowly. "I don't much care to talk about it. But how was I to know? I couldn't see the nerve going. You see I couldn't believe it was all nonsense. If I could I might have seen. But I still think there was something in it—up to a point. Oh, I agree he went mad in the end. It is the only explanation. Something must have snapped in that fine brain, and he saw the little bit more which we call madness. Thank God, you and I are prosaic fellows . . .

"I was going out to Chamonix myself a week later. But before I started I got a post-card from Hollond, the only word from him. He had printed my name and address, and on the other side had scribbled six words—'*I know at last—God's mercy.—H.G.H*' The handwriting was like a sick man of ninety. I knew that things must be pretty bad with my friend.

"I got to Chamonix in time for his funeral. An ordinary climbing accident—you probably read about it in the papers. The Press talked about the toll which the Alps took from intellectuals—the usual rot. There was an inquiry, but the facts were quite simple. The body was only recognised by the clothes. He had fallen several thousand feet.

"It seems that he had climbed for a few days with one of the Kronigs and Dupont, and they had done some hair-raising things on the Aiguilles. Dupont told me that

they had found a new route up the Montanvert side of the
Charmoz. He said that Hollond climbed like a *'diable fou,'*
and if you know Dupont's standard of madness you will
see that the pace must have been pretty hot. 'But monsieur
was sick,' he added; 'his eyes were not good. And I and
Franz, we were grieved for him and a little afraid. We were
glad when he left us.'

"He dismissed the guides two days before his death.
The next day he spent in the hotel, getting his affairs
straight. He left everything in perfect order, but not a line
to a soul, not even to his sister. The following day he set
out alone about three in the morning for the Grèpon. He
took the road up the Nantillons glacier to the Col, and
then he must have climbed the Mummery crack by himself. After that he left the ordinary route and tried a new
traverse across the Mer de Glace face. Somewhere near
the top he fell, and next day a party going to the Dent du
Requin found him on the rocks thousands of feet below.

"He had slipped in attempting the most foolhardy
course on earth, and there was a lot of talk about the dangers of guideless climbing. But I guessed the truth, and I
am sure Dupont knew, though he held his tongue. . . ."

We were now on the gravel of the drive, and I was
feeling better. The thought of dinner warmed my heart
and drove out the eeriness of the twilight glen. The hour
between dog and wolf was passing. After all, there was a
gross and jolly earth at hand for wise men who had a mind
to comfort.

Leithen, I saw, did not share my mood. He looked glum
and puzzled, as if his tale had aroused grim memories. He
finished it at the Lodge door.

". . . For, of course, he had gone out that day to die.
He had seen the something more, the little bit too much,
which plucks a man from his moorings. He had gone so far
into the land of pure spirit that he must needs go further

and shed the fleshly envelope that cumbered him. God send that he found rest! I believe that he chose the steepest cliff in the Alps for a purpose. He wanted to be unrecognisable. He was a brave man and a good citizen. I think he hoped that those who found him might not see the look in his eyes."

The Never-Ending Road

Anonymous

(1913)

Sometimes one wonders whence folk-tales arise; how people, commonplace people apparently, came to have such conceptions, such beliefs; how out of a work-a-day, sleep-a-night world they found the time and the imagination to fashion a world and peoples that never knew the moon and sun. At other times it is all plain enough, and the only really real world is the world of the folk who had the lore. The mind's eyes are readjusted by a spider's thread's breadth, and there is a world transformed, haunted from sunrise to sunrise with unseen presences, good and evil, beautiful and ugly, terrible and transcendent. The child-mind and the untutored mind are perhaps readjusted in this way most readily, but all minds are capable of the readjustment and every mind at some time or another bathes in the light that never shone on sea or land. All this philosophising arises on the Never-Ending Road where to-day, as always, the readjustment comes. It is certainly no ordinary road to possess so singular a power. It is a real road, as the donkey's hoofs and the wheels of the little cart proclaim. But it is not a road of commerce, and few carts raise its dust or disturb with sound the endless acres of purple heather and deep bracken that it threads. It comes out of a wood with the sunrise, it goes into a wood with the sunset, and between the woods are miles and miles—so it seems—of

the road, miles and miles of this east-west thread drawn
by the monks seven centuries ago to link their House with
the sea that brought them fish, that brought them wine,
that brought them news from Rome or Avignon. The road
is haunted, every dip of it, and, believe it or disbelieve it,
white-robed Cistercians still hold the right-of-way. And
not Cistercians only, that is the worst and the best of it.
It is much more difficult to convey the impression of a
haunted road than of a haunted house. It is so open, so
wind-blown, so frank in its reception of travellers. There
is apparently no deception about it. Yet it is in reality
far more terrible at midday than the haunted house at
midnight. The remoteness of help; the sense of solitude;
the probability of ambush, the unfathomable heather, the
gorse and bracken where a host might hide, the occasional
solitary pines, the belts of trees that here and there arch
the road, the great woods that swallow it at either end, if
it have beginning or end, the sound of insect life that in
the noonday silence becomes, or seems to become, clamor-
ous, the startling cry of a frightened bird, the occasional
grim horse—"I never knew a beast I hated so"—the tinkle
of far-off belled cattle: all tend to make the casual wander-
er nervous in spite of himself. Yet how beautiful it all is to
anyone who knows the road! Walking eastward at sunrise
the traveller finds the bees booming over the heather, the
birds darting with lightning wings at every level. Far in
the height the wild geese speed towards the dappled east,
in mid-air the heron press towards shining waters, while
in the homestead under the hill the yard-cat sleeps righ-
teously in the sun. An hour earlier the road saw a different scene. In the dim light the straying cattle cropped the
roadside grass with an uncanny sound—there is nothing
so blood-curdling as the sound of strayed beasts breathing and cropping and moving in the night—bats like bird
ghosts wheeled unevenly, moths flickered in the shade, and

the cat hunted with pricked ears and crouching back, gliding from cover to cover with deadly velvet tread stalking the field mice, awaiting the awakening of the birds. One could watch him moving along the hedgerows as the darkness shimmered into grey: undomesticated, lonely, feline. Then the sun shone out from a glowing purple bank of cloud over the imperial purple of the heather for endless miles, abolishing cat and moth and bat. Or, again, walking westward at evening, the scene is still more lovely. The birds have not the speed of the morning, the cattle move slowly, the long, hot day bends quietly to its end. But the sun sets in splendour, and the long white ribbon of the road shines amid the folding purple of the moor, a purple that deepens and dies in the shadows of dark, threatening woods, or beside white sheets of water. Travellers are rare upon the road toward evening, are scarce indeed all day. Sometimes a small gipsy van lingers, but the children make little noise. True gipsy children never cry, they say. But these dark people, harmless enough, with their strange tongue add to the sense of mystery.

But all this is mere country life: why is the road reputed to be, nay, let us boldly say is, haunted? The old man who sits near the eastern wood all day making sticks, peeling and bending them, is real enough; though why he makes sticks, or for whom, is a mystery. Nor is he more real than the old woman who knits endless somethings by the western wood. Sticks to beat men, halters to hang them, said a herb-gatherer the other day. But he is as mysterious as the people he criticises as he hovers from bog to hill with his basket and his long stride. Yet they are all real people. Besides these three and the gipsies there is the woodcutter, a stern man who has laid low many a great tree, and there is the charcoal burner, a man whose laugh, thin and sibilant, comes down the wind from the woods with his smoke, and two or three wild children who drive the cattle to

pasture. And there is the grey ferryman at the great pond,
still stocked with carp, that breaks the road where the
long sea marsh cleaves the plain. The little homesteads are
ordinary enough and very hospitable, but they all stand
far back from the road. That the way is haunted no one
doubts, but yet it is hard to cite evidence of it. It is the
sum total of the place that terrifies, the looking back at
evening into the black woods from which one has come,
the looking forward over the endless mysterious waste of
perfect beauty. But at any rate one can prove, in a trice,
that the Cistercians, abolished nearly four centuries ago,
are still there haunting in white habit the road they trod
so long. Here is the proof.

On an autumn evening some years since a foot traveller
walking eastward towards a little seaport village crossed
this moor along this road. He had come out of the dark
woods and had gone some two hundred yards on the open
moor when he turned back to admire the fast dying sunset.
He shuddered as his eyes travelled from the sky down to
the gloomy woodland road from which he had just issued.
Then he was suddenly startled by something that he saw.
He was a scholar, and the scene conveyed more to him
than to most men. He saw passing along the road from
the bright moor into the dark wood a small cavalcade of
men riding mules. What struck him first was the costume
of the men, men dressed and armed in fourteenth-century fashion escorting three ecclesiastics, one of whom was
clearly a man of high rank. The second thought was, how
did they get there? He had passed no one. With curious
eyes he watched the party pass along the road into the
wood, where the full moon from the south-east already
cast an avenue of light. Then a strange scene was enacted.
There was no sound, but he was watching a furious struggle. The Bishop and his chaplains and escort had been am-
bushed. That the attacking force consisted of Cistercian

monks there was no manner of doubt, and suddenly he saw
in the heather by a solitary tree not forty paces from him,
watching the fray with keen attention, a man in the white
Cistercian habit. The figure seemed totally unconscious
of his presence. The escort scattered into the woods with
the foe in pursuit. The Bishop lay prone on the ground
in the moonlight, and the figure strode forward and with
lifted hand bent over him. The scene vanished as swiftly as it came, and the spectator found himself alone on
the moor, now flooded with moonlight and edged by the
clean-cut, dark outlines of the woods. He sped on in wonder at the illusion, for so he deemed it to be, and, despite
a deliberate suppression of nervousness, was relieved to
be joined unexpectedly by the herb-gatherer on his way
to the cottage that he shared with the woodman. Told of
the experience, he shrugged his great shoulders, and, wav-
ing his hand round the shining moor, exclaimed: "We are
never lonely on this road. There on that clump were the
Abbey gallows. Down there is the village that the plague
destroyed. Both are places of dead men's bones. Ho! it was
merry work in the olden time." So they strode on, the last
folk over the ferry at the very end of day, and they heard
the charcoal-burner laughing as he, too, went home.

There is a sequel to this evidence of the uncanniness of
the road. The witness searched the extant records of the
monastery for some fourteenth-century evidence of this
scene. There was none, though there were various entries
that showed violent resistance to episcopal visitation. But
one day in his own college library the spectator found a
manuscript that appeared to solve the problem. The college after the Reformation had acquired as a charitable be-
quest certain lands once held by the monastery, and with
the lands passed certain title-deeds and manuscripts. The
manuscript in question was a copy of a document relating to an appeal to the Pope against the right of visita-

tion. In the manuscript there is the significant statement
that the said Lord Bishop was on the morning of the 7th
August, 1350, found dead on the lands of the said House,
he having succumbed to the sweating sickness then prev-
alent, and that such death was wrongfully attributed to
the servants of the said House. The records of the diocese
show that the Bishop, in fact, died of the plague whilst on
visitation. Now the scene had been witnessed on the 17th
August (N.S.). This is a story that suggests new sources for
writing history. But ghosts are not always so kind even on
the Never-Ending Road.

The Bureau d'Echange de Maux

Lord Dunsany

(1915)

I often think of the Bureau d'Echange de Maux and the wondrously evil old man that sate therein. It stood in a little street that there is in Paris, its doorway made of three brown beams of wood, the top one overlapping the others like the Greek letter pai, all the rest painted green, a house far lower and narrower than its neighbors and infinitely stranger, a thing to take one's fancy. And over the doorway, on the old brown beam, in faded yellow letters, this legend ran, "Bureau Universel d'Echange de Maux."

I entered at once and accosted the listless man that lolled on a stool by his counter. I demanded the wherefore of his wonderful house, what evil wares he exchanged, with many other things that I wished to know, for curiosity led me, and, indeed, had it not, I had gone at once from the shop, for there was so evil a look in that fattened man, in the hang of his fallen cheeks and his sinful eye that you would have said he had had dealings with Hell and won the advantage by sheer wickedness.

Such a man was mine host, but above all the evil of him lay in his eyes, which lay so still, so apathetic, that you would have sworn that he was drugged or dead; like lizards, motionless on a wall they lay, then suddenly they darted, and all his cunning flamed up and revealed itself in what one moment before seemed no more than a sleepy and ordinarily wicked old man. And this was the object and trade of that peculiar shop, the Bureau Universel d'Echange de Maux: you paid twenty francs, which the old man proceeded to take from me, for admission to the bureau, and then had the right to exchange any evil or misfortune with anyone on the premises for some evil or misfortune that he "could afford," as the old man put it.

There were four or five men in the dingy ends of that low-ceilinged room who gesticulated and muttered softly in twos as men who make a bargain; and now and then more came in, and the eyes of the flabby owner of the house leaped up at them as they entered, seemed to know their errands at once and each one's peculiar need, and fell back again into somnolence, receiving his twenty francs in an almost lifeless hand and biting the coin as though in pure absence of mind.

"Some of my clients," he told me. So amazing to me was the trade of this extraordinary shop that I engaged the old man in conversation, repulsive though he was, and from his garrulity I gathered these facts. He spoke in perfect English, though his utterance was somewhat thick and heavy; no language seemed to come amiss to him. He had been in business a great many years, how many he would not say, and was far older than he looked. All kinds of people did business in his shop. What they exchanged with each other he did not care, except that it had to be evils, he was not empowered to carry on any other kind of business.

There was no evil, he told me, that was not negotiable there; no evil the old man knew had ever been taken away in despair from his shop. A man might have to wait and come back again next day and next day and the day after, paying twenty francs each time, but the old man had the addresses of his clients and shrewdly knew their needs, and soon the right two met and eagerly changed their commodities. "Commodities" was the old man's terrible word, said with a gruesome smack of his heavy lips, for he took a pride in his business, and evils to him were goods.

I learned from him in ten minutes very much of human nature, more than I had ever learned from any other man; I learned from him that a man's own evil is to him the worst thing that there is or could be, and that an evil so unbalances all men's minds that they always seek for extremes in that small, grim shop. A woman that had no children had exchanged with an impoverished, half-maddened creature with twelve. On one occasion a man had exchanged wisdom for folly.

"Why on earth did he do that?" I said.

"None of my business," the old man answered in his heavy, indolent way. He merely took his twenty francs from each and ratified the agreement in the little room at the back, opening out of the shop, where his clients do business. Apparently the man that had parted with wisdom had left the shop upon the tips of his toes with a happy though foolish expression all over his face, but the other went thoughtfully away, wearing a troubled and very puzzled look. Almost always, it seemed, they did business in opposite evils.

But the thing that puzzled me most in all my talks with that unwieldy man, the thing that puzzles me still, is that none that had once done business in that shop ever returned again; a man might come day after day for many weeks, but once do business and he never returned; so much the old man told me, but when I asked him why, he only muttered that he did not know.

It was to discover the wherefore of this strange thing, and for no other reason at all, that I determined myself to do business, sooner or later, in the little room at the back of that mysterious shop. I determined to exchange some very trivial evil for some evil equally slight, to seek for myself an advantage so very small as scarcely to give Fate, as it were, a grip; for I deeply distrusted these bargains, knowing well that man has never yet benefited by the marvelous, and that the more miraculous his advantage appears to be, the more securely and tightly do the gods or the witches catch him. In a few days more I was going back to England and I was beginning to fear that I should be seasick; this fear of seasickness, not the actual malady, but only the mere fear of it, I decided to exchange for a suitably little evil. I did not know with whom I should be dealing, who in reality was the head of the firm (one never does when shopping), but I decided that neither Jew nor Devil could make very much on so small a bargain as that.

I told the old man my project and he scoffed at the smallness of my commodity, trying to urge me on to some darker bargain, but could not move me from my purpose. And then he told me tales, with a somewhat boastful air, of the big business, the great bargains, that had passed through his hands. A man had once run in there to try and exchange death, he had swallowed poison by accident and had only twelve hours to live. That sinister old man had been able to oblige him. A client was willing to exchange the commodity.

"But what did he give in exchange for death?" I said.

"Life," said that grim old man with a furtive chuckle.

"It must have been a horrible life," I said.

"That was not my affair," the proprietor said, lazily rattling together as he spoke a little pocketful of twenty-franc pieces.

Strange business I watched in that shop for the next few days, the exchange of odd commodities, and heard strange mutterings in corners amongst couples who presently rose and went to the back room, the old man following to ratify.

Twice a day for a week I paid my twenty francs, watching life, with its great needs and its little needs, morning and afternoon, spread out before me in all its wonderful variety.

And one day I met a comfortable man with only a little need; he seemed to have the very evil I wanted. He always feared the lift was going to break. I knew too much of hydraulics to fear things as silly as that, but it was not my business to cure his ridiculous fear. Very few words were needed to convince him that mine was the evil for him; he never crossed the sea, and I, on the other hand, could always walk upstairs, and I also felt, at the time, as many must feel in that shop, that so absurd a fear could never trouble me. And yet, at times, it is almost the curse of my life. When we both had signed the parchment in the spidery back room, and the old man had signed and ratified (for which we had to pay him fifty francs each), I went back to my hotel, and there I saw the deadly thing in the basement. They asked me if I would go upstairs in the lift; from force of habit I risked it, and I held my breath all the way up and clenched my hands. Nothing will induce me to try such a journey again. I would sooner go up to my room in a balloon. And why? Because if a balloon goes wrong you have a chance: it may spread out into a parachute after it has burst, it may catch in a tree, a hundred and one things may happen, but if the lift falls down its shaft you are done. As for seasickness, I shall never be sick again; I cannot tell you why, except that I know that it is so.

And the shop in which I made this remarkable bargain, the shop to which none return when their business is done, I set out for it next day. Blindfold I could have found my way to the unfashionable quarter out of which a mean street runs, where you take the alley at the end, whence runs the cul-de-sac where the queer shop stood. A shop with pillars, fluted and painted red, stands on its near side; its other neighbor is a low-class jeweler's, with little silver brooches in the window. In such incongruous company stood the shop with beams, with its walls painted green.

In half an hour I stood in the cul-de-sac to which I had gone twice a day for the last week; I found the shop with the ugly painted pillars and the jeweler that sold brooches; but the green house, with the three beams, was gone.

Pulled down, you will say, although in a single night. That can never be the answer to the mystery, for the house of the fluted pillars painted on plaster, and the low-class jeweler's shop, with its silver brooches (all of which I could identify one by one), were standing side by side.

The Street
H. P. Lovecraft
(1920)

There be those who say that things and places have souls, and there be those who say they have not; I dare not say, myself, but I will tell of the Street.

Men of strength and honour fashioned that Street: good valiant men of our blood who had come from the Blessed Isles across the sea. At first it was but a path trodden by bearers of water from the woodland spring to the cluster of houses by the beach. Then, as more men came to the growing cluster of houses and looked about for places to dwell, they built cabins along the north side, cabins of stout oaken logs with masonry on the side toward the forest, for many Indians lurked there with fire-arrows. And in a few years more, men built cabins on the south side of the Street.

Up and down the Street walked grave men in conical hats, who most of the time carried muskets or fowling pieces. And there were also their bonneted wives and sober children. In the evening these men with their wives and children would sit about gigantic hearths and read and speak. Very simple were the things of which they read and spoke, yet things which gave them courage and goodness and helped them by day to subdue the forest and till the fields. And the children would listen and learn of the laws and deeds of old, and of that dear England which they had never seen or could not remember.

There was war, and thereafter no more Indians troubled
the Street. The men, busy with labour, waxed prosperous
and as happy as they knew how to be. And the children
grew up comfortable, and more families came from the
Mother Land to dwell on the Street. And the children's
children, and the newcomers' children, grew up. The town
was now a city, and one by one the cabins gave place to
houses—simple, beautiful houses of brick and wood, with
stone steps and iron railings and fanlights over the doors.
No flimsy creations were these houses, for they were made
to serve many a generation. Within there were carven man-
tels and graceful stairs, and sensible, pleasing furniture,
china, and silver, brought from the Mother Land.

So the Street drank in the dreams of a young people
and rejoiced as its dwellers became more graceful and happy. Where once had been only strength and honour, taste
and learning now abode as well. Books and paintings and
music came to the houses, and the young men went to the
university which rose above the plain to the north. In the
place of conical hats and muskets there were three-cornered hats and small-swords, and lace and snowy periwigs.
And there were cobblestones over which clattered many
a blooded horse and rumbled many a gilded coach; and
brick sidewalks with horse blocks and hitching-posts.

There were in that Street many trees: elms and oaks and
maples of dignity; so that in the summer, the scene was
all soft verdure and twittering bird-song. And behind the
houses were walled rose-gardens with hedged paths and
sundials, where at evening the moon and stars would shine
bewitchingly while fragrant blossoms glistened with dew.

So the Street dreamed on, past wars, calamities, and
change. Once, most of the young men went away, and some
never came back. That was when they furled the old flag
and put up a new banner of stripes and stars. But though
men talked of great changes, the Street felt them not, for

its folk were still the same, speaking of the old familiar things in the old familiar accounts. And the trees still sheltered singing birds, and at evening the moon and stars looked down upon dewy blossoms in the walled rose-gardens.

In time there were no more swords, three-cornered hats, or periwigs in the Street. How strange seemed the inhabitants with their walking-sticks, tall beavers, and cropped heads! New sounds came from the distance—first strange puffings and shrieks from the river a mile away, and then, many years later, strange puffings and shrieks and rumblings from other directions. The air was not quite so pure as before, but the spirit of the place had not changed. The blood and soul of their ancestors had fashioned the Street. Nor did the spirit change when they tore open the earth to lay down strange pipes, or when they set up tall posts bearing weird wires. There was so much ancient lore in that Street, that the past could not easily be forgotten.

Then came days of evil, when many who had known the Street of old knew it no more, and many knew it who had not known it before, and went away, for their accents were coarse and strident, and their mien and faces unpleasing. Their thoughts, too, fought with the wise, just spirit of the Street, so that the Street pined silently as its houses fell into decay, and its trees died one by one, and its rose-gardens grew rank with weeds and waste. But it felt a stir of pride one day when again marched forth young men, some of whom never came back. These young men were clad in blue.

With the years, worse fortune came to the Street. Its trees were all gone now, and its rose-gardens were displaced by the backs of cheap, ugly new buildings on parallel streets. Yet the houses remained, despite the ravages of the years and the storms and worms, for they had been made to serve many a generation. New kinds of faces

appeared in the Street, swarthy, sinister faces with furtive eyes and odd features, whose owners spoke unfamiliar
words and placed signs in known and unknown characters upon most of the musty houses. Push-carts crowded
the gutters. A sordid, undefinable stench settled over the
place, and the ancient spirit slept.

Great excitement once came to the Street. War and revolution were raging across the seas; a dynasty had collapsed,
and its degenerate subjects were flocking with dubious intent to the Western Land. Many of these took lodgings
in the battered houses that had once known the songs of
birds and the scent of roses. Then the Western Land itself
awoke and joined the Mother Land in her titanic struggle
for civilization. Over the cities once more floated the old
flag, companioned by the new flag, and by a plainer, yet
glorious tricolour. But not many flags floated over the
Street, for therein brooded only fear and hatred and ignorance. Again young men went forth, but not quite as did
the young men of those other days. Something was lack-
ing. And the sons of those young men of other days, who
did indeed go forth in olive-drab with the true spirit of
their ancestors, went from distant places and knew not the
Street and its ancient spirit.

Over the seas there was a great victory, and in triumph
most of the young men returned. Those who had lacked
something lacked it no longer, yet did fear and hatred and
ignorance still brood over the Street; for many had stayed
behind, and many strangers had come from distance places
to the ancient houses. And the young men who had returned dwelt there no longer. Swarthy and sinister were
most of the strangers, yet among them one might find a
few faces like those who fashioned the Street and moulded
its spirit. Like and yet unlike, for there was in the eyes of
all a weird, unhealthy glitter as of greed, ambition, vin-
dictiveness, or misguided zeal. Unrest and treason were

abroad amongst an evil few who plotted to strike the Western Land its death blow, that they might mount to power over its ruins, even as assassins had mounted in that unhappy, frozen land from whence most of them had come. And the heart of that plotting was in the Street, whose crumbling houses teemed with alien makers of discord and echoed with the plans and speeches of those who yearned for the appointed day of blood, flame and crime.

Of the various odd assemblages in the Street, the Law said much but could prove little. With great diligence did men of hidden badges linger and listen about such places as Petrovitch's Bakery, the squalid Rifkin School of Modern Economics, the Circle Social Club, and the Liberty Cafe. There congregated sinister men in great numbers, yet always was their speech guarded or in a foreign tongue. And still the old houses stood, with their forgotten lore of nobler, departed centuries; of sturdy Colonial tenants and dewy rose-gardens in the moonlight. Sometimes a lone poet or traveler would come to view them, and would try to picture them in their vanished glory; yet of such travelers and poets there were not many.

The rumour now spread widely that these houses contained the leaders of a vast band of terrorists, who on a designated day were to launch an orgy of slaughter for the extermination of America and of all the fine old traditions which the Street had loved. Handbills and papers fluttered about filthy gutters; handbills and papers printed in many tongues and in many characters, yet all bearing messages of crime and rebellion. In these writings the people were urged to tear down the laws and virtues that our fathers had exalted, to stamp out the soul of the old America—the soul that was bequeathed through a thousand and a half years of Anglo-Saxon freedom, justice, and moderation. It was said that the swart men who dwelt in the Street and congregated in its rotting edifices were the brains of a

hideous revolution, that at their word of command many
millions of brainless, besotted beasts would stretch forth
their noisome talons from the slums of a thousand cities,
burning, slaying, and destroying till the land of our fathers should be no more. All this was said and repeated,
and many looked forward in dread to the fourth day of
July, about which the strange writings hinted much; yet
could nothing be found to place the guilt. None could tell
just whose arrest might cut off the damnable plotting at
its source. Many times came bands of blue-coated police
to search the shaky houses, though at last they ceased to
come; for they too had grown tired of law and order, and
had abandoned all the city to its fate. Then men in olive-
drab came, bearing muskets, till it seemed as if in its sad
sleep the Street must have some haunting dreams of those
other days, when musket-bearing men in conical hats
walked along it from the woodland spring to the cluster
of houses by the beach. Yet could no act be performed
to check the impending cataclysm, for the swart, sinister
men were old in cunning.

So the Street slept uneasily on, till one night there
gathered in Petrovitch's Bakery, and the Rifkin School of
Modern Economics, and the Circle Social Club, and Liberty Cafe, and in other places as well, vast hordes of men
whose eyes were big with horrible triumph and expecta-
tion. Over hidden wires strange messages traveled, and
much was said of still stranger messages yet to travel; but
most of this was not guessed till afterward, when the Western Land was safe from the peril. The men in olive-drab
could not tell what was happening, or what they ought to
do; for the swart, sinister men were skilled in subtlety and
concealment.

And yet the men in olive-drab will always remember
that night, and will speak of the Street as they tell of it
to their grandchildren; for many of them were sent there

toward morning on a mission unlike that which they had expected. It was known that this nest of anarchy was old, and that the houses were tottering from the ravages of the years and the storms and worms; yet was the happening of that summer night a surprise because of its very queer uniformity. It was, indeed, an exceedingly singular happening, though after all, a simple one. For without warning, in one of the small hours beyond midnight, all the ravages of the years and the storms and the worms came to a tremendous climax; and after the crash there was nothing left standing in the Street save two ancient chimneys and part of a stout brick wall. Nor did anything that had been alive come alive from the ruins. A poet and a traveler, who came with the mighty crowd that sought the scene, tell odd stories. The poet says that all through the hours before dawn he beheld sordid ruins indistinctly in the glare of the arc-lights; that there loomed above the wreckage another picture wherein he could describe moonlight and fair houses and elms and oaks and maples of dignity. And the traveler declares that instead of the place's wonted stench there lingered a delicate fragrance as of roses in full bloom. But are not the dreams of poets and the tales of travelers notoriously false?

There be those who say that things and places have souls, and there be those who say they have not; I dare not say, myself, but I have told you of the Street.

The Blue City
Frank Owen
(1927)

Hwei-Ti sat in his garden. A gentle breeze was blowing, fragrant with the perfume of peach-blossoms. The sun streamed down warmly. He sighed. It seemed too bad that he had but six months to live. He was wealthy. Money meant no more to him than shriveled lotus petals. Though he were to live hundreds of years he could not exhaust his treasuries. Again he sighed and breathed deeply of the pungent air. Never had he felt in more perfect health, and yet the hand of death was reaching down to grasp him. He was still young. He had not yet reached half the span of ordinary life. He had worked hard to acquire a fortune, so hard that he had forsaken all earthly pleasures. He had never married. He was the last of his family. It was too bad that there was no offspring to carry on the splendid tradition of his old and venerated ancestors.

But now he was about to die. Woo Ling-foh, the prophet, had predicted it and never had his prognostications failed. He had predicted fire and flood, earthquake and plague, and always had his words come true. He had read the stars. His eyes traveled about the skies as though they were set free from his body. To the farthermost realms of space they roamed, and many were the mysteries into which they peered.

Woo Ling-foh and Hwei-Ti had known each other for many years. The old mystic was a most interesting companion and countless were the tranquil hours Hwei-Ti passed listening to his quaint philosophies.

"Of all senses," mused Woo Ling-foh, "that of sight is the greatest. Who really looks with eyes that see? In every man is hidden the shadow of his ancestors. From his shadow he can not escape. Therefore might it not be possible for one to gaze at a man so intently that one could see his ancestors reaching back dimly through the mists of the ages? However, this is purely speculative on my part. I have never had opportunity to pursue this particular road of thought farther. I have been too intent on experimenting with spiritual things. For years this has been my main subject of research, and do you know what I have come to realize? Vision is granted a man only just before his death. At that period his senses are developed to their most superb degree. Animals and people do not see things in the same manner. Visions are of different intensities. For instance, birds can not distinguish blue because of the presence of yellow granules in the retina of their eyes. Numerous animals can distinguish ultra-violet rays which are not apparent to human sight, due perhaps to the fluorescence of their eyes. I merely mention these things in a fragmentary way to emphasize my point. If such things can be, might it not also be possible for one to gaze into the spiritual world if one's vision was sufficiently tuned? Not only is it possible but it has been done. I have wandered through a silent Blue City, a city of peace and contentment and rest, a city of soft whispers and sweet tones, of beauty and rare love. Come with me upon a pilgrimage. You have not long to live, six months at best, and I will take you to realms that will make your passing splendid."

Hwei-Ti was interested. He leaned forward. "Where is this city of which you speak?"

Woo Ling-foh extended his hands. "Who knows?" he said slowly. "Who knows the exact position of anything? Most places exist only if you believe in them enough."

In the early evening the old mystic stopped for Hwei-Ti at his garden. The sun was setting and the rose-tinted lights of late afternoon splashed on the mountains in gorgeous splendor. They walked on and on, without heat or hurry. The air was cool and refreshing, in strange variance to the humid heat of the day that had passed. Gradually the rose-tinted lights faded, giving place to purpling mists as night crept into its own. Onward they continued up a winding mountain-road, a road upon which no other wayfarers walked, a road deserted, sad, rough.

Woo Ling-foh said nothing nor did Hwei-Ti, although it was true that the rich merchant's interest and enthusiasm were raised to a pitch never attained before. He felt, as he climbed up the crooked mountain-road, as though his old life was falling from him, like a shell that had become useless. The future held mystery. He could sense it in the air. Whether it held happiness he did not know. But he doubted it because his uttermost goal was dearth within six months anyway. Still the night's adventure was attractive, and he labored onward up the road beside old Woo Ling-foh, the mystic, who seemed unable to appreciate fatigue. He walked forward without effort despite his age and the steepness of the trail.

Now the mantle of night had fallen completely, the stars gleamed forth. They seemed of immense size, more brilliant than ever before.

Finally they reached the summit of the mountain—a broad, tablelike plateau that faded off into the gray of the night distances. The sky was of a brilliant blue. It seemed to bear down upon the mountain as though it were resting prone against it. The air was keen and fragrant.

It was very light. The stars shone forth in startling splendor.

Woo Ling-foh seized Hwei-Ti by the shoulder. "They are not stars," he whispered; "they are lanterns gleaming from windows m the magical Blue City."

The moon had risen, silver-bright, cool, as sharp-cut as a diamond. Before them stretched a long white road, a road of moonbeams that spread off toward the Blue City.

Woo Ling-foh took Hwei-Ti's hand. "Come," he murmured, and together they set off down the Moon Road that swerved into the skies.

Hwei-Ti's eyes were round with amazement. Could it be possible that they were walking into the very skies? Was he mad? Was even Woo Ling-foh but a figment of his distorted imagination? And yet there was a peace, a quietude about the occasion which was extremely beautiful. If it were madness it were better than his former state. Never had he known such complete tranquility.

Woo Ling-foh still held his arm. "Look clearly," he said softly, "and as your eyes grow accustomed to the azure light you will be able to make out the forms of houses, and perhaps if you are able to tune your vision sufficiently, people also will be apparent to you."

The light was of queer intensity, blue that made one long to slumber, blue that was maddening in its beauty, blue that was like a soft caress. Here and there gray shadows loomed. Hwei-Ti sighed. He was at peace. Dimly through the mists he could see the outlines of houses, charming little houses with happy lanterns glowing in the windows. They were all of blue, not of one tone but of many, suggesting that they were really of variegated colors softened by a glaze of blue.

It was very quiet in that strange city, but not soundless. The solitude was restful. It was like a city in the deep hush of morning before the birds had awakened or the flowers had unfolded to the dawn. Their footbeats made no sound as they passed along, and this was well, for on the fragrant air was the suggestion of sweet singing, as though some lovely lady were crooning love-melodies to the moon. Now the blue trees commenced to stir. They exhaled a sweet fragrance, fragrance of pine and fir, of myrrh and sandalwood. Onward they walked. In the houses the lamps still burned. They glowed gorgeously through the blue maze.

Hwei-Ti sighed. Vision had been granted him at last. All that he had beheld in his entire life dwarfed to naught by comparison to this.

At last they came to a house lovelier than all others. It was by no means a mansion, merely a lovely homelike dwelling with countless flowers growing all about it. Before the door of the house sat a lovely maiden. She was simply dressed in a soft blue costume. Her hair was blue-black. It shone with an exotic sheen in the lantern light that streamed through the window. Her lips were red, made more vivid and startling by the fact that they were the sole bit of color other than blue in the garden. When she smiled, her teeth gleamed white as alabaster.

As Hwei-Ti gazed into her wondrous young face he was thrilled. She was lovelier than any woman his wildest dreams had pictured. She was exquisite. She was divine. It had been the echo of her singing which had given music to the air. It was she who had been crooning to the moon. He stepped forward and bowed toward the ground. Before such beauty he was speechless. All that he desired was to worship before her. He felt as though he were less than the dust at her feet, even though his wealth was boundless. Before the great wealth of her beauty his own wealth faded utterly.

At their approach she glanced up and smiled. One would have imagined that they had been friends always. Hwei-Ti put out his arms and she came to him, with the sweet simplicity of a child. The next moment he had kissed her soft red lips and in that moment he knew that life held nothing better for him than the love of this glorious girl. Again and again he kissed this maiden of the strange Blue City. He did not stop to consider that he had found her by walking down the Moon Road that led into the sky. It was sufficient that she was in his arms, accepting his kisses. It was the zenith hour of existence.

Meanwhile old Woo Ling-foh stood near by, smiling faintly. His old wrinkled face seemed lit by a divine fire. He was patient and he waited.

The girl led the way to a bench beneath a magnolia tree. The scent of blossoms perfumed the garden. And there she sat and sang love-songs to him, sang until his senses reeled for the want of her, sang until the lanterns in the windows one by one flickered out, sang until the soft blue of the city began to fade into the glorious rose-tints of morning.

It was then that Woo Ling-foh's manner changed completely. He glanced about at the pale pink shadows, then he seized Hwei-Ti by the hand and dashed pell-mell up the Moon Road as though all the serpents that hide under the mountains of China were close at their heels. Hwei-Ti tried to protest, but the strength of the aged prophet was phenomenal. By his chaotic manner Hwei-Ti sensed that they were fleeing from some terrible horror. Yet how could horror stalk in the lovely garden of that beautiful girl?

It was sacrilege to credit such a doubt. And if danger existed, were they not cowards to flee from it, sacrificing her to an unknown fate?

At last they arrived at the mountain-top from which they had walked off onto the Moon Road. Woo Ling-foh fell panting to the ground. His lean, gaunt face was colorless. He closed his eyes and moaned and moaned. He had used up all his strength in an effort to escape from the Blue City.

Hwei-Ti was amazed. He could not understand Woo Ling-foh's sudden change of front. The Blue City had been exquisitely peaceful and calm, yet it had aroused panic in the mind of the old mystic. He stood gazing off toward the majestic picture of dawn which was unfolding before him. The last star had expired, not a vestige of the Blue City remained. Gone, too, was the Moon Road, like a night-fog before the West Wind.

He bent over Woo Ling-foh and touched him upon the shoulder. Hwei-Ti was not in the best of tempers. He resented having been torn away from the magnolia garden against his will, from the presence of that little China girl who was more lovely than any vision which his wildest fancy painted.

"Why did you drag me away?" he demanded angrily.

Woo Ling-foh opened his eyes and smiled wanly. "To save you from being crushed by the dawn," he said slowly. "You are still a mortal. The terrific beauty of a rose-dawn in the Blue City would crush you to death. You would be blinded, dazzled by the light, scorched by the glory of the sun. Would you want such a hideous death of beauty? To be blasted by beauty: what more awful fate could ever be devised?"

"But the girl," pleaded Hwei-Ti hoarsely: "What has become of her? Has she been burned beyond recognition? Did we sacrifice her to a death so frightful?"

"No," replied Woo Ling-foh, "we did not leave the girl in danger for she was in truth but a spirit and therefore she was safe in the spiritual Blue City. It has been given you to see that which few men have ever witnessed during their natural lives. You should be content. Because one can not always see the Blue City does not prove its non-existence. For neither can one see with the unaided eye the ultra-violet ray. But enough. Do not dwell too much on the happenings of the night that has passed. It would be unwise. It might unbalance your reason. Too profound meditation has its dangers. That is why no philosopher is entirely sane."

During the weeks that followed, Hwei-Ti sat long in his garden. He brooded over the Blue City. A great melancholy descended upon him. He was in love, in love with a gorgeous girl who lived in a spirit city. Perhaps she had been dead for fifty years. His life lay in ruins. He was very wealthy, but his wealth was not sufficient to bring that wondrous girl to him. He could not have been more despondent if he had been the veriest beggar in the market-place. He lost his desire for food. Sam-shu held no allure. He grew thin and haggard. Old Woo Ling-foh had gone off on a pilgrimage to the South, so he could not accompany him to the city once again.

Weeks rolled by. They lengthened into months. And Hwei-Ti remained in his garden. Desiring, dreaming, yearning for the magic city and the lovely girl.

And he thought of the prediction of the old philosopher, that he would not live six months. He believed it to be true, for he was ill from longing. He was on the threshold of death and he did not care. There was naught left to him in the world. Gold and jewels—what need had he for such worthless baubles? They could not buy happiness.

Then again came Woo Ling-foh.

"I am dying," murmured Hwei-Ti, "and before I finally expire I wish once more to visit the wondrous Blue City."

"I wonder," mused Woo Ling-foh. "I wonder whether death is really death, or is it life? Is it the birth of the soul? For surely when it is set free from the body, to wander untrammeled through the universe, it can not be death. However, vain speculations interest only those who like to spend their hours in such pursuits."

"I wish once more to visit the magical city," repeated Hwei-Ti.

"It would be dangerous," replied Woo Ling-foh. "We escaped with our lives only by the width of a spun golden thread. To return would be to court disaster. You are too emotional. Be content. Wander not into realms that are fraught with danger."

Hwei-Ti sprang to his feet. He seized the old man by the throat. His reason snapped. Slowly his long fingers closed about the lean old throat. "If you do not take me to the mountain-top from which we walked off into the Moon Road," he cried hoarsely, "your life shall end at this moment!"

Woo Ling-foh flung Hwei-Ti's fingers from about his throat. He was not angry at the attack, for he realized that madness was creeping over his friend. He was not afraid, but he acceded to his wishes because he believed that calm death would be preferable to the maniacal existence toward which Hwei-Ti was plunging.

So in the evening he called again at the garden and together they set off toward the mountain-road. Hwei-Ti was very weak. Only his will to reach the Blue City carried him forward. He was overtaxing his feeble strength in this one superb effort, but he did not care. His craving was to be satiated.

When they arrived at the mountain-road, Woo Ling-foh paused. "You must continue onward alone," he said slowly. "The stars do not portend well, so I can not go with you. All my movements are controlled by astrological divinings. That is why contentment and peace are mine."

Hwei-Ti made no protest at the old mystic's desertion. In fact he scarcely heeded it. It was enough that he was nearing the Blue City. His weakness was acute. His throat was parched. His tongue was dry. Time after time he staggered and fell. But ever he rose to his feet and continued onward up the sad, lonesome road. Eventually he reached the summit of the mountain. He breathed painfully. His eyes were wet with tears. He was very weak. But there before him stretched the Moon Road, a street of shimmering silver that swerved off into the Blue City.

As he walked out upon the Moon Road much of his fatigue abated. The cool air laved his tired body as though it were balm. It caressed his wasted cheeks, smoothed away the marks of worry and care. In the windows of the houses the star-lamps gleamed, and gradually he could make out the form of the houses as his vision adjusted itself to the pungent blue. Finally he heard the sound of sweet singing. His heart beat fast. Now he was weak no longer. Love, desire, made him strong.

The next moment he was in the magnolia garden and the wondrous girl was in his arms, crushed to his breast like a beautiful, fragrant flower. Contentment was complete. He kissed her soft lips again and again. Then she pushed him slowly away and continued her singing. But now she sang directly to him, a song that roses sing when their lovers return. It was magic, it was enchantment. Perhaps Woo Ling-foh was right. The Blue City was a spirit world; but if so, what mattered?

Entranced, he lingered in the garden until the rose-tipped shafts of morning crept into the skies. Slowly the blue faded into roseate magnificence. The magnolia trees sighed softly. They swayed in the breeze as though they were awaking. A few of the fragile blossoms fell upon him. The lovely, flowerlike maiden rose to her feet. She took his hand and faced toward the East. An ecstatic expression was upon her face and her soft bosom rose and fell as though she were greatly enthused. Forgotten by Hwei-Ti was the panic that had seized Woo Ling-foh on that other morning when they had fled together from the gorgeous horrors about which Woo Ling-foh talked in whispers. Gone was fear, fear of death, fear of life. Only the rose tints of lovely dawn remained and this girl of songs and dreams.

Slowly the blue faded and the rose, pink, orange glow intensified. From the distance there came a great moaning, a moaning as of the sea booming upon a white coral beach. It sounded like distant thunder. It was the thunder of dawn, the crashing beauty of the sun. Slowly, majestically it loomed into view. Its brilliance was blinding, dazzling. It burned the eyes of Hwei-ti, yet he could not turn them away. One by one the star-lanterns flickered out. His body commenced to tremble. It was the most exalted moment of his life. It was like a journey to the sun. It was a beauty too intense for his poor mind to absorb. He commenced to tremble.

The roar of the waves upon the coral beach intensified. Now the whole city was golden, tipped with rose and orange. The roar was frightful. He felt as though his head were bursting. His eyes pained as though they were on fire. He could not breathe. Moaning he fell to his knees, nor could he rise again. Yet ever he kept, his eyes turned toward the sun. The sun in morning splendor beat upon him, dazzlingly beautiful but ruthless in its intensity. It burned out his eyes. It scorched his body to ashes. It crushed him beneath its glory. When he had borne pain to the uttermost, agony beyond words, the spark of his life flickered out.

All through the rose dawn he lay lifeless at the feet of the lovely girl. Softly she crooned threnodies of love to him. Until at last sunset came, the golden glow gave way to the purpling shadows of evening, then to the pungent blue of night. Gradually the lamps were lighted in the windows. A fragrant breeze cooled the air.

Abruptly the girl stopped singing. She stooped and kissed the cracked, broken lips of Hwei-Ti. He opened his eyes. As he gazed into hers, new strength came to him.

"Come," she whispered softly.

He rose to his feet. Together they sat once more beneath the magnolia tree. The garden had never before seemed more beautiful.

"You will never again have to leave the Blue City," she murmured. "Now we can be together until the very sun doth cool."

"What do you mean?" he asked.

And she replied, "Simply that you came into the Blue City with a material body. But now all that is material has been burned away. The spiritual only remains."

As she finished speaking she commenced once more to sing of old longings and young love. Hwei-Ti folded his hands. He was content. He was at peace.

The Theater Upstairs
Manly Wade Wellman
(1936)

"Look, a picture theater—who'd expect one here?"

Luther caught my arm and dragged me to a halt. We'd been out on a directionless walk through lower Manhattan that evening—"flitting" was Luther's word, cribbed, I think, from Robert W. Chambers. The old narrow street where we now paused had an old English name and was somewhere south and east of Chinatown. Its line of dingy shops had foreign words on their dim windows, and lights and threadbare curtains up above where their proprietors lodged. And right before us, where Luther had stopped to gaze, was a narrow wooden door that bore a white card. CINEMA, it said in bold, plain capitals. And, in smaller letters below: Georgia Wattell.

I was prepared to be embarrassed by that name. Everyone suspected, and a few claimed to know positively, that Georgia Wattell had committed suicide at the height of her Hollywood career because Luther had deserted her. But my companion did not flinch, only drew up that thick body of his. A smile wrinkled his handsome features, features that still meant box-office to any picture, even though they were softening from too much food and drink and so forth.

"Wonder which of Georgia's things it is," Luther mused, with a gayety slightly forced. "Come on, I'll stand you a show."

I didn't like it, but refusal would seem accusation. So I let him draw me through the door.

We had stairs to walk up—creaky old stairs. They were so narrow that we had to mount in single file, our shoulders brushing first one wall, then the other. I was mystified, for doesn't a New York ordinance provide that theaters cannot be on upper floors? There was no light on those stairs, as I remember, only a sort of grayness filtering from above. At any rate, we saw better when we came to the little foyer at the top. A shabby man stood there, with lead-colored eyes in his square face and a great shock of coarse gray hair.

"Admission a quarter," he mumbled in a soft, hoarse voice, and accepted the half-dollar Luther produced. "Go on in."

With one hand he pocketed the coin and with the other drew back a dark, heavy curtain. We entered a long hall, groped our way to seats—we were the only patrons, so far as I could tell—and almost at once the screen lit up with the title: THE HORLA, by Guy de Maupassant.

"Creepy stuff—good!" muttered Luther with relish, then added some other comment on the grisly classic. What with trying to hear him and read the cast of players at the same moment, I failed in both efforts. The shimmering words on the screen dissolved into a pictured landscape, smitten by rain which the sound apparatus mimicked drearily. In the middle distance appeared a cottage, squat and ancient, with a droopy, soft-seeming roof like the cap of a toadstool. The camera viewpoint sailed down and upon it, in what Luther called a "dolly shot." We saw at close quarters the front porch.

Two women sat on the top step, exchanging the inconsequential opening dialog. Georgia Wattell seated at center with her sad, dark face turned front, was first recognizable. Her companion, to one side and in profile, offered to our view a flash of silver-blond hair and a handsome, feline countenance.

"It's Lilyan Tashman," grunted Luther, and shut up his mouth with a snap. He might have said more about this uneasy vision of two dead actresses talking and moving, but he did not. A third figure was coming into view at the left, shedding a glistening waterproof and a soaked slouch hat. My first glimpse of his smooth black hair and close-set ears, seen from behind, struck a chord of memory in me. Then his face swiveled around into view, and I spoke aloud.

"This can't be!" I protested. "Why, Rudolph Valentino died before anybody even dreamed of sound pic—"

But it was Valentino nevertheless, and he had been about to speak to the two women. However, just as I exclaimed in my unbelieving amazement, he paused and faced front. His gaze seemed to meet mine, and suddenly I realized how big he was on the screen, eight or ten feet high at the least. Those brilliant eyes withered me, his lip twitched over his dazzling teeth—the contemptuous rebuke-expression of an actor to a noisy audience.

So devastatingly real was that shadowy snub that I almost fell from my seat. I know that Luther swore, and that I felt sweaty all over. When I recovered enough to assure myself that my imagination was too lively, Valentino had turned back to deliver his interrupted entrance line. The show went on.

So far there was nothing to remind me of de Maupassant's story as I had read it. But with Valentino's first speech and Georgia Wattell's answer the familiar plot began. Of course, it was freely modified, like most film versions of the classics. For one thing, the victim of the invisible monster was not a man but a woman—Georgia, to be exact—and it seemed to me at the time that this change heightened the atmosphere of helpless horror.

Valentino might have done something vigorous, either
spiritual or physical, against de Maupassant's Horla. Georgia Wattell, with her sorrowfully lovely face and frail little
body, seemed inescapably foredoomed.

The remainder of the action on the porch was occupied
by Georgia's description of the barely-understood woes
she was beginning to suffer at the Horla's hands. Miss
Tashman as her friend and Valentino as her lover urged her
to treat everything as a fancy and to tell herself that all
would be well. She promised—but how vividly she acted
the part of an unbeliever in her own assurance! Then the
image of the porch, with those three shadows of dead players posed upon it in attitudes of life, faded away.

The next scene was a French country bedroom—curtained
bed, *prie-dieu* and so on. Georgia Wattell entered it, un-
fastening her clothing.

"Ho!" exploded Luther somewhat lasciviously, but I
did not stop to be disgusted with him. My mind was wres-
tling with the situation, how items so familiar in themselves—lower New York, the motion picture business, the
performers, de Maupassant's story—could be so creepy in
combination.

Well, Georgia took off her dress. I saw, as often before,
that she had a lovely bosom and shoulders, for all her fra-
gility. Over her underthings she drew an ample white robe,
on the collar of which fell her loosened dark hair. Kneeling
for a moment at the *prie-dieu,* she murmured a half-audi-
ble prayer, then turned toward the bed. At that moment
there entered—just where, I cannot say—the Horla.

It was quite the finest and weirdest film device I have
ever seen. No effect in the picture versions of *Frankenstein*
or *Dracula* remotely approached it. Without outline or
opacity, less tangible than a shimmer of hot air, yet it gave
the impression of living malevolence. I felt aware of its

presence upon the screen without actually seeing it; but how could it have been suggested without being visible? I should like to discuss this point with someone else who saw the picture, but I have never yet found such a person.

It was there, anyway. Georgia registered sudden and uneasy knowledge of it. Her body shuddered a trifle inside the robe and she paused as if in indecision, then moved toward the bed. A moment later she moaned wildly and staggered a bit. The thing, whatever triumph of photo-dramatic trickery it was, enveloped her.

She went all blurred and indistinct, as though seen through water. Doesn't de Maupassant himself use that figure of speech? Then the attacking entity seemed to pop out into a faint approach to human shape. I could see shadowy arms winding around the shrinking girl, a round, featureless head bowed as if its maw sought her throat. She screamed loudly and began to struggle. Then Valentino and Miss Tashman burst into the room.

With their appearance the Horla released her and seemed to retire into its half-intangible condition. I, who had utterly forgotten that I saw only a film, sighed my inexpressible relief at the thing's momentary defeat, then whispered to Luther.

"I don't like this," I said. "Let's get out, or I won't sleep tonight."

"We stay right here," he mumbled back, his eyes bright and fascinated as they kept focused on the screen.

Valentino was holding Georgia close, caressing her to quiet her hysterics and speaking reassuringly in his accented English. Lilyan Tashman said something apparently meant for comedy relief, which was badly needed at this point. But neither Luther nor I laughed.

Georgia suddenly cried out in fresh fear.

"It's there in the corner!" she wailed, turning toward the spot where the Horla must be lurking.

Both her companions followed her gaze, apparently seeing nothing. For that matter I saw nothing myself, though I well knew the thing was there.

Valentino made another effort to calm her.

"I'll put a bullet into it, darling," he offered, with an air of falling in with her morbid humor. "In the corner, you say?"

From his pocket he drew a revolver. But Georgia, suddenly calming her shudders, snatched the weapon from his hand.

"Don't!" she begged. "How can a bullet harm something that has no life like ours?"

"Here, don't point that gun at me!" begged Miss Tashman, retreating in comic fright.

Georgia moved forward in the picture, looming larger than her companions. "You can't kill spirits," she went on, tonelessly and quite undramatically. "Bullets are for *living* enemies."

She gazed out upon us.

Right here is where the whole business stopped being real and became nightmare. Georgia moved again, closer and closer, until her head and shoulders, with the gun hand lifted beside them, filled the screen. She looked as big as the Sphinx by then, but grim and merciless as no Sphinx ever was. And her enormous, accusing eyes weren't fixed upon me, but upon Luther.

My inner self began arguing silently. "That's odd," it said plaintively. "A gaze from the screen seems to meet that of each member of the audience. How can she be looking *past* me at—"

Georgia spoke, between immense, hardened lips, in a voice that rolled out to fill the whole theater:

"Jan Luther!"

And she swelled bigger, bigger beyond all reason, too big for the screen to contain. Suddenly there were only the hand and the gun, turned toward us like a cannon aimed point-blank.

Luther was on his feet, screaming.

"You can't!" he challenged wildly, "You—why, you're only a shadow!"

But the screen exploded in white light, that made the whole hall bright as day for just the hundredth part of a second. After that I was trying to hold Luther erect. He sagged and slumped back into his seat in spite of all I could do. Blood purled gently down his face from a neat round hole in his forehead.

I glanced wildly at the screen. The picture had shrunk back to ordinary dimensions now, showing again the bed-room, the three performers and everything else exactly as it had been.

Georgia was offering Valentino his pistol again. "Thanks, Rudy," she said.

I suppose I must have run crazily out of there, for my next memory is of panting the story in broken sentences to a big blue-coated policeman. He frowned as I tried to tell every-thing at once, then came back with me to the street with the foreign-labeled shops. When I couldn't find the door and its lettered card he laughed, not very good-naturedly, and accused me of being drunk. When I tried to argue he ordered me to move along or go to jail and sleep it off.

I haven't seen Luther since, nor heard from him. There has been plenty in the papers about his disappearance, though several editors have put it down as a publicity stunt. Three times recently I have gone into the part of town where I lost him, and each time I have seen, at a lit-tle distance along a sidewalk or across a street, the white-haired, leaden-eyed man who admitted us to the theater. But, though I always tried to hail him, he lost himself among the passers-by before I reached him.

At length I have decided to stay away from there altogether. I wish I could stop thinking about the affair as
well.

The Street That Wasn't There
Clifford D. Simak and Carl Jacobi
(1941)

Mr. Jonathon Chambers left his house on Maple Street at exactly seven o'clock in the evening and set out on the daily walk he had taken, at the same time, come rain or snow, for twenty solid years.

The walk never varied. He paced two blocks down Maple Street, stopped at the Red Star confectionery to buy a Rose Trofero perfecto, then walked to the end of the fourth block on Maple. There he turned right on Lexington, followed Lexington to Oak, down Oak and so by way of Lincoln back to Maple again and to his home.

He didn't walk fast. He took his time. He always returned to his front door at exactly 7:45. No one ever stopped to talk with him. Even the man at the Red Star confectionery, where he bought his cigar, remained silent while the purchase was being made. Mr. Chambers merely tapped on the glass top of the counter with a coin, the man reached in and brought forth the box, and Mr. Chambers took his cigar. That was all.

For people long ago had gathered that Mr. Chambers desired to be left alone. The newer generation of townsfolk called it eccentricity. Certain uncouth persons had a different word for it. The oldsters remembered that this queer looking individual with his black silk muffler, rosewood cane and bowler hat once had been a professor at State University.

A professor of metaphysics, they seemed to recall, or some such outlandish subject. At any rate a furore of some sort was connected with his name . . . at the time an academic scandal. He had written a book, and he had taught the subject matter of that volume to his classes. What that subject matter was, had long been forgotten, but whatever it was had been considered sufficiently revolutionary to cost Mr. Chambers his post at the university.

A silver moon shone over the chimney tops and a chill, impish October wind was rustling the dead leaves when Mr. Chambers started out at seven o'clock.

It was a good night, he told himself, smelling the clean, crisp air of autumn and the faint pungence of distant wood smoke.

He walked unhurriedly, swinging his cane a bit less jauntily than twenty years ago. He tucked the muffler more securely under the rusty old topcoat and pulled his bowler hat more firmly on his head.

He noticed that the street light at the corner of Maple and Jefferson was out and he grumbled a little to himself when he was forced to step off the walk to circle a boarded-off section of newly-laid concrete work before the driveway of 816.

It seemed that he reached the corner of Lexington and Maple just a bit too quickly, but he told himself that this couldn't be. For he never did that. For twenty years, since the year following his expulsion from the university, he had lived by the clock.

The same thing, at the same time, day after day. He had not deliberately set upon such a life of routine. A bachelor, living alone with sufficient money to supply his humble needs, the timed existence had grown on him gradually.

So he turned on Lexington and back on Oak. The dog at the corner of Oak and Jefferson was waiting for him once again and came out snarling and growling, snapping at his heels. But Mr. Chambers pretended not to notice and the beast gave up the chase.

A radio was blaring down the street and faint wisps of what it was blurting floated to Mr. Chambers.

". . . still taking place . . . Empire State building disappeared . . . thin air . . . famed scientist, Dr. Edmund Harcourt. . . ."

The wind whipped the muted words away and Mr. Chambers grumbled to himself. Another one of those fantastic radio dramas, probably. He remembered one from many years before, something about the Martians. And Harcourt! What did Harcourt have to do with it? He was one of the men who had ridiculed the book Mr. Chambers had written.

But he pushed speculation away, sniffed the clean, crisp air again, looked at the familiar things that materialized out of the late autumn darkness as he walked along. For there was nothing . . . absolutely nothing in the world . . . that he would let upset him. That was a tenet he had laid down twenty years ago.

There was a crowd of men in front of the drugstore at the corner of Oak and Lincoln and they were talking excitedly. Mr. Chambers caught some excited words: "It's happening everywhere. . . . What do you think it is. . . . The scientists can't explain. . . ."

But as Mr. Chambers neared them they fell into what seemed an abashed silence and watched him pass. He, on his part, gave them no sign of recognition. That was the way it had been for many years, ever since the people had become convinced that he did not wish to talk.

One of the men half started forward as if to speak to him, but then stepped back and Mr. Chambers continued on his walk.

Back at his own front door he stopped and as he had done a thousand times before drew forth the heavy gold watch from his pocket.

He started violently. It was only 7:30!

For long minutes he stood there staring at the watch in accusation. The timepiece hadn't stopped, for it still ticked audibly.

But 15 minutes too soon! For twenty years, day in, day out, he had started out at seven and returned at a quarter of eight. Now . . .

It wasn't until then that he realized something else was wrong. He had no cigar. For the first time he had neglected to purchase his evening smoke.

Shaken, muttering to himself, Mr. Chambers let himself in his house and locked the door behind him.

He hung his hat and coat on the rack in the hall and walked slowly into the living room. Dropping into his favorite chair, he shook his head in bewilderment.

Silence filled the room. A silence that was measured by the ticking of the old-fashioned pendulum clock on the mantelpiece.

But silence was no strange thing to Mr. Chambers. Once he had loved music . . . the kind of music he could get by tuning in symphonic orchestras on the radio. But the radio stood silent in the corner, the cord out of its socket. Mr. Chambers had pulled it out many years before. To be precise, upon the night when the symphonic broadcast had been interrupted to give a news flash.

He had stopped reading newspapers and magazines too, had exiled himself to a few city blocks. And as the years flowed by, that self-exile had become a prison, an intangible, impassable wall bounded by four city blocks by three. Beyond them lay utter, unexplainable terror. Beyond them he never went.

But recluse though he was, he could not on occasion escape from hearing things. Things the newsboy shouted on the streets, things the men talked about on the drugstore corner when they didn't see him coming.

And so he knew that this was the year 1960 and that the wars in Europe and Asia had flamed to an end to be followed by a terrible plague, a plague that even now was sweeping through country after country like wild fire, decimating populations. A plague undoubtedly induced by hunger and privation and the miseries of war.

But those things he put away as items far removed from his own small world. He disregarded them. He pretended he had never heard of them. Others might discuss and worry over them if they wished. To him they simply did not matter.

But there were two things tonight that did matter. Two curious, incredible events. He had arrived home fifteen minutes early. He had forgotten his cigar.

Huddled in the chair, he frowned slowly. It was disquieting to have something like that happen. There must be something wrong. Had his long exile finally turned his mind . . . perhaps just a very little . . . enough to make him queer? Had he lost his sense of proportion, of perspective?

No, he hadn't. Take this room, for example. After twenty years it had come to be as much a part of him as the clothes he wore. Every detail of the room was engraved in his mind with . . . clarity; the old center leg table with its green covering and stained glass lamp; the mantelpiece with the dusty bric-a-brac; the pendulum clock that told the time of day as well as the day of the week and month; the elephant ash tray on the tabaret and, most important of all, the marine print.

Mr. Chambers loved that picture. It had depth, he always said. It showed an old sailing ship in the foreground on a placid sea. Far in the distance, almost on the horizon line, was the vague outline of a larger vessel.

There were other pictures, too. The forest scene above the fireplace, the old English prints in the corner where he sat, the Currier and Ives above the radio. But the ship print was directly in his line of vision. He could see it without turning his head. He had put it there because he liked it best.

Further reverie became an effort as Mr. Chambers felt himself succumbing to weariness. He undressed and went to bed. For an hour he lay awake, assailed by vague fears he could neither define nor understand.

When finally he dozed off it was to lose himself in a series of horrific dreams. He dreamed first that he was a castaway on a tiny islet in mid-ocean, that the waters around the island teemed with huge poisonous sea snakes . . . hydrophinnae . . . and that steadily those serpents were devouring the island.

In another dream he was pursued by a horror which he could neither see nor hear, but only could imagine. And as he sought to flee he stayed in the one place. His legs worked frantically, pumping like pistons, but he could make no progress. It was as if he ran upon a treadway.

Then again the terror descended on him, a black, un-imagined thing and he tried to scream and couldn't. He opened his mouth and strained his vocal cords and filled his lungs to bursting with the urge to shriek . . . but not a sound came from his lips.

All next day he was uneasy and as he left the house that evening, at precisely seven o'clock, he kept saying to himself: "You must not forget tonight! You must remember to stop and get your cigar!"

The street light at the corner of Jefferson was still out and in front of 816 the cemented driveway was still boarded off. Everything was the same as the night before.

And now, he told himself, the Red Star confectionery is in the next block. I must not forget tonight. To forget twice in a row would be just too much.

He grasped that thought firmly in his mind, strode just a bit more rapidly down the street.

But at the corner he stopped in consternation. Bewildered, he stared down the next block. There was no neon sign, no splash of friendly light upon the sidewalk to mark the little store tucked away in this residential section.

He stared at the street marker and read the word slowly: GRANT. He read it again, unbelieving, for this shouldn't be Grant Street, but Marshall. He had walked two blocks and the confectionery was between Marshall and Grant. He hadn't come to Marshall yet . . . and here was Grant.

Or had he, absent-mindedly, come one block farther than he thought, passed the store as on the night before?

For the first time in twenty years, Mr. Chambers retraced his steps. He walked back to Jefferson, then turned around and went back to Grant again and on to Lexington. Then back to Grant again, where he stood astounded while a single, incredible fact grew slowly in his brain:

There wasn't any confectionery! The block from Marshall to Grant had disappeared!

Now he understood why he had missed the store on the night before, why he had arrived home fifteen minutes early.

On legs that were dead things he stumbled back to his home. He slammed and locked the door behind him and made his way unsteadily to his chair in the corner.

What was this? What did it mean? By what inconceivable necromancy could a paved street with houses, trees and buildings be spirited away and the space it had occupied be closed up?

Was something happening in the world which he, in his secluded life, knew nothing about?

Mr. Chambers shivered, reached to turn up the collar of his coat, then stopped as he realized the room must be warm. A fire blazed merrily in the grate. The cold he felt came from something . . . somewhere else. The cold of fear and horror, the chill of a half-whispered thought.

A deathly silence had fallen, a silence still measured by the pendulum clock. And yet a silence that held a different tenor than he had ever sensed before. Not a homey, comfortable silence . . . but a silence that hinted at emptiness and nothingness.

There was something back of this, Mr. Chambers told himself. Something that reached far back into one corner of his brain and demanded recognition. Something tied up with the fragments of talk he had heard on the drugstore corner, bits of news broadcasts he had heard as he walked along the street, the shrieking of the newsboy calling his papers. Something to do with the happenings in the world from which he had excluded himself.

He brought them back to mind now and lingered over the one central theme of the talk he overheard: the wars and plagues. Hints of a Europe and Asia swept almost clean of human life, of the plague ravaging Africa, of its appearance in South America, of the frantic efforts of the United States to prevent its spread into that nation's boundaries.

Millions of people were dead in Europe and Asia, Africa and South America. Billions, perhaps.

And somehow those gruesome statistics seemed tied up with his own experience. Something, somewhere, some part of his earlier life, seemed to hold an explanation. But try as he would his befuddled brain failed to find the answer.

The pendulum clock struck slowly, its every other chime as usual setting up a sympathetic vibration in the pewter vase that stood upon the mantel.

Mr. Chambers got to his feet, strode to the door, opened it and looked out.

Moonlight tessellated the street in black and silver, etching the chimneys and trees against a silvered sky.

But the house directly across the street was not the same. It was strangely lop-sided, its dimensions out of proportion, like a house that suddenly had gone mad.

He stared at it in amazement, trying to determine what was wrong with it. He recalled how it had always stood, foursquare, a solid piece of mid-Victorian architecture.

Then, before his eyes, the house righted itself again. Slowly it drew together, ironed out its queer angles, readjusted its dimensions, became once again the stodgy house he knew it had to be.

With a sigh of relief, Mr. Chambers turned back into the hall.

But before he closed the door, he looked again. The house was lop-sided . . . as bad, perhaps worse than before!

Gulping in fright, Mr. Chambers slammed the door shut, locked it and double bolted it. Then he went to his bedroom and took two sleeping powders.

His dreams that night were the same as on the night before. Again there was the islet in mid-ocean. Again he was alone upon it. Again the squirming hydrophinnae were eating his foothold piece by piece.

He awoke, body drenched with perspiration. Vague light of early dawn filtered through the window. The clock on the bedside table showed 7:30. For a long time he lay there motionless.

Again the fantastic happenings of the night before came back to haunt him and as he lay there, staring at the windows, he remembered them, one by one. But his mind, still fogged by sleep and astonishment, took the happenings in its stride, mulled over them, lost the keen edge of fantastic terror that lurked around them.

The light through the windows slowly grew brighter. Mr. Chambers slid out of bed, slowly crossed to the window, the cold of the floor biting into his bare feet. He forced himself to look out.

There was nothing outside the window. No shadows. As if there might be a fog. But no fog, however, thick, could hide the apple tree that grew close against the house.

But the tree was there . . . shadowy, indistinct in the gray, with a few withered apples still clinging to its boughs, a few shriveled leaves reluctant to leave the parent branch.

The tree was there now. But it hadn't been when he first had looked. Mr. Chambers was sure of that.

And now he saw the faint outlines of his neighbor's house . . . but those outlines were all wrong. They didn't jibe and fit together . . . they were out of plumb. As if some giant hand had grasped the house and wrenched it out of true. Like the house he had seen across the street the night before, the house that had painfully righted itself when he thought of how it should look.

Perhaps if he thought of how his neighbor's house should look, it too might right itself. But Mr. Chambers was very weary. Too weary to think about the house.

He turned from the window and dressed slowly. In the living room he slumped into his chair, put his feet on the old cracked ottoman. For a long time he sat, trying to think.

And then, abruptly, something like an electric shock ran through him. Rigid, he sat there, limp inside at the thought. Minutes later he arose and almost ran across the room to the old mahogany bookcase that stood against the wall.

There were many volumes in the case: his beloved classics on the first shelf, his many scientific works on the lower shelves. The second shelf contained but one book.

And it was around this book that Mr. Chambers' entire life was centered.

Twenty years ago he had written it and foolishly attempted to teach its philosophy to a class of undergraduates. The newspapers, he remembered, had made a great deal of it at the time. Tongues had been set to wagging. Narrow-minded townsfolk, failing to understand either his philosophy or his aim, but seeing in him another exponent of some anti-rational cult, had forced his expulsion from the school.

It was a simple book, really, dismissed by most authorities as merely the vagaries of an over-zealous mind.

Mr. Chambers took it down now, opened its cover and began thumbing slowly through the pages. For a moment the memory of happier days swept over him.

Then his eyes focused on the paragraph, a paragraph written so long ago the very words seemed strange and unreal:

> Man himself, by the power of mass suggestion, holds the physical fate of this earth . . . yes, even the universe. Billions of minds seeing trees as trees, houses as houses, streets as streets . . . and not as something else. Minds that see things as they are and have kept things as they were. . . . Destroy those minds and the entire foundation of matter, robbed of its regenerative power, will crumple and slip away like a column of sand. . . .

His eyes followed down the page:

> Yet this would have nothing to do with matter itself . . . but only with matter's form. For while the mind of man through long ages

may have moulded an imagery of that space in which he lives, mind would have little conceivable influence upon the existence of that matter. What exists in our known universe shall exist always and can never be destroyed, only altered or transformed.

But in modern astrophysics and mathematics we gain an insight into the possibility . . . yes probability . . . that there are other dimensions, other brackets of time and space impinging on the one we occupy.

If a pin is thrust into a shadow, would that shadow have any knowledge of the pin? It would not, for in this case the shadow is two dimensional, the pin three dimensional. Yet both occupy the same space.

Granting then that the power of men's minds alone holds this universe, or at least this world in its present form, may we not go farther and envision other minds in some other plane watching us, waiting, waiting craftily for the time they can take over the domination of matter? Such a concept is not impossible. It is a natural conclusion if we accept the double hypothesis: that mind does control the formation of all matter; and that other worlds lie in juxtaposition with ours.

Perhaps we shall come upon a day, far distant, when our plane, our world will dissolve beneath our feet and before our eyes as some stronger intelligence reaches out from the dimensional shadows of the very space we live in and wrests from us the matter which we know to be our own.

He stood astounded beside the bookcase, his eyes staring unseeing into the fire upon the hearth.

He had written that. And because of those words he had been called a heretic, had been compelled to resign his position at the university, had been forced into this hermit life.

A tumultuous idea hammered at him. Men had died by the millions all over the world. Where there had been thousands of minds there now were one or two. A feeble force to hold the form of matter intact.

The plague had swept Europe and Asia almost clean of life, had blighted Africa, had reached South America . . . might even have come to the United States. He remembered the whispers he had heard, the words of the men at the drugstore corner, the buildings disappearing. Something scientists could not explain. But those were merely scraps of information. He did not know the whole story . . . he could not know. He never listened to the radio, never read a newspaper.

But abruptly the whole thing fitted together in his brain like the missing piece of a puzzle into its slot. The significance of it all gripped him with damning clarity.

There were not sufficient minds in existence to retain the material world in its mundane form. Some other power from another dimension was fighting to supersede man's control and take his universe into its own plane!

Abruptly Mr. Chambers closed the book, shoved it back in the case and picked up his hat and coat.

He had to know more. He had to find someone who could tell him.

He moved through the hall to the door, emerged into the street. On the walk he looked skyward, trying to make out the sun. But there wasn't any sun . . . only an all-pervading grayness that shrouded everything . . . not a gray fog, but a gray emptiness that seemed devoid of life, of any movement.

The walk led to his gate and there it ended, but as he moved forward the sidewalk came into view and the house ahead loomed out of the gray, but a house with differences.

He moved forward rapidly. Visibility extended only a few feet and as he approached them the houses materialized like two dimensional pictures without perspective, like twisted cardboard soldiers lining up for review on a misty morning.

Once he stopped and looked back and saw that the grayness had closed in behind him. The houses were wiped out, the sidewalk faded into nothing.

He shouted, hoping to attract attention. But his voice frightened him. It seemed to ricochet up and into the higher levels of the sky, as if a giant door had been opened to a mighty room high above him.

He went on until he came to the corner of Lexington. There, on the curb, he stopped and stared. The gray wall was thicker there but he did not realize how close it was until he glanced down at his feet and saw there was nothing, nothing at all beyond the curbstone. No dull gleam of wet asphalt, no sign of a street. It was as if all eternity ended here at the corner of Maple and Lexington.

With a wild cry, Mr. Chambers turned and ran. Back down the street he raced, coat streaming after him in the wind, bowler hat bouncing on his head.

Panting, he reached the gate and stumbled up the walk, thankful that it still was there.

On the stoop he stood for a moment, breathing hard. He glanced back over his shoulder and a queer feeling of inner numbness seemed to well over him. At that moment the gray nothingness appeared to thin . . . the enveloping curtain fell away, and he saw. . . .

Vague and indistinct, yet cast in stereoscopic outline, a gigantic city was lined against the darkling sky. It was a city fantastic with cubed domes, spires, and aerial bridges and flying buttresses. Tunnel-like streets, flanked on either side by shining metallic ramps and runways, stretched endlessly to the vanishing point. Great shafts of multicolored light probed huge streamers and ellipses above the higher levels.

And beyond, like a final backdrop, rose a titanic wall. It was from that wall . . . from its crenelated parapets and battlements that Mr. Chambers felt the eyes peering at him.

Thousands of eyes glaring down with but a single purpose.

And as he continued to look, something else seemed to take form above that wall. A design this time, that swirled and writhed in the ribbons of radiance and rapidly coalesced into strange geometric features, without definite line or detail. A colossal face, a face of indescribable power and evil, it was, staring down with malevolent composure.

Then the city and the face slid out of focus; the vision faded like a darkened magic-lantern, and the grayness moved in again.

Mr. Chambers pushed open the door of his house. But he did not lock it. There was no need of locks . . . not any more.

A few coals of fire still smouldered in the grate and going there, he stirred them up, raked away the ash, piled on more wood. The flames leaped merrily, dancing in the chimney's throat.

Without removing his hat and coat, he sank exhausted in his favorite chair, closed his eyes then opened them again.

He sighed with relief as he saw the room was unchanged. Everything in its accustomed place: the clock, the lamp, the elephant ash tray, the marine print on the wall.

Everything was as it should be. The clock measured the silence with its measured ticking; it chimed abruptly and the vase sent up its usual sympathetic vibration.

This was his room, he thought. Rooms acquire the personality of the person who lives in them, become a part of him. This was his world, his own private world, and as such it would be the last to go.

But how long could he . . . his brain . . . maintain its existence?

Mr. Chambers stared at the marine print and for a moment a little breath of reassurance returned to him. They couldn't take this away. The rest of the world might dissolve because there was insufficient power of thought to retain its outward form.

But this room was his. He alone had furnished it. He alone, since he had first planned the house's building, had lived here.

This room would stay. It must stay on . . . it must. . . .

He rose from his chair and walked across the room to the book case, stood staring at the second shelf with its single volume. His eyes shifted to the top shelf and swift terror gripped him.

For all the books weren't there. A lot of books weren't there! Only the most beloved, the most familiar ones.

So the change already had started here! The unfamiliar books were gone and that fitted in the pattern . . . for it would be the least familiar things that would go first.

Wheeling, he stared across the room. Was it his imagination, or did the lamp on the table blur and begin to fade away?

But as he stared at it, it became clear again, a solid, substantial thing.

For a moment real fear reached out and touched him with chilly fingers. For he knew that this room no longer was proof against the thing that had happened out there on the street.

Or had it really happened? Might not all this exist within his own mind? Might not the street be as it always was, with laughing children and barking dogs? Might not the Red Star confectionery still exist, splashing the street with the red of its neon sign?

Could it be that he was going mad? He had heard whispers when he had passed, whispers the gossiping housewives had not intended him to hear. And he had heard the shouting of boys when he walked by. They thought him mad. Could he be really mad?

But he knew he wasn't mad. He knew that he perhaps was the sanest of all men who walked the earth. For he, and he alone, had foreseen this very thing. And the others had scoffed at him for it.

Somewhere else the children might be playing on a street. But it would be a different street. And the children undoubtedly would be different too.

For the matter of which the street and everything upon it had been formed would now be cast in a different mold, stolen by different minds in a different dimension.

Perhaps we shall come upon a day, far distant, when our plane, our world will dissolve beneath our feet and before our eyes as some stronger intelligence reaches out from the dimensional shadows of the very space we live in and wrests from us the matter which we know to be our own.

But there had been no need to wait for that distant day. Scant years after he had written those prophetic words the thing was happening. Man had played unwittingly into the hands of those other minds in the other dimension. Man had waged a war and war had bred a pestilence. And the

whole vast cycle of events was but a detail of a cyclopean
plan.

He could see it all now. By an insidious mass hypno-
sis minions from that other dimension . . . or was it one
supreme intelligence . . . had deliberately sown the seeds
of dissension. The reduction of the world's mental power
had been carefully planned with diabolic premeditation.

On impulse he suddenly turned, crossed the room and
opened the connecting door to the bedroom. He stopped
on the threshold and a sob forced its way to his lips.

There was no bedroom. Where his stolid four poster
and dresser had been there was greyish nothingness.

Like an automaton he turned again and paced to the
hall door. Here, too, he found what he had expected. There
was no hall, no familiar hat rack and umbrella stand.

Nothing . . .

Weakly Mr. Chambers moved back to his chair in the
corner.

"So here I am," he said, half aloud.

So there he was. Embattled in the last corner of the
world that was left to him.

Perhaps there were other men like him, he thought.
Men who stood at bay against the emptiness that marked
the transition from one dimension to another. Men who
had lived close to the things they loved, who had endowed
those things with such substantial form by power of mind
alone that they now stood out alone against the power of
some greater mind.

The street was gone. The rest of his house was gone.
This room still retained its form.

This room, he knew, would stay the longest. And when
the rest of the room was gone, this corner with his favorite
chair would remain. For this was the spot where he had
lived for twenty years. The bedroom was for sleeping, the

kitchen for eating. This room was for living. This was his last stand.

These were the walls and floors and prints and lamps that had soaked up his will to make them walls and prints and lamps.

He looked out the window into a blank world. His neighbors' houses already were gone. They had not lived with them as he had lived with this room. Their interests had been divided, thinly spread; their thoughts had not been concentrated as his upon an area four blocks by three, or a room fourteen by twelve.

Staring through the window, he saw it again. The same vision he had looked upon before and yet different in an indescribable way. There was the city illumined in the sky. There were the elliptical towers and turrets, the cube-shaped domes and battlements. He could see with stereoscopic clarity the aerial bridges, the gleaming avenues sweeping on into infinitude. The vision was nearer this time, but the depth and proportion had changed . . . as if he were viewing it from two concentric angles at the same time.

And the face . . . the face of magnitude . . . of power of cosmic craft and evil. . . .

Mr. Chambers turned his eyes back into the room. The clock was ticking slowly, steadily. The greyness was stealing into the room.

The table and radio were the first to go. They simply faded away and with them went one corner of the room.

And then the elephant ash tray.

"Oh, well," said Mr. Chambers, "I never did like that very well."

Now as he sat there it didn't seem queer to be without the table or the radio. It was as if it were something quite normal. Something one could expect to happen.

Perhaps, if he thought hard enough, he could bring them back.

But, after all, what was the use? One man, alone, could not stand off the irresistible march of nothingness. One man, all alone, simply couldn't do it.

He wondered what the elephant ash tray looked like in that other dimension. It certainly wouldn't be an elephant ash tray nor would the radio be a radio, for perhaps they didn't have ash trays or radios or elephants in the invading dimension.

He wondered, as a matter of fact, what he himself would look like when he finally slipped into the unknown. For he was matter, too, just as the ash tray and radio were matter.

He wondered if he would retain his individuality . . . if he still would be a person. Or would he merely be a thing?

There was one answer to all of that. He simply didn't know.

Nothingness advanced upon him, ate its way across the room, stalking him as he sat in the chair underneath the lamp. And he waited for it.

The room, or what was left of it, plunged into dreadful silence.

Mr. Chambers started. The clock had stopped. Funny . . . the first time in twenty years.

He leaped from his chair and then sat down again.

The clock hadn't stopped.

It wasn't there.

There was a tingling sensation in his feet.

Tunnel Terror

Allison V. Harding

(1946)

They were at first glance, a strange Mutt and Jeff pair. To some slouch-hatted, poorly dressed client of Ed's "Express Diner," there seemed little on the surface between the big man in work clothes and his small bright-eyed companion.

In a way, their friendship was an accident. It had started at Oceanside High School. Big Bill Van Hooten and little Tom Mead. Van Hooten with the muscles, Mead with the brains, making up in gray matter what he lacked in bulk. And the two got along, or maybe it was a conspiracy of the expedient, for certainly Big Bill was too dumb to get far even on his muscles and Tom too small, likewise.

They'd drifted apart the way people do after high school, and Van Hooten got a job with a trucking company. Pulling at a wheel and loading crates were nearer to high-school football and baseball than sitting at an office desk somewhere. And anyway, remember, he was, as Joe Ferro, boss of the Acme, used to say with a significant finger-tapping at his forehead, "Thick!"

And Tom, just naturally it seemed, ended up on the Big City *Courier*. You know, that's that big almost-orange stucco building facing the wharves downtown where the presses go day and night, turning out five-inch headlines on everything from crime to scandal.

The two men lived in Oceanside though, and at night they'd meet often in the diner. Not to say much perhaps, because there wasn't always a lot to say, but just to be together for a moment like out of habit from old days and then go off with "G'nights" to their respective rooms.

Big Bill's father and mother had both been old beyond figuring when Tom first remembered them and they had been dead for several years. Let's see now, they died a couple of years before the tunnel went through from Oceanside to the city. All Tom knew of family was his aunt, who'd brought him up and seen him through high school and— he was glad of this, kind of like a repayment—to the first day he'd landed the job at the Big City *Courier,* and she said in an old tired voice full of tears, "I'm so glad for you, Tommy."

But the happiness of this added only a few more months to her life and then she was gone and he was as alone as Big Bill. So there didn't need to be much said at Ed's diner, but tonight there was. Big Bill was talking, wagging his massive head.

"It's Joe Ferro," he complained. "Can't please that guy, Tom. Always kickin'."

The little man continued to stare disinterestedly into the brown mud of his coffee, discouraging the thin cream from collecting on the top with the end of his cruller.

"I came through with some oranges this morning from upstate and Joe, he gets poking around in the back, and he says to me, he says, 'Bill, what the hell's the idea? Lot of these things are spoiled. Whatja do, float 'em across the river,' and he's making out like I dumped 'em in salt water on purpose."

It was a long speech for Bill, and he thumped his ham fist on the diner counter, making Ed, the proprietor, look up.

When the two men finished their evening meal and parted, Tom noticed the worried look in his big friend's eyes. He slapped him on the back and walked a ways home with him. It was no use, he thought to himself, letting either a trucking foreman or a city editor get you down.

The next night Tom was first of the two at the diner. He wondered with an amused anticipation whether Big Bill had taken his advice given last night, "Aw, poke him one if he gets tough, fellah."

He heard steps outside the diner, a heavy tread up the wooden stairs to the car and Van Hooten came in.

"Hiya," said Ed from behind the counter automatically, not looking up from apron-polishing a plate.

But the big driver didn't answer. And in his eyes as he lumbered across the diner towards the small man, Tom saw something that looked out of place there—fear! The hulking trucker settled heavily on the next stool.

"How's it?" said Tom.

Automatically Van Hooten started to eat the food the counter man placed before him, but slowly without relish. Mead knew his friend too well to push the conversation. He could see that a struggle was going on in the big inarticulate driver. Bill pushed back his pie plate only half finished.

"Let's get out of here," he said, and wordlessly Tom followed.

Outside they walked along the dusk-streaked avenue. It was a poor section of the industrial town, hard by the river, and the damp, moist smell was as much a part of Oceanside as the red-brick factory chimneys, the poor run-down houses, and Ed's "Express Diner." The sound of their leather heels on the stones echoed hollowly from the buildings on either side as the men walked. Finally, abruptly, Big Bill spoke up.

"Had more trouble with Ferro today, Tommy."

"Whyn't ya sock him?" was Mead's comeback.

"I'm still hauling for the grocery account," went on Van Hooten, his tan brow wrinkled up perplexedly, "and Ferro blames me. Things I don't have nothin' to do with."

"What happened?"

"Well, I made my usual run up to Bureau Market and came back with a load of lettuce. I 'specially watched 'em load it in at the market. Looked like mighty good stuff to me. We get back here and whadda think I got in there?"

"What?"

"Seaweed!"

The two men stopped under a street lamp.

"Some kind of joke, huh?"

"Naw," persisted Van Hooten. "There's lettuce in the crates but a lot of old dirty green salt water seaweed too, and Ferro gives me the devil."

"Well," said Tom Mead after a moment's thought, "what's it to do with you? You're just the trucker. You don't contract for any of this food or buy it or even load it at the market."

The big man nodded. "That's what I told Ferro, Tommy, but there's sumpin' else. I been thinkin'. 'Member I told you about oranges yesterday soaked with sea water?"

The reporter bobbed his head.

"I figure it's to do with me coming through—the tunnel! Don't you get it, Tommy? Those funny things are happening in the tunnel."

Mead grinned. "Are you kidding, big boy? Whaddya think, that the seaweed and salt water just dropped through all that steel and concrete into your truck? Whaddya think, the river's got a grudge on you, Bill?"

The big man looked wise. And scared.

"It's the river," he whispered, as though two blocks away it might hear him. "It's what's in it, Tommy. What's in it down at the bottom where the tunnel goes!"

The reporter's first reaction was to laugh, but you don't laugh at a friend. Especially when "scared" is standing out all over him.

"You think I'm crazy," the big man put in, almost as though intuitively sensing the other's thoughts, "but I'm not. I got something to show you, Tommy. Will you come up to my room right now?"

Mead followed unquestioningly. As they walked through the dark streets, he found himself worried about his big friend. Does a trucker overwork and have to take a vacation? Well, why not? Maybe Bill had lugged a bit too much of that junk through the tunnel.

They climbed the steps to Van Hooten's fourth-floor room. Tom had been up before. It was plain, neat. No books he'd ever seen. Just a few magazines. Nothing to take much brain work or imagination. But after Big Bill's latch key had let them in, Mead noticed an old trunk in the middle of the room. It was dark-colored with a rusty hinge that squeaked as Van Hooten lifted the cover. For a moment Tom thought romantically of a pirate's treasure chest. He felt that inside certainly there would be crossed cutlasses on top of doubloons.

Instead, there came the fragrance of old clothes and then the clothes themselves. Precious few, belonging to Big Bill's parents. With a tenderness that was pathetic in one so large, Bill took the dresses and suits out. Mead found himself marveling at the culture of the Old World. These people, or their people before, had been somebodies in Holland across the sea. At the bottom of the trunk was a book, its yellow cloth cover stained with the passing of the decades. It was labeled simply with the flourishing strokes of an ancient dress hand, "Van Hooten."

The trucker did not offer the volume but took it on his knee as he sat by the table light, and again the reporter's eye noted the incongruity of the scene. The huge trucker in his rough work clothes, his big gnarled hands caressing a book that looked centuries old. And then he spoke and it seemed his harsh voice took on a softer quality. "Some of my people, Tommy, were about the first in this country. It tells all about them in this book." He frowned down at the pages before him and turned them idly, "About Peter Minuet and New Amsterdam and the Dutch fighting the English. It's kind of like school history books but it's my family."

The two sat quietly for a moment and then Van Hooten sighed.

"Take it," he said extending the book. "Take it and read it, Tommy. You'll see what I'm thinking."

Mead placed the book carefully in a paper.

"Sounds mighty interesting, Bill. You never told me anything—"

Van Hooten waved his hand. "These things you don't think about until something makes you. If they can be forgotten, they're better forgotten. You read the book, Tommy. It'll tell you."

The reporter rose. "For you I'll be glad to. Don't worry now, Bill. So what if they're blaming you for some crates of bad oranges and hauling seaweed instead of lettuce. I can find a spot for you at the paper."

The pleasantry was not appreciated. Van Hooten stood in the center of the room, looking not exactly at Mead but through him, beyond him, as though at those other people who'd once been a part of the things in the trunk, those others of his kin. It gave Tom the creeps, and with a quick good night he turned and left, with the wrapped book under his arm.

The reporter hurried his steps home, and once in his own room took forth the old volume, settling himself on the frame bed with the table lampshade tilted. For some of the letters in the took were nearly illegible with age. As he turned the pages, idly reading here and there, his interest dissolved somewhat and he began to wonder what it was Van Hooten had wanted him to read. It was seemingly the usual family record of trystings and marriages, births and deaths. Here was a notation concerning the first branch of the family to come from Holland to the New Land.

His eyes sharpened as he read on. The meticulous and penned letters spelled out words of adventure of the early days of the middle seventeenth century, of sea battles with the English. The name of Hendrik Van Hooten attracted Mead. Big Bill's father was a Hendrik Van Hooten and he'd heard the name before. Surely a direct antecedent of the burly trucker. The words on the yellowed brittle pages seemed to come alive. Ancient and stilted as the phraseology might be, the tale was one of excitement and blood. Hendrik Van Hooten the First had been junior master on a Dutch ship that had fought valiantly in and around the waters of New Amsterdam.

But the pages implied that "English, or other interests" had got to members of the crew. There had been the surrender of large tracts of east-coast land to the Britishers in the early 1860s, and Van Hooten, against the advice of his own blood cousin, had suddenly destroyed his ship in the river rather than go out into the bay and surrender it and its cargo to the enemy men-of-war.

The story continued. Van Hooten had blown the bottom of his ship out with dynamite and the Dutch vessel had plunged to the bottom with all hands. Some said, the diary reported, that old Van Hooten himself had escaped, but this was not known for sure. Certain it was though, that from that time on there had been hatred in the divided ranks of the family.

An old-world curse had been leveled at Hendrik Van
Hooten—"For him this river shall ever be closed by the
doings of his own evil hand, nor shall it be passed over nor
up and down for any purpose, sayeth the curse," and the
diary gave a day and year in the late middle seventeenth
century.

The family history went on then to affairs of birth and
marriage. The details of events so all-important to those
concerned and so trivial to an outsider. Tom was about to
lay the book aside when another item caught his attention.
It concerned another Hendrik Van Hooten who had been
lost in the river one stormy night and presumed to have
died. His body was later recovered, washed up opposite
the city at Oceanside. The pages commented pithily that
the poor doomed man was "purple in color, swollen, his
mouth choked full of seaweed, showing that this was no
ordinary act of God but the workings of the Van Hooten
curse."

Mead closed the volume then and lay back to consider it
possibilities. Certainly the old wives' tales had affected his
friend's rather simple mind. The recent seaweed-in-the-
lettuce episode, of course, recalled to Big Bill the ominous
words in the family volume about an earlier Van Hooten.
Tom lay awake for some time that night, enthralled with
these pages from the past. As a youngster, Big Bill had
probably been imbued with wild tales of the family curse,
and even in the unimaginative soil of his mind, the legends had stock. Mead fell asleep considering the somewhat
irrelevant aspect of what a splendid newspaper feature the
whole yarn would make.

The next day he did his copy at the office and covered
an afternoon sporting event for the paper, but all the time
his thoughts were on Big Bill. He was waiting in Ed's diner
again when their meeting time rolled around. Van Hooten's eyes were less troubled this time and he nodded at

the diner proprietor, one or two other familiar customers, and Tom. Mead handed him the paper-wrapped volume.

"Well," Bill asked. "Whatja think of that?"

"It's interesting," answered the reporter. "It would make a nice Sunday feature story but you don't believe that curse business, do you? Why, they've practically given up that idea in the movies!"

Van Hooten shook his head. "It's no kid, Tom. This business is real."

"Aw, stop it, big boy," the reporter chortled. "You think the Van Hooten curse is reaching out of the river for you, huh?"

The look on the big driver's face straightened Mead's smiling lips, though.

"You can laugh, Tom, but it's all true. That river's bad for us of the Hendrik Van Hootens."

The look of worried conviction on the plain square face of the driver was almost comical. Lord, thought Mead to himself. I never thought a physique like that could have an *imagination*. The other toyed with the salt cellar for a moment, and then, "Did I ever tell you about my father, Tom?"

Mead nodded, "Well, some. He seemed to be a grand old gentleman."

"Did I tell you about how he died?"

"People die," reasoned the reporter. "He was a mighty old fellow, Bill."

"No, it wasn't any act of God," persisted the big driver, "but like the curse said. You didn't know much about it, Tom, at the time. The doc said my father took sick from the shock of my mother dying but nobody thought . . . nobody thought he was going to die, and if I hadn't been away from home, I never would've let the doc do what he did, 'cuz I would've *known*.

"See, he thought my father should come in to City Hospital and he got an ambulance and everything to take him. Across the river. Do you get it, Tom? On the ferry and during the trip a squall came up. That's how the doc explained it to me. He just died sudden and unaccountably."

Mead looked doubtful. He blurted out, "I suppose there was seaweed around too."

"That's right," said Van Hooten. "Seaweed there on the ambulance bed where he lay, 'cuz the doc told me and he wouldn't lie or make things up not knowing anything about our family and the river being after us!"

The two were silent for a minute and then Mead asked, "How did today go, Bill?"

"Okay," said the trucker. "1 was working over to the border of the state, didn't go near the river all day. Tomorrow though, I gotta go through, Joe Ferro says."

The next day Mead made time to go to Oceanside City Hall and look through the death certificate archives. There, sure enough, was one made out to Big Bill's father, Hendrik Van Hooten. The death did take place on the Oceanside-Big City ferry in a hospital ambulance and the laconic comment of the attesting physician was, "Shock." That, of course, fit in neatly with the legend of the Van Hooten curse but might also be, and to his mind was beyond question, just a coincidence. With sudden inspiration he looked up at the clock, on the wall of the record room. It was three. He still had some time before he was needed back at the newspaper office and he quickly phoned the Acme Trucking Company.

He got someone gruff, uncommunicative, disagreeable, as he imagined Joe Ferro probably was. The replies were laconic but he gathered that Big Bill Van Hooten was picking up canned goods stock at the North Street Depot at the outskirts of Big City. He was due back here sometime after six. Yes, the loading took an hour or so.

Mead tore out of the City Hall, hopped a cab, and directed the hack driver to the food depot. They started through Oceanside streets, headed towards the river past the big orange brick "breather," through the toll gate of the tunnel and into its illuminated tube, the tires swishing damply on the red-brick road surface. As they sped through its length, Tom could not help but think of the legend of the Dutch ship that had gone down to nestle somewhere near in the river bed. He noted grudgingly his own feeling of relief when the cab poked its nose up out of the underground like a mole. Sunshine slanting down into the opening of the tube which they were approaching was a welcome sight.

In twenty more minutes they reached the North Street Depot, and Tom's heart leaped at the sight of the big red Acme truck. Bill was in the driver's seat even as Tom threw a bill to his cab driver and sprinted.

"Hey," he yelled, "I'm hitching a ride with you back!"

Big Bill hesitated for a second, then threw open the door of the cab and grinned.

"Hiya, Tom," he said. "Glad to see you. Did the *Courier* fire you?"

Tom slid onto the leather seat beside the burly driver, and the big motor surged forward in first gear. Van Hooten sent the vehicle into the highway traffic expertly. They took a road downward that traversed the river. The last of the sun sliding into the west warmed Tom's face. He turned and looked at Big Bill. The driver's huge hands were knotted on the black steering wheel. His massive body was set and his eyes squinted ahead. There was a white look around his mouth.

And suddenly Mead spoke, "Why don't you quit your job, Bill? If there's sumpin' that bothers you, it's not worth it. I know to tell another guy his worries is nothing doesn't do much good. There's not many truckers better than you, kid. You could hook on with a company anywhere in the city probably. How about it?"

Bill turned for a minute and looked at his companion, trouble in his eyes.

"I've thought of that, Tom. I don't like it, this that I have to do, but somehow something kind of draws me like a magnet. Like today. We're going back through the tunnel and I don't want to, yet I do. D'ya understand? I can't explain it better'n that."

Mead turned his face away again and gazed at the river, his forehead wrinkled perplexedly. The drone of the tires took on a sharper quality as the truck ground up an incline and then slowed for a red light. Van Hooten set the tonnage rolling again expertly, and they weaved into the line of cars jockeying for the tunnel entrances.

Somehow, inexplicably, tension grew in Mead. It was absurd, he reasoned with himself, absurd to let the old wives' legends and crazy ideas of another affect oneself.

Before he could reason further, the truck had wound its serpentine way into the slow lane of the truck tube. They started down the decline, the concrete giving way to the red brick of the tunnel. Ahead, the white tile sides and inset lights stretched. Truck traffic was light at this time of day and they seemed alone. A solitary policeman stood just inside the opening on the catwalk to the left. The heavy ply tires of the truck began to swish damply as the roadway slanted downward.

Bill switched on fender indicator lights and the dash dials. The thunder of the motor reverberated back from the light walls. The truck used up its coasting speed and hit the straightened-out level of the tunnel. Tom found himself peering ahead intently, looking for something, he knew not what, and he jerked his eyes away from the dim tube ahead. He turned then to look at Bill and the driver grinned back. But despite the welcoming smile, the reporter saw that the big fellow was keeping tight rein on himself. The inside side lights slipped by monotonously and Mead suddenly became conscious of the biting pressure of his fingernails against his palms. He had been sitting stiffly with tightly clamped fists. The truck droned on, and except that here and there a patch of fog, made up perhaps of exhaust fumes as yet undispersed by the air intakes, the red composition road tube stretched harmless before them.

Actually, the entire trip through the tunnel takes but seven or eight minutes, but Tom felt he had been underground for half an hour under tons of water and surrounded by the dim, deep mysteries of the river bottom. Silent, brooding secrets that allowed for no solution.

Tom's mood changed abruptly as the truck crawled into increased engine life, taking up the load as the long slope leading upward began. "Well," he remarked loudly above the road and reverberations of the vehicle. "Wasn't much to that, kid."

It was the first word either of them had spoken since going in at the Big City entrance. Van Hooten smiled back and, visibly, strain had left him too. With a grinding of gears, the truck stuck its square nose up and rumbled its way out the Oceanside end of the underwater highway. Now that they were out, the whole of the episode seemed ridiculous to Tom Mead and he said as much to Big Bill as they slid to a corner a block away from the newspaper office.

That night the big trucker did not show up at Ed's diner, and Mead ate alone. He waited for some time after he'd finished, then decided to take in a movie. Outside the theater though, he stopped. He'd go by Van Hooten's anyway and see what the trucker was up to.

It was dark by the time he walked the several blocks. The steps creaked ominously as he climbed the flights to

Big Bill's. He knocked on the door. There was no answer.
He tried again louder. Finally, just as he was about to turn
away, he heard a step from within and fumbling hands on
the lock. The door swung open then and the driver stood
in front of him, his hugeness unsteady, his eyes dilated.
He jerked his head almost imperceptibly for Tom to come
inside. Then with actions that were swift in spite of their
unsteadiness, he quickly relocked and bolted the door.

Mead knew immediately that the big man had been drinking, but there was something in him more than that. More
powerful than alcohol. For the reporter had seen Van Hooten drinking before and it merely served to accentuate his
usual boisterous, rollicking nature. Tonight the man who
slumped into the chair in front of the reporter had been
drinking, yes. But he was also mortally afraid. Mead knew
his friend of old well enough to realize that a blunt de-
mand for explanation would not serve. Van Hooten would
speak when he was ready and not before.

Big Bill leaned in the chair for a time, his face working, his mouth forming syllables, words, that were given
no sound but stayed like the ghosts of unspeakable things
in the mind. Finally, his eyes rolled toward the ceiling,
heavenward, and he gasped.

"I've sent for him."

"Sent for who?" said Mead in a small voice.

There was no answer, only the strange disquieting
workings of the man's face before him. Mead stood up and
crossed to his friend. He shook him, first gently and then
harder, but there was no satisfactory response from the big
man.

"C'mon, snap out of it," said the diminutive reporter.
He felt angry with Van Hooten, an emotion that was probably akin to the long-standing friendship he'd had with
the trucker.

"Get ahold of yourself, Bill. Who's coming? What's all this mumbo-jumbo stuff about? You'll be seeing the ghost of Joe Ferro next."

But the driver was insensitive to the appeals and Mead let go of his shoulder.

"He's coming," Van Hooten said again through thick lips. "I've sent for him and he's coming."

It was then that Mead noticed the candle standing in the melt of its own wax on the far side of the floor. Beside it the volume that he had so recently thumbed through in his own room. More—crossed sticks and a pile of ashes on the floor. The Van Hooten volume was open, and when Mead peered down he saw a heading in a towards-the-back-of-the-volume page labeled, "Exorcise of the Curse." Tom bent closer and read, "—and for all these matters of the past, the present, and the future, the judge shall be the one before the first Van Hooten, keeper of these magic powers and bestower of both good and evil as justice may require—"

Mead was interrupted by the sound of a step from behind. Big Bill was almost on him as the reporter spun. Bill brushed the small man aside and stooped for the book. In his eyes Mead had seen the angry red fire of temper. Mead reached for the book again but Van Hooten shoved him away, this time brutally so that his friend fell heavily, and then, with an animal sound took a match out of his pocket and held it to the book. The crisp pages took quickly, and in a moment, the volume was a flaming square on the floor.

Mead had pulled himself into a chair and was watching. As suddenly as it had come and as the flames of the book died, the anger drained from Van Hooten's face. He moved over to where Tom sat, laid a heavy hand on the reporter's shoulder.

"I'm sorry, Tom," he mumbled, and then as a propitiatory gesture, he brought over a bottle of liquor and set out two cups, motioning the smaller man to join him.

They drank then and the time slipped past. Finally
Mead lifted his wrist to look at the watch there after what
seemed like hours. It was after midnight. Van Hooten was
again slumped in the chair on the other side of the room,
the worse for their several drinks on top of what he'd had
earlier in the evening. Mead himself was sleepy from the
liquor, and the single-yellow bulb burning on the center
table was conducive to drowsiness.

Against his will and better judgement Mead found his
eyelids dropping. He would force his head upward, look
around the room, and make plans for getting to his feet
and leaving, but the drowsiness came back and it was so
comfortable. Big Bill was sleeping—a little nap wouldn't
hurt.

The next thing he knew, Tom Mead awoke, his back
cramped in the uncomfortable wooden chair and the light
of the room now subtly different. The center bulb had
gone out but still there was illumination, strange yellow
suffused with green streaked the room. He turned his head
slowly to limber the stiffness in his neck, and as his head
swerved to the left, his eyes focused, incredulously at first,
on a figure that sat silently at the far end of the room.

Tom tried to force himself upward in the chair but it
was as though a heavy weight bore him down. The figure
was of a man, incredibly old, with parchment-yellow face
and elaborate ancient clothes.

Mead's unbelieving eyes then noticed that on the old
man's knee rested a cutlass, rusty with age but once probably of fine workmanship. As he watched, powerless to
move a muscle or speak, Mead saw the figure rise and
start toward the center of the room—towards him. The
strange greenish-yellow light caught the guard hilt of the
cutlass and reflected bleakly for a moment, and then the
old wax-like figure passed on by and Mead forced his eyes

to follow the apparition's course. The aged figure stopped in front of Big Bill, extended the cutlass, and then with an inexorable gentleness lifted one of Big Bill's huge hands, relaxed in sleep, and carefully curled the fingers over the finely made cutlass.

Then slowly the figure turned and moved with measured tread back past the reporter over to the far end of the room where the fire had been, where the ashes still were. And suddenly, Tom Mead was overcome with the appalling nature of his experience. His senses swam. Things grew black for a moment or many minutes. He could not tell, when again his eyes opened.

But the figure was gone and he was alone in the room with the still-sleeping Van Hooten, and the first streaks of dawn were touching the plain yellow papering of the room. The big man had not moved. His hands still hung slackly, and there was no sign of the cutlass that Mead had seen in his dream—for a dream it certainly must have been. Soundlessly, Mead straightened his tie and shrugged himself into his coat, quietly tiptoeing to the door and letting himself out.

It was a chill early dawn with a dampness that permeated even to a man's soul. Clouds scudded across the horizon in the early sky. Mead shivered and rubbed the heel across his cold cramped back. From a few blocks away a river vessel hooted, and the sound was not reassuring. He made his way to Ed's diner and downed three cups of black coffee, one after another. Then he headed for the newspaper office.

The girl in the front office raised her eyebrows questioningly as Mead came in. He had not been that early to work since his first month with the sheet. Reports of a three-alarm fire came in later in the morning and the city desk sent him north to cover the story. After he'd filed his

paragraphs from the scene of the blaze, Mead turned the
Courier sedan back towards home.

Storm clouds were blackening the sky now and the
wind whistled at the sedan window. Suddenly, a compel-
ling thought made Mead pull to the nearest drugstore. He
placed a toll call to Oceanside, gave his name, and got
gruff Foreman Ferro again. Sure, Big Bill had reported in
to work that morning. Else he would have been fired. Get
it! Yeah, he was over in Big City. He'd gone over early and
was coming back through the tunnel in the afternoon with
a shipment.

Tom slammed up the receiver and sprinted for his car.
Up north here there was no tunnel but the mid-river bridge
was only a few miles distant. He jazzed the *Courier* auto
across and headed towards the outskirts of Big City on the
other side. His memory of the previous night loomed large
in his mind as the day grew darker and more ominous. The
strange actions of Big Bill, the startlingly realistic image
of the old man of another age. And then one conclusion
that had slowly crept into his consciousness sometime
during the day. That was, that all the accidents so-called
that had happened to the Van Hootens on the river since
the curse was laid had come on bad days when the tempestuous black elements had conspired as it were to cloak an
even greater danger.

Mead found himself racing the car along the roads that
led into town, and by his very hurry, he realized he was
tacitly accepting the legend, in part if not all. Anyway,
he wanted to keep Big Bill from that tunnel run. But he
sent his car lurching into the food depot just too late. Van
Hooten had left for the south a few minutes earlier, he was
advised. Undeterred, Mead took up the chase and rocketed
the protesting sedan down the roads in pursuit.

Roaring up to an intersection he saw the Acme truck
disappearing around a far corner. He speeded up even more

and gained on the next incline. He tooted frantically but
the truck gave no notice of acknowledgment. Twin lines
of traffic developed then around an excavated place in the
highway. For a moment, Mead was able to draw abreast
and he yelled at Big Bill but the truck driver stared frozen-
ly ahead, set and unnatural. In a moment more, moving
traffic had jockeyed the red truck ahead.

Just before they reached the tunnel, the traffic slowed
and stopped. Quickly Tom swerved the newspaper's sedan
to the roadside, hopped out and ran. He caught the guard
rail on the rear of the truck just as the cars started in motion again. Straining mightily, he pulled himself upright
as the vehicle gathered speed, and with furious twisting
got the back van door open and let himself inside where
he fell sprawling midst the crates.

Picking himself up he scrambled forward and came
to the glass-paneled portion that separated him from the
driver's compartment. He hammered on the pane but the
thick stiff neck and back of Van Hooten ahead paid no
heed. Through the glass and out the truck's sides the reporter could see they were nearing the tunnel entrance,
and as he looked, the day's blackness suddenly gave way to
rain and the quickening tempo of drops on the steel roof
lent strength to his blows on the panel. But Big Bill never
so much as looked around. And then past the toll gates,
the truck picked up speed and swung careeningly into the
curving decline of the tunnel entrance.

Mead gave up his attacks on the thick glass and looked
frantically around for some sort of heavy object. The crates
were heavy but too large for one man to lift, and there
seemed to be nothing else.

As he searched, the sound of raindrops on the roof increased—the sudden realization of this made him straight-
en with a gasp. For they were in the tube. There could be
no rain here! There could be no water—but river water!

Mead crowded forward again, peering through the pane and the cab into the tunnel. It was not his imagination that the roadway ahead was darker, almost obscured in a green-yellow mist. Even the white-tiled sides and the set-in lights seemed many yards away instead of a few feet. His breath began to catch in his throat. The dampness made each inhalation a heavy task. But Van Hooten, as though transfixed, sat woodenly at the wheel and the truck roared on into the misty shadows of some unspeakable hell.

Mead felt it then. From the torrent of water that fell on the roof, his upturned face caught a drop or two and it came to him with a new horror. The sudden sharp salt taste. That could mean only one thing. Dear Lord, the tunnel was going! She'd sprung a leak and they'd be drowned down here. Trapped under tons of water in their own white-tile and red-brick tomb!

The truck slackened speed so abruptly then that it threw Mead to his knees. He felt his way in the gloom along the floor and crawled to the back opening. His pulses were pounding as he forced the metal frame open, and as he did, a wet slimy substance, not water exactly but heavier, much heavier than air, slipped in around him with chill octopus fingers, and he seemed to be swirling out into the dim green-yellow streaked light of the under-water highway. The sound of the truck's motor had long ago been lost, for the swishing and plopping and splashing was heavier, noisier. Mead thought of Van Hooten sitting in his cab. He struggled a few steps forward but his body seemed not to obey him.

It was as though he were floating, that last step of consciousness before, ether-like, you float into a swirling blackness.

He did not know afterward exactly what happened but somehow he crawled, staggered, or swam his way out of that tunnel hell. He was treated by an ambulance surgeon at the mouth of the tunnel where he collapsed, and by that time word of the tragedy inside the tube had come out.

It was a confrere of his from the *Courier* who told him, big-eyed, self-important, not sparing him because of his friendship with Big Bill or the experience he'd just been through. Van Hooten was dead, sitting there in his truck, unaccountably, that is, by all the laws of logic.

There is nothing briefer than a police investigation of a death that has no forthright logical explanation, but what explanation could you have for a man who had died of drowning sitting at the wheel of his truck in the middle of a tunnel, seaweed in the cab? And yet, of course, no one could drown in a perfectly sound tunnel.

Port of Authority officials hastily put out statistics of the number of million cars that had transversed the tunnel without accident. Then too, there was no logical explanation for the cutlass that was found in Bill Van Hooten's right hand, grasped tightly, its blade stained red with fresh blood, not his own obviously, for there wasn't a mark on him anywhere.

Tom Mead's part in the whole episode was considered thoroughly unimportant and the official verdict was "Heart attack." Mead was let go after some questioning and testimony brought forth his friendly relationship with the deceased. His only memento from the episode, the clothes he had had on, rotted now, a few months later, from soaking they'd received from the vengeful salt river water—where none could possibly be!

LIGHT SPIRITS

*Horrific Specters, Comedic Shades,
and Criminous Phantasms in
Vintage Periodical
Ghost Stories*

Also Available

Coachwhip Publications

CoachwhipBooks.com

Also Available

Coachwhip Publications

CoachwhipBooks.com

Also Available

Coachwhip Publications

CoachwhipBooks.com

CATS OF SHADOW,
CLAWS OF DARKNESS

Stories of Were-Cats, Ghost Cats,
and Other Supernatural Felines

Also Available

Coachwhip Publications

CoachwhipBooks.com

ANCIENT
HAUNTS

The Stoneground
Ghost Tales
by E. G. Swain

Tedious Brief Tales
of Granta and Gramarye
by Arthur Gray

Also Available
Coachwhip Publications
CoachwhipBooks.com

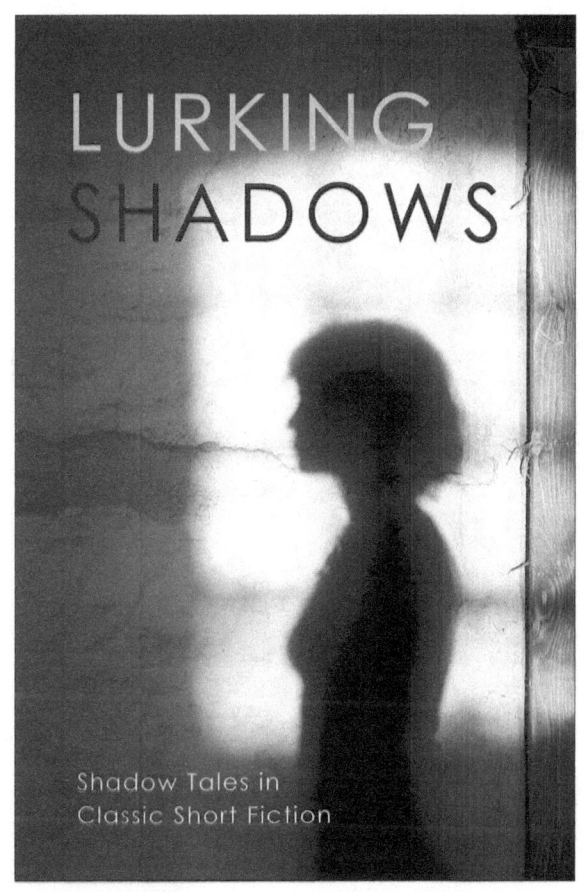

Also Available

Coachwhip Publications

CoachwhipBooks.com

Also Available
Coachwhip Publications
CoachwhipBooks.com

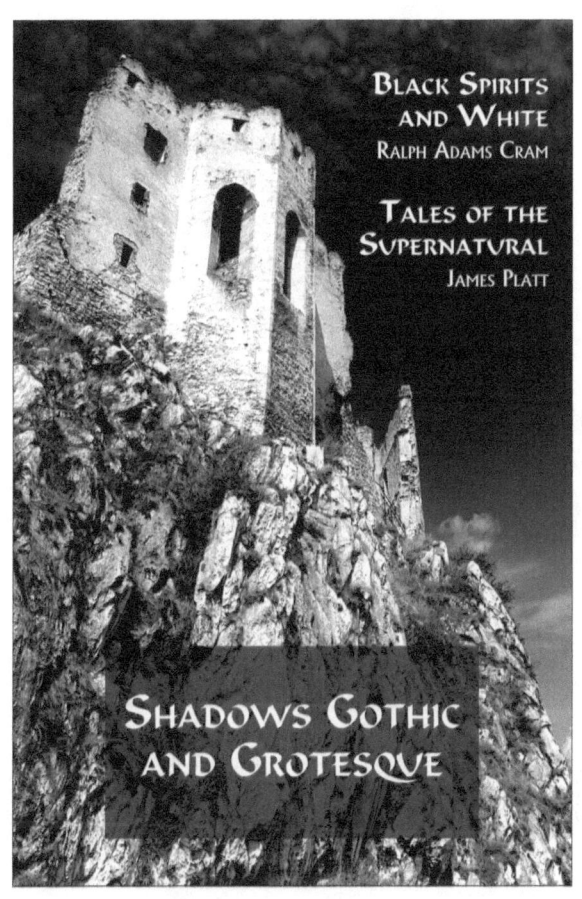

Also Available

Coachwhip Publications

CoachwhipBooks.com

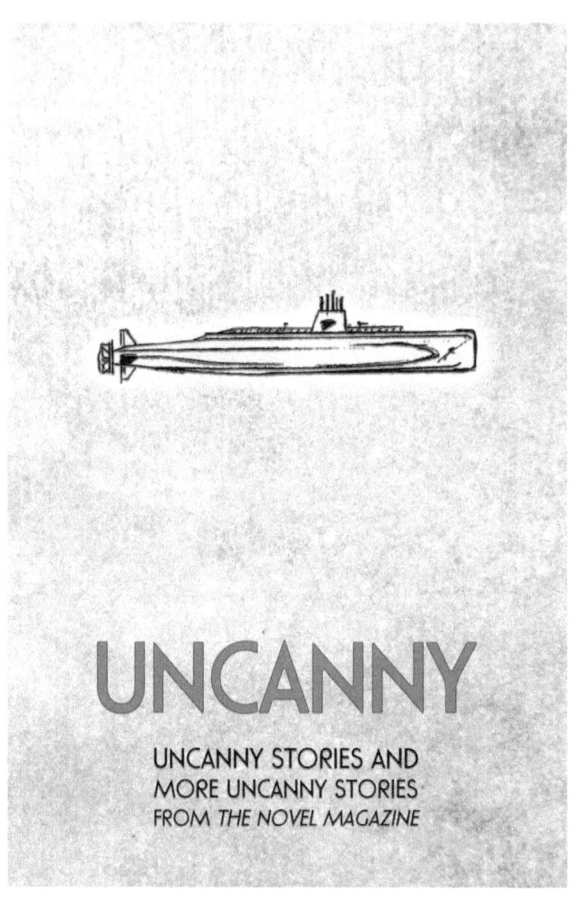

UNCANNY STORIES AND
MORE UNCANNY STORIES
FROM *THE NOVEL MAGAZINE*

Also Available
Coachwhip Publications
CoachwhipBooks.com

LONELY HAUNTS

Also Available
Coachwhip Publications
CoachwhipBooks.com

www.ingramcontent.com/pod-product-compliance
Lightning Source LLC
Chambersburg PA
CBHW020823260626
47169CB00003B/801